GW01397913

COUNTING
IN
DANISH

CELIA BERGGREEN

CRANTHORPE
—MILLNER—
PUBLISHERS

Copyright © Celia Berggreen (2024)

The right of Celia Berggreen to be identified as author of this work has been asserted by them in accordance with section 77 and 78 of the Copyright, Designs and Patents Act 1988.

All rights reserved. No part of this publication may be reproduced, stored in a retrieval system, or transmitted in any form or by any means, electronic, mechanical, photocopying, recording, or otherwise, without the prior permission of the publishers.

Any person who commits any unauthorised act in relation to this publication may be liable to criminal prosecution and civil claims for damages.

This book is a work of fiction. Names, characters, places and incidents are either products of the author's imagination or are used fictitiously. Any resemblance to actual events or locales or persons, living or dead, is entirely coincidental.

First published by Cranthorpe Millner Publishers (2024)

ISBN 978-1-80378-213-3 (Paperback)

www.cranthorpemillner.com

Cranthorpe Millner Publishers

Printed and bound by CPI Group (UK) Ltd
Croydon, CR0 4YY

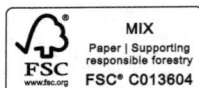

MIX
Paper | Supporting
responsible forestry
FSC® C013604
FSC
www.fsc.org

In loving memory of Celia, who lives on in these pages, but most of all in our hearts.

CHAPTER ONE

I stand in the kitchen doorway. Bonfire smoke drifts across our untidy garden, and an acrid smell of burning hangs in the air. There's something about the light at this time of year; the way the days start and end so uncertainly. The fading November afternoon, the pungent scent of wet leaves, a late lone bird calling from the stark black skeleton of the beech tree: I almost can't bear the sudden swoop of sadness. I watch my father as he marshals the scattered leaves on the grass into restless heaps.

He looks back at the house and lifts a hand, but he turns away before I can raise my arm to wave back. He's working with such purpose that tears fill my eyes and my throat constricts. After heaping the leaves together in the corner of the garden, near where the old climbing frame used to be, he stops for a moment, leaning on the rake, as the rapid fall of dusk makes it hard for him to see and carry on.

'Time to admit defeat, I guess!' he calls up the garden, to where the light from the kitchen behind me sends a long shadow sprawling onto the patio. 'What do you think, Jess? Cup of tea?'

I clench and unclench my fingers, digging them into the palms of my hands. How can I do this to him? How can I tell him what I wanted to say? Since last spring he's lurched from day to day, just like the rest of us. Something as simple as sweeping the leaves takes all his inner strength, and yet he still somehow manages to prop us both up, Mum and me. And the boys. All of us.

I turn back into the house. If only everything could be as simple as making tea. If only there were an easy way to tell him what I've decided.

*

Late last night, Sophie came into my room and perched cross-legged on the end of my bed. Ever since she was little, for as long as I can remember, it had always been her favourite way to sit. Her toes peeped round under her knees, so I could see the familiar purple and blue nail varnish, painted on alternate toes, that was beginning to chip at the edges.

'It's going to be OK, you know,' she whispered.

I clutched the duvet around me, up to my chin. My heart battered my chest so hard it hurt, in that kind of silent way when you want to be able to tell someone about it, but feel too embarrassed. Sophie would have understood, of course she would. But now, she was a part of the fear.

'Sophie?' I swallowed. 'Sophie! What... what are *you* doing here?'

My sister Sophie, who loved cats but was frightened of dogs, who only ate an orange when every last thread of pith had been peeled away, and who had watched E.T. maybe twenty times, but hated sci-fi films, sat watching me.

'Hey,' she said. 'Don't be scared, Jessie.'

She stretched out a hand towards me, her thin fingers heavy and crowded with those shiny silver rings she wore like a kind of armour.

I stared at her. Sophie, who could swim like a fish but still thought she might drown, who liked fudge but not toffee, and who loved running, very fast, through rain. Here she was, glancing round my bedroom, her eyes moving impatiently from one thing to the next. She tucked her hair behind her ears and that gesture, which I used to find so annoying, was reassuringly familiar. In one swift, easy movement she uncurled herself to dart across the floor and examine the laptop on my desk:

'Wow, Jess! This is smart! I've not seen this before!'

She gave me a long hard look, as if suddenly suspicious that I might be hiding something else from her. Sophie, who always got straight A's without appearing to do any work, and who was very good at singing the words to most of the songs we knew, but all slightly wrong and vaguely off-key, and whose hands now passed silently over and through my laptop; I could see her fingers floating into the keyboard and her hands appeared behind the screen as if it were just glass.

'Jessica.' Sophie came closer and crouched down next to me. 'Jessie.'

I tried to feel her warm breath on my face.

3

'Jessie,' she said again. 'It's all right. It's cool. Mum will be fine. She really will. I'll be looking out for her. And Dad.'

There was no warm breath. I reached out a tentative hand towards my sister, my beloved twin. So many questions, so many thoughts, jostled for position in my head, but as I faltered on the first, Sophie vanished. I thought she smiled. I ached for her then; the pain of missing her sliced through me. Sophie, who ate Christmas tree chocolates and always left the empty wrappers hanging on the branches, who loved Winnie the Pooh but not the Disney version, who never spoke to strangers when she was a little girl, and who had died, alone, on some waste ground behind the old telephone exchange. Last spring.

*

This evening, early, I go down to the kitchen. I'm full of resolve, my mind clear, my motives prepared. Better, I've decided, to talk to my mother first. She's the one, after all, who has most to lose from what I'm going to say.

Jessie. It's all right. And Mum will be fine.

Dad will be sad, of course he will, but still, it won't be the same for him. I know I'll come back, so it's not like it would be forever. He won't be losing me for ever.

'Mum?'

She's chopping a red pepper; it seems to be taking all of her concentration.

'Mm hmm?' She doesn't look up, but she's wearing her attentive "I'm-listening-but-not-looking" face.

I hoist myself up onto the opposite worktop, alongside the toaster, breadbin and mugs. It's always been my preferred place for a discussion of any sort, ever since I've been old enough to lever myself up there. Mum glances across, and then reaches for a green pepper. The soothing smell of slow frying onions wafts from the pan on the hob.

'I'm going to go. I've decided. To Denmark.' I watch my mother's face as I speak, and she watches the peppers. She finishes chopping the last one, puts down the knife with careful precision next to the chopping board, and pushes her hair away from her face with the heel of her hand.

'To find Per,' I add, in case I need to be clearer.

'I thought you would, Jess.' Her voice shakes; a stone drops into the pit of my stomach. Something more, surely – there must be something more she could say?

Mum picks up the bowl of peppers, slides them into the simmering pan of onions, and stands there staring as they steam and hiss. She takes a wooden spoon and begins, very slowly, to stir and turn the vegetables.

'Mum, I— I know this is going to be really, really difficult for you... but Sophie...' I take a breath. 'Sophie and I had been talking about it for, well, ages. You know we had. And now...'

After uni? What d'you think, Jess? We can use Grampy's money, can't we? Good idea or what?

I waver, uncertain what to say next, unable to read my mother's expression.

'And now what? Now it's just you, so maybe we won't notice? Is that what you think?' Mum turns round to look straight at me. My eyes fill; I try to swallow the urge to cry. My mother's gaze is steady.

'No,' I whisper. 'No, it's not that. Of course it's not. I just... it's just something I have to do. I don't know why – well, I do, but I hoped that Dad, well, that you'd both understand. I think he will, don't you?'

Mum turns back to the hob, opens the old, battered canister that she's kept flour in for as long as any of us can remember, then gives her head a little shake, replaces the lid, and picks up instead a tin of chopped tomatoes. She fixes the can opener to the top of it, and starts to open the tin.

'What do you want me to say, Jess? That I'm happy for you to go...?' Her voice trails away and she grasps the handle of the pan, shaking in the tomatoes. 'Have you really thought it through? I mean, *really*? You have no idea...' She stirs the mixture with sudden vigour.

'No idea about what, exactly?' I press my fingers against the thin edge of the worktop, feel it cutting into my skin. I can hear my voice rising, and struggle to remember all the things I'd meant to say, all those things Sophie and I had endlessly debated.

There's got to be youth hostels or something, hasn't there, Jess? That would be good. What about cheap flights? Can you get cheap flights d'you suppose?

Before I came into the kitchen, I'd arranged the careful explanations in my head. Now they tumble around with abandon. I close my eyes, tight, and I start to count silently, pressing my fingers in turn for each number.

6

When I reach ten, I look again at Mum, and she's reached across to the windowsill and is tearing some basil leaves from the pot of herbs that stands there. The heady scent floats in the air. She adds the shredded leaves to the pan.

'Jess.' She leans back against the counter, and her words are more measured. 'Jessie.' Her eyes hold mine and she searches my face. I know I must look stricken.

'I just don't want you... hurt, maybe, or, I don't know, disappointed. Even if you found him, after all this time, even then, *he doesn't know*, remember? Are you going to suddenly appear and announce who you are? Is he going to believe you? Why would he? How will you find him? How will you get there? Where will you stay?'

'Don't you think I've thought of all those things already? For God's sake, Mum, I'm not a child! I am capable of working things out. Do you honestly think I'm not going to spend... hours, days, weeks, months, even! Planning it, researching. Sophie and me, we'd already... well, we'd already done some stuff. Together.'

Denmark! Do you know anything about Denmark, Jess? Bacon? Yeah! Lots of bacon! Pastries? They must make those. But where is it, exactly?

Geography was never Sophie's strong point.

On an impulse, I slide off the worktop and go over to put my arms around my mother, burying my head against her shoulder. We stand wrapped together like that for a moment, a mutual comfort blanket, and then Mum reaches back and turns off the heat on the hob.

'We'll talk about it properly.' She holds my shoulders as if they are her most precious possession, and shakes her head a little as she meets my eyes. 'But later. Not now. Supper's nearly ready. The boys will be down any minute. Can you wait, Jess? Just for a bit? I need time too. Just to have a think.'

'I'll lay the table.' I move away to rummage for cutlery in the dresser drawer. 'Sorry, Mum. Of course we can talk later. I've waited this long, I can wait a bit longer. There's a lot to decide... I'd really like your help. Yeah, of course you need some time.'

Sometimes, the grief rises up like a tsunami, threatening to overtake us, toss us around like pieces of wreckage, abandon us on some high, unreachable rock. Sometimes it laps around the edges, nudging and worrying, still there, but biddable. Making plans for the future is the only way I can feel Sophie is with me still; it's important not to lose sight of what we had decided together. The grief doesn't disappear, but it's more manageable. And in my head, I can hear Dad's familiar mantra: 'Whatever makes you happy, girls. You've only got one life. So enjoy!'

CHAPTER TWO

We loved to hear the story of how our mother met Mike. As we grew up and grew older, it seemed the very essence of romance, of chance, of uncontrived circumstance. A real-life love story.

'If you hadn't walked along that street...!' There was glee in Sophie's voice. Our parents glanced at each other, smiling. It was as if they, too, could never quite believe the way things had happened.

'And seen the photo place,' I added, anxious to play my own part in the familiar story.

'Ah well, it was destiny, girls. Your Mum and I, we were just meant to meet.'

It was a story of "ifs" and "buts".

Laura, our mother, hurrying to work, and taking what she hoped was a short-cut, convinced as she was that she would otherwise be late. Life back then was one big hurry. We lived with my grandparents, John and Frances, in the rambling Victorian villa in Altrincham where Mum had grown up. Now Sophie and I were growing up there too. But it was Mum who cared for us in the mornings, dressing us, brushing our hair and making our breakfast, all in a whirl of activity while she herself showered and dressed, made sandwiches for lunch, checked her bag and left instructions for our day with Gran and Grampy. So every morning she seemed out of breath as she kissed us goodbye.

'Jessica's turn to be first today, Sophie. No, no, now, no fuss! You were first yesterday. Bye my lovelies, bye, love you both.' The door would bang behind her, and we would hear her feet running down the path. 'Late, late again! Oh God, always late!'

Then the house would settle around us, our messy remains of breakfast cleared, tired rumpled beds smoothed and coaxed into readiness for the night, and our day with Gran, with its comforting blend of routine and outings and activities, would begin.

Until the day of the short-cut down an unfamiliar road when, as Mum checked her watch and hitched her bag under her arm, she noticed, across the street, a photographer's studio.

Coming out of her college several hours later, her bag even heavier now with the typed opinions of twenty sixth-formers on the Peasants' Revolt, she resolved to find the studio and have a look in the window.

'And if you hadn't...' Dad would say at this point in the story.

'If I hadn't, I wouldn't have seen your Special Easter Prices sticker.' Mum always started to giggle at this point.

'But Mum,' Sophie would interrupt, 'don't forget, you didn't know, you just thought, what a lovely surprise for Gran and Grampy. A photo of me and Jess! So you thought you'd just go in and ask.'

'But it was all booked up!' I added. 'No spaces left.' I loved the melodrama of this particular part of the story.

Then we had to hear of how, when they so nearly didn't meet, fate intervened, and someone whose child had measles cancelled a sitting.

'If they hadn't...'

'But they did!'

The best episode was still to come. One cold morning in the Easter holidays, our mother, flustered and of course a little late, had to negotiate our twin buggy through the narrow studio doorway.

'Can I help you?' That was Clancy, Dad's receptionist at the time: Clancy of the scarlet lips, nose ring and spiky purple hair, raising an already surprised eyebrow even higher, and glancing up from her perusal of a celebrity magazine. For some reason, this had disconcerted Mum even more.

'A portrait sitting... we're booked, my little girls, that is, are booked for the Easter Special. Sorry, sorry if we're late...' As she stooped to release us both from the buggy, Sophie scrambled out, and with a delighted crow of laughter, ran past a speechless Clancy and in through the door behind her desk marked: "DO NOT ENTER! PHOTO SESSION IN PROGRESS!"

It wasn't in progress, as it turned out. The studio had been empty except for a startled Mike, who scooped up the joyous Sophie and carried her back to join us, before introducing himself and taking us through to start our session.

We were two years old then, Sophie and I, and our memories of that momentous day are not our own. We've borrowed them over the years, from the long-winded reminiscences of our parents – both of them so good at spinning tales – and we've made them ours.

'I thought you and Clancy must be an item!' Mum would muse. 'And how boring I must have seemed to you in comparison. Not to mention having two small people in tow. Pretty brave you were, really, thinking about it.'

'But not as brave, by and large,' Dad would add, winking at Sophie and me, 'as if I'd actually been going out with Clancy...'

When they married, two years later, Dad adopted us, Sophie and me. We always knew he wasn't our real father, but, as far as we were concerned, he became our proper Dad. "Daddy" when we were little, "Dad" as we reached teenage years.

'Not your *biological* father.' Mum was always very clear about the distinction, about using the right words. There was a difference, she said, between a real father and a biological one. Anyone could be a biological father, but not everyone could be a real one.

That took a special sort of person.

We were lucky, all three of us, that Dad had turned out to be one of the special sort. There was also another difference, she said. A difference between love at first sight, and the gradual recognition that this was the person you wanted to spend the rest of your life with. Sometimes it was the same thing. But often it wasn't.

Sophie believed only in love at first sight. Anything else was boring, in her view. Sophie, who liked Marmite, but not jam, and loved Wuthering Heights...

Heathcliff! Imagine!

And Peter Pan...

Although I'd hate to not grow up, wouldn't you, Jess? I just can't wait!

And was frightened of clowns, or anyone in a mask...

So creepy.

And who slept with Lucas Fleming on her sixteenth birthday.

A year after our parents married, Alex was born. We adored him. And two years later, we adored Toby too. The boys annoyed us a lot of the time as well: they crawled or staggered over our games of Happy Families, or Snap, or Pairs, as we arranged the cards with care all over the floor; they scrawled and scribbled over cherished pictures; they screamed and cried when we were watching our favourite programmes; and they took our mother's attention, when before it had been just for us. But despite these aggravations, we loved them. We competed over which little brother liked which of us best, we dressed them up like dolls, and we instigated elaborate games of make-believe, where they always had to play the supporting roles.

When we went out with Mum, the boys in the double buggy Sophie and I had once shared (now somewhat past its best) and the two of us holding onto one side each, there would always be someone who stopped to admire us, the perfect little family.

'So different!' Every time, at least one passer-by would make that comment.

And every time Mum would respond, 'Yes. They *all* take after their father.'

Then on she would march, the humour of the situation carving, when no one could see, an irrepressible grin on her face. Her two little boys with their dark curly hair, and her blonde, blue-eyed daughters.

Then, back then, we never understood.

CHAPTER THREE

After supper, it's Toby's turn to load the dishwasher. Dad has stayed in the kitchen to help him, impervious as ever, it seems, to the clatter of cutlery and plates and the endless complaining. My mother's getting ready for her book group meeting. She spends some time searching for the book she needs to take, and leaves in her usual hurry.

I wonder whether she'll unburden herself to the group. They're mostly old friends of hers, people who've seen each other through all the highs and lows of parenting. Several of them are friends Mum made once we'd moved to the village, and who now have teenage children of my brothers' ages. I've known them all, as they have known me, for a large part of my life. I think my mother uses the group as a kind of therapy. Each monthly meeting since Sophie died has been a brief beacon in her storm of grief; an escape from the black cloud of reality that hovers at home. For a few hours she can almost forget. But it never disappears completely: that stark fact of having only three children where before she'd had four.

15

'You'll never guess,' she'll tell them tonight, 'what Jess wants to do.'

They'll then throw her their lifelines: 'No! I don't believe it!' and 'Oh Laura! You poor thing!' and 'You're *so* strong, Laura. How do you manage?' And rescued, she can bob along in her choppy sea of emotion, buoyed up by her friends' support, saved briefly from the clammy depths of despair. I sound cynical, I think, but if I'm honest I'm glad for her. Glad my mother has friends who, even if they didn't – couldn't – understand, at least listened without judgement. Because in our family, we all need that.

Some of my friends never found the words. I could see how upset they were; I could see the sympathy in their eyes. But lacerated as I was with my own misery, so much worse than theirs, I wasn't able to give them an easy opening. So mostly we avoided the subject. My closest friends – Polly, Karen, and Em – reached out to me. Wordless, often, they seemed to know what to do. They hugged me, or held me, and they listened when I needed to talk.

Now, as I wander into the living room, I hear the thumping on the stairs which indicates that Toby has, in his view at least, finished his dishwasher chores, and is disappearing into his bedroom. A soft click in the hall tells me that my father has gone into his studio and closed the door. But Alex is stretched along one of the sofas, playing with his phone, a contrived look of careless concentration on his face. He gives a grunt, and swings his legs onto the floor so that I can share the sofa. It's the best one for watching television. That's what I want. I want to immerse myself in the mindless wash of a programme. That way I won't have to make any decisions, or ponder any dilemmas – at least for the rest of the evening.

'Where's the remote?' I ask.

Alex grunts again. It's an unintelligible sound. I turn to look at him.

'Alex?'

'What? What's the matter?' His eyes never leave his phone.

'The remote. Are you sitting on it?'

Above us comes the familiar creak of floorboards from Toby's room. Alex shifts a little and feels with his hand around the sofa. 'Nope.'

While I get up and start moving papers and magazines off the floor, picking up an old apple core, an empty mug and some CDs and putting them on the coffee table, he fiddles a little more with his mobile.

'Jess?'

I look at him again, properly this time. He's texting. His thumbs move rapidly, and his brow furrows with the absorption of the task. What's happened to him? What's happened to that small boy with the big grin and unruly hair? When did his legs grow so long that they seem to fill the floor in front of him? His voice, too: when did those constant comments and that babbling stream of questions requiring instant and definitive answers dry up, and when were they replaced by these monosyllabic croaky grunts? Some time since last spring, while we've all been immersed in a trench of despair, Alex became simply my brother and stopped being my little one.

'Jess?' he says again, avoiding my gaze. 'What you were saying to Mum. In the kitchen. Earlier.'

I straighten the papers on the table into an unnecessary pile of precision.

'Yeah? What about it?'

His attention is fixed on the phone. 'Just, I heard you. That's all.'

I sit down on the small space of sofa next to him and curl my legs under me.

'And...?'

A trumpeting sound signals that his text has been answered. He frowns as he starts to read the message, and then a slow grin restores the old Alex. The one I thought we'd lost. It occurs to me that at least one of his friends must manage more than a grunt of communication. Perhaps Alex does, too, when he's typing. Just not when he's speaking.

'You're going away.' His voice is gruff.

'Well, for a bit. Just to – you know – try and find Per.' I attempt to sound nonchalant. 'We'd been planning it, Sophie and me. But I'll be back.'

I uncurl my legs and find I'm sitting on the lost remote control.

'It seems like...' Alex puts down his phone, leans forwards with his elbows on his knees, rubs his face with his hands, then runs his fingers into his hair and stares at nothing on the carpet in front of him.

'What? Seems like what?'

My thumb is poised over the TV control; it's rare for me to have first choice of a programme.

'First Sophie, now you. It seems like... everyone's going, and no one cares. What's going to happen, Jess?' A tear runs down his face, and he brushes it away with the back of his hand. 'Don't you think it's kind of selfish, wanting to go now? After everything that's happened?'

With deliberate care I put down the control.

'Yeah, it could seem like that, I suppose, but Sophie's gone, Alex, and...' I take a few deep breaths, '... and this is something I just have to do. For me. But it's for Sophie too. She's never coming back, but I told you, I'll be back. Of course I will.'

I find it hard to look at him. I pull out a cushion from behind me, and hug it against my chest.

'I see her sometimes.' Alex's voice is very small.

'What?'

He's dropping his phone from one hand to the other.

'Sometimes, she walks past my bedroom door. Or she's just standing out in the garden, and then she goes.'

'Alex,' I shift closer and reach out my hand. 'Alex, that's just... I think that's just because you want to see her. It's like... a memory of her. It's OK though. It's OK.'

He pulls his knees up to his chin away from my hand, so his arms are clasped tight around them, and mumbles indistinctly, 'Sometimes it's you, Jess. Sometimes I think it's Sophie, but it's just you.'

What do I know?

I think I have a monopoly on grief, but here we are, all of us, trying to find our own little path through the wilderness Sophie has left behind. After she died, everything changed, yet life stayed the same. We still had to eat: my parents still had to shop, and cook food that at first no one wanted. Alex and Toby went back to school, and after a while I went back to Warwick for the last few weeks of my second year there. And life went on. It's just that Sophie, who liked sugar on strawberries but not cream, who had practised every day for three weeks when she was ten until she could walk on her hands right across the kitchen floor, and whose earrings never matched "*just because*", isn't here anymore.

For a while, Alex and I remain silent. He doesn't resist when my arm creeps round his shoulder. Then he gives a great shuddering sigh.

'I just miss her,' he mutters. 'Really, really miss her. And now... you're going too.'

'But I told you. I'll be back. Of course I will.'

We hear Toby moving across his room upstairs, then his footsteps on the landing, and then the rhythmic thuds that indicate his rapid descent down the stairs two at a time, and three at the bottom.

I ruffle Alex's hair. 'Oh well, luckily, you won't miss *me* at all! Or only in a good way. Hey, guess what?' I say, and I reach out to snatch up the remote. 'We are *so* not going to watch football tonight.'

After a moment we both laugh.

*

The area of wasteland where Sophie's body was found was cordoned off.

In other circumstances we would all have found the police activity compelling. And the media attention – that might even have been thrilling. But that would have been for a life less cherished. A life unmourned. Now we only longed for them all to go away, and let us get on with missing Sophie.

They had found a carrier bag, they said, nothing in it apart from an empty packet of mixed nuts. There were also a couple of beer cans, drained of any liquid, and Sophie's shoes – her favourite, but very uncomfortable, shiny heels. They lay abandoned near where Dad had found her body.

At first, we were questioned quite closely by detectives. They quizzed me gently and carefully, but I was left haunted by the thought that her death was somehow my fault, that I could have said or done something differently, and Sophie would still be alive. My worst fear was that she'd somehow guessed my secret, the one I thought I'd hidden from her so well.

I still believed that any minute now, she'd stroll in and she'd be alive; there would be no blue and white striped tape and it would all have been some sort of mistake.

They asked Dad for his account of what had happened. Every last detail.

And they spoke to Lucas Fleming for a long, long time.

We had to look in Sophie's room. Clothes that she'd rejected for that evening lay abandoned on her bed and on the

21

floor. A cheese sandwich with one bite out of it, and a mug of cold tea – filmed with a thin veil of stale milk – stood on her chest of drawers, bleak reminders of Mum's determination that we should always have something "sensible" to eat before we went out.

They wanted to know if she'd kept a diary and, if so, where it would be. I stayed silent.

'Jess, lovey, if you know, if you can find it... it's only to help.' My mother spoke like everyone else: no sharp edges, a joyless weight to her words, their borders dulled by grief. 'If they have to look, the room – Sophie's room – will get turned upside down. We don't want that.'

There was a diary. It was one of those old-fashioned five-year ones, which she'd started in 1998, the year we were going to be sixteen, after she'd been given it for Christmas. It was in her room, in an old biscuit tin. It had a lock and a key, and the key was somewhere else. But I knew it wouldn't help. What Sophie wrote in her diary rarely resembled the truth, I'd decided. So why would we want people reading a fantasy?

*

I walk between headstones whose inscriptions have become as familiar to me as the shop signs in our village. "Florence, beloved wife of Arthur", "Clementine, taken to live with the angels", "In loving memory of Gladys Mary, a very dear wife and mother" and "Marcus, who fell asleep too soon". Above me, the rooks never cease their relentless cawing, flapping out from the bare branches with a slow steady beating of wings into the grey desolate sky.

I follow the tarmac path and turn down to the grassy area between the graves, taking a route that is now as unchanging and instinctive as any in my life. The wet grass is brushed flat by other footsteps, other recent visitors to the cemetery. The marks of the living, while the dead lie silent and unmoving beneath them. I carry a watering can filled with fresh water from the tap by the gate, and a bag of evergreens cut from our garden and the hedge in the lane outside.

Sophie is sitting by the grave, cross-legged on the damp ground. She tucks her hair behind her ears with her usual impatience.

'What kept you?' she says. 'You've been ages.'

I drop the bag of greenery and put down the watering can on the grass.

'Stuff,' I reply. 'What do you think? Places to go...'

'... people to meet,' she chimes, and then: 'Wow! I like it! So *that's* why...'

I reach my hand up to my hair. It feels very odd to have lost the swing of it when I move my head; odd to have a fringe, and nothing covering my ears.

'Very neat!' Sophie is admiring. 'Very urchin and all that. Who was, you know...?'

'Audrey Hepburn.' We loved the old classic films. 'It was time for a change, I guess, and it means I look...'

'Less like me.'

We've so often been able to finish each other's sentences. She stares at me with an odd expression. There is a silence.

From the field next to the cemetery a dog barks, and a cloud of birds fly chattering into the air before descending again into the hedgerow. Over the Downs, to the south, a raw sun filters through the dank mist and casts a brief low light over the gravestones. It's only three o'clock, nearly the shortest day. Beyond the perimeter bushes, a thin spiral of smoke creeps cautiously upwards. I can smell the burning garden waste, the scent of it pungent in my nostrils. I tip the stuff I've brought out of the bag.

Our parents created Sophie's grave with care. My mother chose a soft pearly grey for the stone, rejecting the black marble suggested to us as being most resilient to the elements. "Our beloved Sophie" it announces at the top. We'd all agreed on the wording, and the inscription below was hewn with a deliberate disjointed unevenness. If you were passing you would have to stop and read it carefully, letter by letter. Word by word. It's unpredictable, like the person it commemorates.

I crouch down to remove the dead flowers from the little vase in the middle of the grave. 'I got you ivy, and laurel, and holly,' I say, 'and some of these. Dad says they're Christmas roses, but they've got some proper name too, I can't...'

I look up. Sophie has gone. The grass where she's been sitting glistens with drops of moisture, the blades uncrushed.

I still can't believe that for the rest of my life, whatever I do and wherever I go, Sophie, whose favourite colour was blue, and who liked eating mussels but not snails, will always be only here.

CHAPTER FOUR

'Always wanted,' Mum would assure us whenever asked. '*So* wanted. Just not... *planned.*'

Sophie and I had endless discussions about our conception and arrival in the world, especially as we became older and turned into teenagers. We grew up surrounded by people – our parents and grandparents – who loved and cared for us, but what we really needed to know about was our absent father and, more especially, why he was absent. As far as we were concerned, Mike was our dad, our "real" father. Not some anonymous, long-lost Scandinavian. It was more about understanding our heritage. We never used those words of course, but the unspoken reality, the meaning, hovered between us. It formed the lynchpin of our plans.

So we found it harder to accept our mother's vague explanation as the years went by, her assertions that it had all been for the best. Sophie refused to believe there could be a rational explanation.

He was some sort of nutter, Jessie, I bet! We've probably had a narrow escape. Let's hope it's not genetic!

Our mother, when pushed, insisted that she hadn't wanted to tell him, this mysterious boyfriend. He had had all his life before him, she said, and ambitions, and plans, and none of that would have included one child, let alone twins.

'But what about you?' Sophie demanded. 'You had plans too and... and all that.'

We were sitting round the kitchen table with Mum one spring evening, soon after our fifteenth birthday. An assortment of photos from the last couple of years was spread in front of us, while we tried to decide which ones to keep and put in albums.

Mum picked up a picture of Alex and Toby, triumphant on skateboards, taken just before Toby fell off and broke his arm. She gazed at it.

'Yes, I did,' she admitted. 'But my plans were... adaptable.'

For someone who, in other circumstances, so loved to spin a yarn, my mother could be maddening in her reluctance to be pressed. Little by little, piece by piece, Sophie and I had knitted together fragments of information over the years. We started to acquire a long, straggling, woolly biography. We had learned his name, Per – sounding like Peer, but spelt differently – and where he came from, and how they met as students in Mum's final year, and how much they had meant to each other.

Kind of weird, Jess, that his name's pronounced like that. Like Brighton Pier! Well, rather appropriate, I guess...

Sophie had thought this quite hilarious when she was younger.

But what we found unbelievable was that, after all this time, Per still didn't know about us.

Now Sophie was pushing back her chair abruptly and running out into the hall and up the stairs. I pressed my face into my hands, and in my head, I started to count; I knew exactly what Sophie would have in her hand when she came back into the kitchen. Mum and I heard the bedroom door slam shut behind her as she thundered back down again, clasping a photo in a small metal frame.

'Look at him, Mum, look at him,' Sophie was insisting. I stopped counting, and lifted my head. Sophie was pushing the picture in front of our mother.

'I know, Sophie.' Mum sounded weary. 'I know.' She was still holding the photo of Alex and Toby; she put it down.

'You gave us this. Don't you remember? Ages and ages ago! You gave us this because we kept asking you. We kept saying – what did he look like?'

'And it's us,' I said quietly. 'He looks like us, or rather, *we* look like him. A bit.'

Mum ran her hands through her hair, and sighed. 'Quite a lot. I think you both look very like him. Which is... great.'

I hooked my legs round under my chair and looked across at Sophie before I said, 'Don't you regret it? Don't you ever think...?'

Mum covered my hand with one of hers, and then did the same with Sophie. 'No!' she said. 'No regrets. But we were lucky, weren't we, that I had Gran and Grampy? I couldn't have done it without them.' She picked up the picture of the boys again, and studied it. 'And lucky,' she added, 'that I met Mike. That he became your dad. A lot of life is like that, I guess. You think it's going one way, and then – whoops! Something happens.'

'Like us.' Sophie had put down the picture of Per, and was concentrating on building a house with other photos, propping them against each other like cards. They kept falling over.

'Yes. Like you two. Now,' my mother's voice became brisk, 'quick, before Dad and the boys get back from football. Which ones out of this lot, do you think?'

*

I push open the little wooden gate that still hangs in the slightly lop-sided way that it always has done, and I walk up the path to my grandparents' house.

I know where my grandmother will be, and as I follow the path round the side of their cottage to the back, I can see her in the wooden summerhouse at the end of the garden. The earlier frost still silvers the parts of lawn untouched by the watery sunshine.

She looks up as I approach, a smile replacing the studied concentration on her face, puts down her brush, and moves her glasses up onto her head. I close the door behind me with care.

'Jess! What a lovely surprise! Your hair! Oh, I love it, it really suits you so short.'

It's nearly as cold in the summerhouse as it is outside. I can see Gran's words forming delicate wispy clouds as they come out of her mouth. She's swathed in layers of scarves, a wool jacket tight over the top of a thick sweater, her feet encased in furry boots, a fleecy hat pulled down over her ears, and fingerless gloves on her hands.

'Gran!' I reach over to touch her fingers. 'It's freezing! *You're* freezing!'

She picks up the brush again, settles her glasses back on her nose, and turns to her easel. 'Have to make the most of the light at this time of year, Jess. You know that.'

I move to stand next to the small electric heater that she uses only sparingly, and I peer over her shoulder at her latest painting, the one in progress. She has drawn an untidy sketch already, and is filling in the outlines with a thin wash of watercolour. It's a family playing on a beach, kites swooping above them, boats dipping on the waves, a large seagull in the foreground.

'Picture book commission?' I guess out loud.

'Mm.' She's frowning now as she moves the brush across the paper, the colours merging and blending with a deliberate untidiness.

Sophie and I owned copies of every single picture book Gran had illustrated when we were younger. We loved to leaf slowly through each one, trying to spot a resemblance to us in some of the different characters she portrayed.

This girl is one *of us, Jess. Probably me. I think it looks more like me.*

I lean back against the paint-splashed table that stretches the length of the back wall, taking care not to move any of the jumble of half-finished sketches that litters the surface. 'Gran? Have you got a minute?'

She squints sideways at me. 'A minute? Or a bit more?'

I make an apologetic face.

'Pop into the house, Jess. Grampy's in there somewhere. Make us all a coffee and I'll be with you in two shakes.'

In the kitchen, brushes and pencils litter the work tops, together with odd half-finished pictures that have managed to escape from her summerhouse studio, squeezed tubes of oil paint, and bits of charcoal. Fleeting smudgy portraits of Sophie and me and the boys are stuck up haphazardly on the walls, although some have migrated to unexpected empty corners of different rooms around the cottage. Besides being an illustrator, Gran exhibits paintings in small local galleries and shops, and her work in progress is often scattered around the house. She likes experimenting too, with different types of material. I move a heap of assorted pieces of textured fabric – coarse-woven cloth, corduroy, thin silky stuff, and hessian – and gather them into a pile next to a tray of feathers and sand and torn tissue paper, so that I have room to fill the kettle and switch it on.

I can hear someone moving in the next room, and wander in there to find my grandfather poring over one of his old road atlases. Some of Gran's paintings and pictures are stacked up at one end of the table; a hoard of Grampy's atlases fills the remaining space. Dust motes hover and float in the streaks of sun slanting through the window as he turns the pages. Without looking up, he waves a hand, and then beckons me over. 'Do you see, Jessie? This road here. Look at it! Do you see how it used to run? Round the hills, look, by the river. Beautiful, beautiful.'

'And now, Grampy?' I know of old my expected response, and before he answers, I hear Sophie.

Well! Now! That's it, isn't it? Bloody – excuse my French – great motorway. Straight through the lot!

He closes the book with a sigh, adding another small cloud of dust to join the specks whirling and scurrying in the sudden draught. 'Now? That's the trouble, Jessie. You've said it. Now? Bloody – excuse my French – steaming great motorway. Straight through, Jessie, straight through the lot.' He shakes his head with a slow sadness. 'Nobody cares any more. Our countryside – pff! Just being swallowed up!'

My grandfather's passion is maps. For as long as I can remember they've jostled for space on shelves, sprawled over the table, and crowded the walls. Every type of map you can imagine has squeezed its way into the cottage somewhere. Framed prints of old English counties march up the staircase wall, crammed next to family photos, and elbowing Gran's abstract oils for entitlement to space. Ordnance survey maps, squashed into a bookcase, have become so creased that it's almost impossible to see any roads or symbols along their folds. The road atlases, some many decades old and recording routes long since vanished or hidden, are usually packed on a shelf in the hall (because, 'You never know,' Grampy would say. 'Never know when they might be needed. There they are, all ready. Just in case.' Just in case of what, nobody ever quite understood). Now they're teetering on the table.

'John? John! Is Jess with you?'

We hear Gran calling from the kitchen, and as we go back to find her, my grandfather puts his arm round my shoulders, giving me a small tight hug. 'So good to see you, Jessie. Always so good.' His voice breaks a little.

*

When Sophie still hadn't come home, and there had been no phone call, no text, Mum had called Gran and Grampy. My grandparents were night birds, they usually stayed up late, but they would only expect a phone call at that time of night to be some sort of worrying news; as my grandfather answered, I could hear the anxiety etching his voice as it boomed out from the receiver.

'It's OK, Dad, nothing to worry about, really. Sorry to bother you so late. We were just wondering... Sophie? She's not with you, is she?'

They had wanted to drive over straight away. They were persuaded against it, but only with difficulty. In the end it was Dad – the adored son-in-law, the rock, the anchor – who had to speak to them, reassure them, explain they were most help staying in their own home, just in case.

That had always been one of Grampy's favourite sayings. Most of his reasons for many of his actions were "just in case".

33

Now, we could hear his tone rising. 'Just in case? Just in case what, Mike? You don't think…?'

'I don't think anything,' Dad said, with a calmness I couldn't believe he was feeling. 'There's going to be a perfectly simple explanation, and so there's no point you two coming all the way over here. We'll let you know as soon as she's back.'

Gran had taken the phone then. 'Mike, have you tried ringing her? Her mobile…'

Dad ran his hand through his hair, and he tugged it as if that way he could root out his worry and his fear, as well as his frustration at pointless questions. He gazed up at the ceiling as if some hope or inspiration would float down and everything would be put back to normal, and Sophie would walk in the door.

Oh, I'm sure I told Jess – sorry! You weren't worried, were you?

I could hear him struggling to keep his voice even. 'Of course, Frances. Of course we have. She's not answering. Jess keeps trying. We'll let you know.'

He handed the phone back to Mum, and turned to me. 'Are you absolutely sure…?'

I was gripping my mobile with both hands, tight, tight. I looked down at it again, pressed re-dial, and held it to my ear.

'Dad, what… she was fine. I told you. She said she'd be just a minute. She needed to speak to Lucas, she said. Just for a moment.' I held the phone again between my hands; Sophie's voicemail could be heard cutting in.

As Mum replaced the handset, Dad took his jacket off the peg in the hall. 'You two stay here. She must be somewhere, had an accident maybe. Fallen over. Don't worry.'

My mother sat down on the stairs, her arms wrapped around herself. 'OK. But as soon – as *soon* – as you find her, phone us. Got your phone?'

The front door closed, quietly; I went to sit next to my mother, wedged beside her on the third step. I closed my eyes, and in my head, I began to count.

*

I'm not sure what I expect my grandparents to say, but they sit in silence for what seems like forever.

I'm holding my mug of coffee. In the time it's taken to tell them my plans, it has cooled enough to start drinking. Their mugs sit in front of them on the kitchen table, untouched. I press my lips together in an effort to keep quiet and shift a little on the hard wooden chair.

My grandfather clears his throat, a sure sign he's finding it difficult to know how to start. 'Well, Jessie, you know...' He tails off.

My grandmother has already taken off her boots and left them by the back door, and thrown her jacket over the back of an empty chair. Now, as she sits down, she peels off her gloves, and pulls off her hat, and puts them on the radiator next to her. Then she readjusts her glasses on her nose, and peers at me with an earnestness I find unsettling.

'You know, we've only ever wanted what's best for you, Jess dear. I think that's what Grampy is trying to say. You must know, don't you, that we've already heard a little about your plans. Your Mum rang... yesterday?' She looks across the table at Grampy for confirmation.

He nods, and clears his throat again. 'We want you to be happy. And if you really think this is going to make you happy, then go. Go and find this man. But we're terribly...' and his voice trails away again.

'Terribly worried, Jessie darling, that it won't make you happy.' Gran raises her eyebrows at my grandfather and his little nod back to her confirms what he's left unsaid. 'After all this time... it's not as if you don't have a simply wonderful dad already. Are you sure you want to go and find a stranger, and then be... well, bitterly disappointed, perhaps?' She picks up her mug to take a mouthful. 'I'm afraid we just think it's madness, really. After everything. Everything that's happened.'

'But that's just it!' I blurt out. 'That's the whole point! After everything that's happened! After Sophie died, is what you mean. Why doesn't anyone just say that? *After Sophie died*. She died...' I can hear my voice begin to quiver, and I take a breath. '... But *I'm* still here, and this is what we planned. *We planned to go and find him*. So... what? I just forget about that? He's our father, for fu— for heaven's sake! There's part of us, of me, that's just him. I can't help it if nobody likes that fact, but it is a fact. I want to know things. *We* wanted to know things. I want to know what he looks like, and where he lives, and what he does, and… does he have children? Other children? What's his favourite food, does he like jazz, or… I don't know…'

I bury my head in my hands for a few seconds before facing my grandparents again. They're both quiet and still, their expressions unfathomable.

'It's not like it's our fault. None of this was ever our fault.' I've started to shake now, and I stop speaking and put my mug down before I spill it, and stare with impotent fury at the table because none of this is my grandparents' fault either. Of course I know that.

My grandmother gets up from her chair, moves round the table next to me and puts her arm round me. She holds me fast for a few seconds, and presses her cheek against my head. My grandfather reaches out with both his hands – the hands that first showed me how to ride a two-wheeler without falling off, and held out maps to show me how much bigger the world is than you could imagine, and helped me hold binoculars so that I could see every detail on a jay's feathers – and he grasps my hands with his, now brown-spotted with age I realise suddenly, and stops mine from trembling.

'I'm sorry,' I whisper. 'I'm sorry. I didn't mean…' I shut my eyes to try and blink back the tears.

'Jessie, you don't need to be sorry,' my grandfather says. 'Does she, Frances? We didn't mean to upset you. We just want to be sure… and your Mum, she wants you to be sure… that you know what might happen. If you find him. Per.' He speaks the name with difficulty, distaste almost.

I look at him then. Gran has gone over to the kettle to make another drink. She's measuring teaspoons of granules into clean mugs, as if she's already forgotten we have three in front of us. Her back is straight and eloquent in restraint.

'Grampy?' I say, 'I thought... you never met him? Did you? Per?'

My grandfather shakes his head, as if unable to answer me. Gran turns round from the counter, a steaming mug in her hand.

'But... you must know about him,' I persist. 'Mum must have told you stuff. Didn't she? Why didn't she tell him about us? You must know why. Don't you?'

As I speak, I wonder why Sophie and I never asked that question before, why we only pestered Mum, never my grandparents. Did we imagine they were oblivious? That they had just changed their whole lives around to accommodate us all those years ago, without needing to know why the father of their expected grandchildren was so significant by his absence, an unknown, unknowing presence lurking always in the background of our lives.

'It was a very tricky time, Jessie.' My grandmother has come back to sit down with us, carrying the fresh drinks on a tray, and setting it down, a little of the hot liquid spilling over the sides of the mugs as she does so. My grandfather sighs, leans back in his chair, and folds his arms with an expression of resignation.

'Well, it was, John!' Gran exclaims, shooting him a fierce look. 'Very tricky. Your Mum came home, after her graduation, and everything was tickety-boo, lots of job applications being sent off, and then she thought maybe she'd travel instead for a bit, before getting a proper job, sorting out a career, and then wham! We found out – well, she told us one evening – that you two were on the way. Except, it wasn't "you two" then.'

'Just the one we thought, at first,' Grampy interrupts. 'And that was...'

My grandmother gets in first, and says swiftly and firmly, '... *Lovely* news! In a way. But... not what we were exactly expecting, was it, John?'

Some of this is familiar. The repeated tales over the years of the delight of our arrival, the sudden admission to hospital where we were delivered by a hurried caesarean section, the exclamations over our respective sizes (Sophie rather large, and me a little smaller), the way our grandparents had had to change not only their lifestyle but also their home, and revert to a life they must have thought they'd left behind twenty years before. Then there were the assertions by everyone – Mum, Gran and Grampy, even Uncle Tim, our mother's beloved older brother – of how we were wanted. So wanted. Just not planned.

('Not in my room!' Uncle Tim would exclaim in mock horror when he visited. 'You two aren't still staying in *my* room, are you?'

'It's not your room now,' we'd giggle, 'you've got your own house.'

He'd clasp his head in despair, and then scoop us up, one under each arm, and whirl us round until we were nearly sick with excitement, and fear, and the thrilling dizziness of it.)

'Mum never told you?' I say now. 'Mum never told you anything about him? About Per?'

My grandparents exchange glances. I can sense the tension in the air between them, and I hear Sophie:

You know what? They're about to tell you something we don't know. Good on you, Jess!

Then my grandmother says, 'It's not really up to us, Jess. You must realise that.'

My grandfather, with forced jollity, adds, 'All turned out for the best! Didn't it? We wouldn't have wanted it any other way in the end, would we, Frances?'

For a minute, all three of us stare into space and say nothing because, of course, nothing's turned out for the best. Sophie died – you could never say that was something any of us wanted. That familiar feeling of guilt starts to creep over me again, shrouding me with a nameless despair, whispering that it was somehow my fault. There must have been something I could have said or done. Maybe I should just have told her, come straight out with it. How bad could that have made things? I'll never know, of course.

Grampy is still leaning back in his chair, arms across his chest. He looks uncomfortable, as though he'd like to escape the whole situation and disappear for a while into another world, into the haven of his maps. Follow an uncomplicated trail, maybe, along a road uncluttered with stones and potholes and deep crevasses. I catch Gran's eye, and she gives me a small, worried smile across the table, her arms propped along the edge of it as if supporting not only her body but all her thoughts.

'They were very much in love,' she says, with a slow deliberation.

My grandfather is unable to stop a derisive snort. Gran and I both turn to him.

'They were, John,' Gran insists.

'Mum always said...' I begin, and then: 'Grampy, there's something you're not telling me and it isn't fair.' I glance across at Gran again. 'I know you're being loyal to Mum. I know you think it's not your place... but if it affects me, and I'm his daughter, and if I'm going to go and find him, then don't I have a right to know?' I take a deep breath.

'You need to ask Laura,' Gran mumbles, twisting her hands together in front of her. 'You need to ask your mother.'

My chair scrapes the floor with a harsh protesting screech as I stand abruptly. 'Well, I will. I'll go right now and...'

Grampy holds out his arm, so that I'd need to push past him to leave the kitchen. 'Hey, hey. Not so hasty. You've got to realise, Jess, this is a difficult time for us all. Not just you. It's stirred up lots of old memories, you deciding to go like this. We know you and Sophie always talked about it, but still...'

I stay standing, reluctant to either leave or wait. Undecided.

'The thing is, Jessie, your Mum... well, she did tell him. She did tell Per she was pregnant.' Gran's eyes have filled with tears, and she takes off her glasses and rubs her hands over her face.

I grab my chair again and sink down onto it with care while I stare at my grandmother. I think that if I keep staring and not saying anything, then the scene will unravel and rewind, and none of what she has just told me will be true.

'Why?' I ask, after a while. 'Why hasn't Mum ever said? All this time... so, he knows. Per knows about us and he's never...'

'It's not quite that simple,' Grampy intervenes, but I'm not listening.

I'm staring out of the kitchen window, and I can see Sophie perched on the rickety old garden table, her bare feet planted on the bench part. She lifts her head slowly and raises her eyebrows when she sees me looking. She's mouthing something at me, using exaggerated, over-large movements of her lips.

So, what now? That's a bit of a shocker, isn't it?

I frown. Gran and Grampy follow my gaze.

'That squirrel again!' says Grampy, pushing back his chair with unexpected vigour to stand up and rush over to the door. 'That pesky squirrel!'

When I switch my eyes back to the garden table, Sophie has gone.

CHAPTER FIVE

That year, the year when we were four and our mother married Mike, spring had arrived in a litter of sudden vicious spats of rain against the windows. Our grandparents told us, in later years, how unexpected gusts tore the newest leaves and vulnerable twigs off the trees, and hurled them around until at last they lay sodden on the ground as the wind died away. But then the uncertain flurries of rain gradually waned, and as the weather warmed it slid slowly towards May and on into a bright cloudless June. The days stretched, sun-drenched, from dawn to dusk, and life remained constant for Sophie and me. We continued to live with our grandparents while Mum moved into Mike's flat over his photographic studio and they set up home together. Every day, Mum hurried from work, arriving – usually with Mike – in time to get us ready for bed, and stay until we were asleep.

One evening, early in June, we had clambered into bed, under a thin sheet that covered each of us against the hot humid night. Puddles of sunlight dappled the sheets and the carpet

43

until Mum banished them by closing the heavy curtains. She bent down in the gloom to hug each of us in turn.

'Where are you going now?' I demanded.

'You know where,' said Mum. 'Downstairs, to have something to eat with Gran and Grampy.'

'And then?' said Sophie, her voice muffled as she lay half under her sheet.

'You know that too.' Mum turned to smile at her. 'Home with Mike.'

'Daddy,' I muttered.

'Daddy, yes. He is your Daddy now.'

'Can we come too? Why can't we come?' Sophie knelt up on her bed, and fixed Mum with a steely gaze. 'He's got us bunk beds, so we can now. I'm sleeping on the top one, remember.'

'No,' Mum sat down on the edge of my bed, 'I don't remember. I think you were going to take turns, weren't you, Jessie?'

I nodded emphatically, saying, 'But we'll miss Gran and Grampy. Won't we, Sophie?'

My mother smoothed back my hair from my face, and gave me a quick kiss. 'You'll still see them lots. Don't worry, Jessie. Now, time to sleep. Love you both.'

'To the moon...' Sophie's voice sounded from the other side of the room.

'All the way to the moon,' Mum whispered.

'And back.' It was a chorus, as the bedroom door closed nearly shut.

*

'... Plenty of time,' Grampy was saying, 'for the girls to join you. In a while. When things have settled down.'

'Settled down?' We could hear Mum fighting to control her voice. 'How can things settle down? As they are now?'

'Your dad's right,' came Gran's soothing voice. 'You could do with some time on your own now. Just the two of you.'

'Now,' our dad was saying, 'or later. It doesn't make much difference, does it? Laura spends every minute she can back here, seeing Sophie and Jess.'

There was a silence.

Upstairs, I had woken to find Sophie's bed empty. I'd tiptoed out onto the landing and crouched next to my sister, our faces squashed against the banisters, our hands gripping the struts tightly.

'They're arguing,' I whispered. 'About us.'

'Not arguing,' Sophie corrected me, in hushed tones. 'Having a discussion. That's what Gran calls it.'

We listened to the rise and fall of voices from downstairs.

'Never mind us,' our mother was saying, 'what about you? You've had us all living here, we've turned your lives upside down. Don't you want to get back to how you were?'

'After everything...' Our grandmother's voice was distinctive with its soft southern vowels, its lack of Manchester twang.

'... We just think you could do with time together, time alone.'

45

'Were you listening to Mike?' Mum's voice was rising in its fury. 'Have you any idea how difficult it is, dividing my time between two homes? Besides, they really need to be with us now. That's what they want. They were just asking me about it tonight.'

Then Dad, the peacemaker, the negotiator, added, 'It's not that Laura isn't grateful, you do know that.'

'We don't want gratitude.' Grampy was speaking so low, so quietly, that we both held our breath to hear him properly.

'... Loved it. Loved having you here. You know that. Those two little girls... We'll miss them, Laura.' There was a catch to Gran's words, an unnatural spike in her tone.

'Mum.' Our mother's voice sounded fierce, desperate. 'Have you been listening to us? At all? *Of course* I know you'll miss them. Of course I do. Of course I know how much you've done, but we need to all be together now.'

'They'll be back to see you,' Dad added. 'You won't have time to miss them! We've worked really hard to make a bedroom for them. They've seen it.'

'They love it!' Mum interrupted. 'But that doesn't mean they won't love coming back here, and staying here sometimes...'

'When it suits?' We could hear an edge in Gran's voice.

Grampy was saying, 'We're all getting over-heated here. Shall we leave this for now...?' when Sophie, her eyelids beginning to droop, lost her grip on the banister strut, and sat back suddenly on the wooden floor. Downstairs, the kitchen door, which had been only slightly ajar, was pushed open, and the voices stopped abruptly.

Jerked back to life like marionettes, Sophie and I scampered across the landing into our beds, lying breathless while we waited for our hearts to stop pounding.

'I don't like it,' I whispered, 'when they argue like that.'

'Why can't Dad just move in here?' Sophie had never understood how this couldn't happen; she had asked often, and never been given a satisfactory answer.

'We need to be a family.' I repeated what our mother had told us.

Sophie turned over, curled on her side, her sheet huddled round her, her voice sleepy, 'Well, we still can.'

*

I walk home slowly from my grandparents', unable to process and understand what they've just told me, needing time on my own to think. If Per has known about us all this time, why has he never tried to make contact? My mouth tastes sour with this new knowledge, and I can feel a familiar knot in my stomach. Perhaps, after all, it's pointless going to find him. Maybe I'm chasing a dream that's potentially a nightmare?

I find Dad and Toby in the kitchen. My father is making some soup, while Toby plays with a small juggling ball, rolling it from one shoulder to the other across his back, balancing it on one foot before flicking it neatly to the other, and then heading it carefully into one hand. He starts to repeat the routine when he sees me walk in.

'Whoa!' he says. 'Did you see that, Jess? Skill or what? Have a go!' He tosses the ball over to me and I drop it.

'Yeah!' He punches the air. 'Pathetic. Did you see, Dad?'

Dad looks up and notices my face; he's always been good at reading emotions. 'I saw you nearly land the ball on my vegetables,' he says to Toby. 'Leave your sister alone for a minute. I think she needs a bit of peace and quiet. Anyway, I thought the rule was no playing football inside?'

Toby holds up the juggling ball. 'What? Is this a *football*? No rule against this. And I have to practise. Coach says...'

I drop onto a chair at the table and lay my head on my arms, so my voice sounds muffled. 'Toby,' I say, 'just give it a break.'

Dad replaces the lid on the saucepan, and says, 'Jessie? You OK?'

I sigh. 'Yeah. Just... well, I've been at Gran and Grampy's.'

He comes to sit opposite me. 'Problem?'

I feel as if I've never needed Sophie so much. Then I remember that I still think that at least once a day. I shrug. 'It's fine. Don't worry.'

'Dad!' Toby yells. 'Soup! It's boiling over!'

He leaps up. 'Toby! It's not beyond the realms of possibility that you could...'

While Dad's turning down the heat, and mopping the spilled liquid, Toby straddles the vacant chair instead, and looks at me with the earnest expression he's had since he was a baby, both expectant and curious. 'Jess?'

I stand up slowly, ready to go up to my room. This doesn't seem the right time after all to have a discussion with my father. 'What?'

He's rolling the ball along the edge of the table, pinging it with one finger to the other hand, and back. Behind us, I can hear Dad still stirring the soup, and the clatter of bowls and spoons as he gets things ready for lunch.

'Aren't you excited?' Toby glances up, and then quickly down again as the ball nearly rolls off the table. 'Close thing!' He catches it.

'Excited?' I play for time. I know I'm being unfair to him, unkind even. But I need to use the right words, answer his questions with care.

'Denmark!' he exclaims. 'That is *so* cool! Do you think you'll find him? Per? Wow! Can I come?' His voice drops a little, and he squints over his shoulder at our father, who's prodding the vegetables in the saucepan and apparently oblivious to our conversation. 'I wish I could,' he mutters, and covers the little red and blue ball with his hand.

I sink down again and look at him, and remember the conversation I had with Alex, only the day before. Already my life seems to have cantered ahead of itself, measuring its steps in units of disbelief and shock, so that yesterday seems to belong to a different era, one where I still had a specific dream to pursue, not this new, shattered one. I need to pick up the fragments of the dream, and somehow fit them back together, but in a different shape.

'Have you been talking to Alex?' I ask Toby.

He shrugs. 'Yeah, course.'

'You know you can't come with me, Toby.' I speak softly. 'You've got school, and anyway...'

'Anyway, he's your dad,' Toby fills in. He's staring at me, and his eyes brim with tears. 'Not mine. He's yours.'

Then we chime together, 'Biological dad!' because that's what Mum has always said.

The urge to go round the table, wrap my arms around him and make everything all right is overwhelming. To breathe in his boy smell, and hug him close. I have to resist with a great effort, mainly because in my head I can hear his practised 'Yuk!'

Instead, I stand up, and I repeat what I said to Alex: 'I'll be back, Toby. You can't get rid of me that easily.' I turn round and catch a glimpse of my father's back at the hob, expressive in its determined silence, and I ask, 'Need any help, Dad?' Although what I really want to do is apologise.

Apologise? For what? None of this is your fault, Jess. And you're only planning to do what we always said. Just a bit earlier. And without me.

'I'm sorry, Dad,' I whisper. 'I'm so sorry. None of this is your fault. None of it. But I do really need your help.'

My father looks up from the pan, and replaces the lid on it. He scans my face, and he says, very quietly, 'Toby. Hop off for a bit. Why don't you take a football outside for a kick around? Lunch isn't nearly ready yet.'

We both settle down on the kitchen chairs, and I tell him about going to find Per, which of course he already knows. I repeat what I've found out from my grandparents.

50

'Did you know?' I demand. 'Did you know all this time? Why hasn't anyone ever told us?'

He doesn't answer immediately, then he gives me one of his quizzical looks. 'I can't answer that, Jessie. It's not up to me. You know that.'

'What was she thinking?' I'm beginning to shake; I can hear the fury in my voice. 'It's... obscene!'

'Jessie,' Dad grips my hand. 'No.'

'Don't tell me,' I speak through gritted teeth. 'Don't tell me to calm down!'

'I wasn't going to. It's... unfortunate that you've found out like this, but...'

'There is no way,' I glare at him now, 'no way that you can make this all right. I should have known. I *do* know. I always think you're like, the voice of reason, but when it comes down to it, you always back her up. Always.'

'Back who up?' My mother's voice comes through the hall. 'What's happened?'

I clench my fists, so my nails dig into my palms, and I hiss, 'What now? What do you suggest I do now, Dad?'

As Mum walks into the kitchen, he says, calm, unhurried, 'I think you go and find him. Per. I think you go and find him, and you tell him that your father, your English father, is very grateful to him.'

I have to force myself to glance over at my mother. She's standing staring out of the window.

'Laura,' says Dad, 'I've made the soup.'

'I can see.'

51

'After lunch, I think Jess needs to talk to you. There's a few things she needs to get straight in her head, before she goes to Denmark.'

Mum stays, still and quiet, gazing outside where the weak winter sun has finally edged its way over most of the frostbitten grass, and she whispers, 'Very grateful for what, Mike? What are you so grateful to Per for?'

'Oh, I think you know, Laura. I'm sure you do.'

CHAPTER SIX

That summer, the one after our fourth birthday, Dad adopted us. We became Mortimers: Sophie and Jessica Mortimer. That summer, too, our mother became pregnant with Alex, but it was early yet for the heaviness and lethargy that increased as her belly swelled with a life that was separate from us. That summer, we were unaware of a possible rival for our parents' attention; we remained the only stars in our family constellation.

A truce had been called on the battles that had started to dominate each evening. Our grandparents had conceded that our new little family's priority should be to all live together, however much of a struggle they felt it was for Mum to cope with such a different life. So we moved, eventually, out of our grandparents' house, the home where we had always lived, and into our new father's flat. We had bunk beds, a glorious acquisition, crammed into what Dad had always called his "junk room". We shared our space with a dusty guitar with two broken strings, boxes of papers, teetering piles of books, and lumpy black bin bags.

'Well, I like it here best,' Sophie said. 'Don't you, Jess?'

'Not best,' I admitted, a hint of uncertainty in my voice. 'Because I like it at Gran and Grampy's too.'

'But I like living here,' Sophie said, 'and then going back to Gran and Grampy. And finding all the things we've left there.'

The flat was not too far from our grandparents' place, close enough to visit often, and Sophie was right, we both loved returning to our old home. During term time Gran and Grampy continued to help out with caring for us on a regular basis while Mum was teaching. We searched, each time we visited, for confirmation of a previous existence. There was the sandpit, just out of sight behind the old woodshed, only now the sand toys were clean and tidy in a lidded box. There was the climbing frame and swing, the grass underneath sparse and trodden, with barely enough time to grow in between visits. Paints and crayons and paper were stacked neatly in a cupboard in our old bedroom, along with all the toys that couldn't quite be fitted into the flat.

Sometimes it seemed as if an eerie quiet had settled over the rambling old house, a bleak tidiness tucked in the edges of every room. It still felt like the home we knew and loved, the place where we had started to grow up, a constant and familiar haven; but it took a little while each time to reassert our positions there.

*

'We want to come too!' Sophie had announced one Sunday, spotting a planned expedition underway by our grandparents.

'Please!' I added, always the one to remember the correct way to make a request.

'Gran and Grampy are escaping,' said Mum. 'There's no room for you two this time.'

'Next week, girls,' Grampy promised. 'Why don't you come with us next week?'

We loved being allowed to join those weekend excursions. The roads and lanes that Gran and Grampy always chose to travel on were ageless, unchanging: thin throwbacks to a quieter era. Every Sunday Grampy planned the journey with the same meticulous care and precision he applied to his clients' cases at his solicitor's practice in Altrincham. Gran, usually adorned with a floating scarf, long dangling earrings and, if the sun shone, a straw hat, would pack a picnic: ham sandwiches, her famous charred wedges of flapjack, and whatever fruit was ripe in the garden. Her art box and easel would be stowed alongside the picnic basket, the tartan rug and folding chairs whose canvas seats were growing so frayed and holey that if you sat in them there was always the delicious possibility you might fall through.

On a few occasions, the pleas to our grandparents were answered, and off we would go, waving to Mum with triumph from the back seat, off on a magical mystery tour. As much a mystery to our grandfather, according to Gran, as it was to us. She always drove.

'That's how we work best,' Grampy declared when asked. 'I'm the navigator; your gran's the pilot. We're a team.'

He would open the required map with a flourish. On most excursions we ended up munching our sandwiches several miles away from the planned destination, Gran doing her best to sketch a very different view from the one she'd imagined. Undeterred, Grampy would brush the crumbs off his trousers, finish the last drop of tea from the thermos flask, and unfold the map again, with the air of a hero undaunted by defeat.

'Now, where I think we went wrong, Frances,' he would say, 'was not taking that little lane I mentioned, the one you were a bit dubious about. But never mind, never mind. A quick detour, that's all this is. We like a challenge, don't we, girls?'

Sophie and I, engrossed in dipping ripe strawberries into a plastic box of caster sugar, then slowly rolling them round with our tongues and letting them dissolve in our mouths, would nod with enthusiasm, juice spilling down our chins. We would lie back on the scratchy travelling rug, and squint up at a cloudless sky, our bare legs scraped by stiff spikes of grass poking up through the worn wool, while the basket and our grandmother's box and the faded but unbroken chairs were piled back in the boot.

Picnics with our parents usually involved some location where Dad wanted to take pictures. He had plans beyond his portrait studio. He was ambitious for success. So there was always somewhere different to explore. One day we might go to the hills, and while he set up a variety of bewildering equipment, Sophie and I paddled in becks, shrieking with anticipation of the icy cold water before our toes had even dabbled in it and making wispy posies of wild flowers and heather for our mother. Other weekends we'd drive to North Wales and spend hours on windy beaches, building castles and hurling pebbles out to sea while my father took endless photos of gulls on the rocks, or a wave as it broke on the shore.

The summer stretched before us, and that year it was full of long, hot days. We woke at night sticky with the heat, and once Mum's holidays had started, we spent hours in our grandparents' garden, jumping in the paddling pool and running through the waterfall of Grampy's sprinkler while he lamented the state of his lawn.

One weekend, our flat oppressively airless in the early morning, Mum packed a picnic, and we scurried around looking for our swimming things, buckets and spades, excited at the prospect of a promised day at the beach.

'Hats!' Mum reminded us.

'I hate my hat!' Sophie shouted. 'It just makes me *too hot*!'

Mum's voice dropped. 'Then we can't go, Sophie, sorry. It's much too hot today, lovey, the sun will burn you, make you feel ill. You have to wear one.'

'I don't care! I don't care! At all!'

'Well, that's OK. That's fine,' our father intervened. 'Just Jessie, then. She can be in the special photo I'm taking today by herself.'

As it happened it wasn't a day for taking photos. Out of the shade of the beach umbrella, standing on the hot sand or burning rocks, the light was too intense, the glare of it blinding. It wasn't really a day for spending much time at the beach at all. Sophie didn't mention once how hot her head was under her hat. After about an hour, our parents packed everything up and drove homewards, inland, to find a shady spot for lunch.

'The rest, as they say, is history!' Sophie loved to announce, years later, when regaling friends with the story.

Because in the end, the photo that changed all our lives wasn't of gulls, or waves, or hills, or the sun sparking off a tumbling stream on the moors, but a hurried, impromptu snap of Sophie and me playing on the edge of a wheat field while Mum was packing up the remnants of the picnic. We were running along beside the tall yellowing stalks, the ripe dusty heads of grain swaying above us. As we dodged in and out of the hard scratchy stems, my father captured that blurred impression, a brief image of joyfulness as we turned, laughing at each other, and I reached out to catch my sister.

He called it "Corn". Anyone who knew him would instantly recognise that it was a deeply ironic title, and when he entered the picture in a prestigious photographic competition and won, it became the image of the year. It was made into posters and greeting cards and different sized prints; for a while it was what everyone wanted to hang in their home. And although it didn't make our family's fortunes, it did change our lives. Winning the competition gave my father some freedom to decide what he really wanted to do, and where our lives should lead. Eventually, he accepted a job lecturing in photography, which gave him the opportunity to do his own work and complete the commissions that poured in after the photo became famous.

We moved down south, from the little terraced house in Altrincham where we'd lived after leaving Dad's increasingly cramped flat, to a village near Brighton, where Dad would be working, and into a larger, more spacious home. One that would accommodate us all, now that new baby Toby had joined the family after Alex. It was an old house, ramshackle and shabby, and our parents had grand plans for doing it up – renovating and redecorating and improving it – but somehow, apart from essential repairs and updating, they never found the time to do more, and grew used to it the way it was. As the walls filled up with the photos, paintings and prints that charted our family's lives, the house became indisputably ours. There was something rather comforting about its slightly down-at-heel appearance.

For our grandparents, accustomed as they had been to our family living only a few streets away, the journey down from Cheshire to visit us now seemed several hours too many. It wasn't long before they moved too, downsizing at the same time, to a cottage on the outskirts of our Sussex village. Life for Sophie and me resumed its regular satisfying tempo.

*

We eat lunch together in a silence broken only by Toby's oblivious comments.

'Jesus, Tobe, just shut it, can't you?' Alex growls at him, slurping his soup and gulping down his bread, making it clear that he wants to escape, as soon as possible, the poisonous atmosphere in the kitchen.

A threatening bunch of unanswered questions hovers in the air above us like a menacing rain cloud. Poke it, I think, and we'll all be drenched by its toxic shower. I dip my spoon in and out of my soup a few times before putting it down, and then I crumble my bread into several small grey pieces.

'Great soup, Dad,' says Toby, with unremitting cheerfulness.

'Thanks, Toby,' my father replies. He's eating his with what I feel is unnecessary haste and enthusiasm. My mother has hardly touched hers.

'Jess, if you're not going to...' Toby begins.

'Yeah, yeah.' I scrape my chair back, and hand him my bowl. 'I just need...'

I grope my way out of the room and fumble with the door into the loo that always sticks. I finally ram down the handle, stumble in, and slam the door shut behind me. I lean against it and slide down onto the floor, the tiles cold against my legs, and listen to the thump of my heart. Beside me, in a jumble, lie all the trainers and shoes and boots that have failed to fit neatly onto the shoe rack, and above them hangs our usual haphazard collection of coats and jackets. I breathe in a mixture of odours: sweaty feet, dried mud, dampness and fresh air. I want to stay in this little room, safe in its small space, and never have to confront all the unknown hidden truths that I know I must hear.

Through the closed door come the indistinct but heated murmurings of my family, probably discussing the best thing to do. Presently, I hear the bang of a door, and feet on the stairs, and faint music. I prop my head against the wall and close my eyes. I want to open them and find the world tilted back on its relentless voyage through time. I want to be out with Sophie again, that night all those months ago, out with Sophie and Karen, Polly and Em. If I open my eyes, won't it all have been a dream; the worst kind, but over? Sophie would be here after all, here even now. I start to count, but when I take my hands away from my face, I'm staring at the wall opposite, and that photo rocks into slow focus.

We have it still. Over the years it's been moved to several different locations around the house, but now it hangs in here, in the same thin black frame. It shares its space with other masterpieces: "My family" by Toby, aged three, and "Gran and Grampy" by a five-year-old Alex – my grandfather instantly recognisable by a pair of huge, over-sized glasses, and Gran wearing earrings so large she should surely have toppled over with the weight of them. There's one of Sophie's quirky photos: assorted wellington boots wearing sunglasses. And there's a pen and ink sketch I drew of the ancient apple tree in the garden, before it fell in last year's winter storm. It's a picture I hate but which my mother loves for some reason.

Friends – family friends who've known us for years – sometimes visit this cloakroom and emerge later making comments like, 'That photo! Still recognise it anywhere!' or,

'Great place to hang that picture, Mike, after it's made your fortune!'

Other visitors, people who come to the house for the first time, will say, 'The photo? In your loo? Always really liked it! Have you had it long?' or, 'So iconic, that picture. How long ago would that have been, do you think?' and, 'Those little girls, in that photo. Makes you wonder where they are now, doesn't it, and whether they're still as gorgeous?'

I gaze at the photo now, so familiar I no longer see it properly, and I yearn to go back. I want to step into that picture, and smell the heat and the dust and feel the spiky stems of wheat on my bare legs and the sun on my arms, and this time when I reach out I want to catch Sophie. Catch her and hold her tight, carry her into the present and never let her go. I close my eyes and count in fives, and when I reach sixty the trembling has almost stopped.

Mum's tapping at the door.

'Jess? Jessie? Are you all right? Open the door, lovey. Please.'

CHAPTER SEVEN

People put flowers on the waste ground near where Sophie had died. The police had cordoned off a large area with blue and white tape. Bunches of daffodils, sprays of freesias and carnations, limp posies of early wildflowers, single roses, all sorts, adorned the perimeter or were tied higgledy-piggledy on the straggling wire fence that was supposed to keep out trespassers. There were messages too, scribbled or printed on torn off sheets of paper, and left with several of the floral tributes: "Miss you, Sophie!" read one, "Never forgotten" and "Taken 2 soon". There were lots of them.

Mum and I walked down there, late in the afternoon, a couple of days after Sophie's body was found; it seemed like a hideous ritual that had to be endured. I knew neither of us wanted to go, but some sort of compulsion to see the place where Sophie was last alive had made us walk down our lane and into the High Street, then left down Furnace Lane to the old telephone exchange building, functional and red brick, and along the side of it past the brambles and through long wet grass to the ground behind. It took us ten minutes, maybe a little more; I remember I looked at my watch. Ten minutes, I thought. Ten minutes between Sophie living and dying.

When we saw what people had brought, we stopped. Close beside me, I could feel Mum shaking.

'Who's done this?' she whispered. 'Who do they think they are?'

I let go of her arm and stooped down to read some of the tributes.

'Some of them are Sophie's old friends,' I said, 'people we were at school with. Some I – I don't know. I don't know who they are. It's just something people feel they have to do. They feel terrible, I suppose, and...' I stopped to brush away the tears with the heel of my thumb. 'I guess it makes them feel better.'

Almost some kind of talisman, I was thinking, to ward off the bad luck of losing your own child, or sister, or friend, and I tried to swallow the grief that was waiting so patiently for its moment to catch me off guard. It would force me into one of those ghastly grimaces over which I had no control. The screeching: those dreadful noises that didn't belong to me, animal sounds, welling up from deep inside me. I'd heard Mum at home too – terrible, terrible wailing noises, wild and unearthly and uncontainable.

Now she was walking along beside the tape, making exaggerated detours around the flowers and messages. I breathed deeply a few times, fighting to control the tremors. My face was wet.

'This was such a bad idea,' I called over to her. 'Why have we come?' What, I thought, were we trying to prove?

A thin drizzle began to mist the air and we turned up our hoods, hunched into our coats. Bigger drops fell, splashing on to the scraps of paper. Some of them had been covered in plastic, but most of the others started to curl at the edges, and the writing was smeared until you could no longer read what they said. Rain spattered the flowers, hitting the cones of paper and drenching the petals: they began to droop. Soon they would die. They couldn't last long against this onslaught.

There was a police van parked inside the stripy tape, but only a couple of police were visible, moving methodically along the edges of the waste ground and poking in the hedge.

As we turned to go, one of the officers came over. He touched his cap. We didn't recognise him but when he spoke his voice had that familiar respectfulness and consideration in its tone that we had already come to expect. They all sounded like that.

'I'm sorry to intrude,' he murmured. 'Mrs Mortimer, Jess. But when we saw you here we wondered if you could throw any light on this. We found it this morning. Just lying in the grass over there.' He nodded in the direction and held out a mask for us to inspect, a cheap plastic mask, the sort you might buy for a Halloween party, or to frighten your neighbours. It was green, with thickly arched eyebrows and painted blood running down from its open mouth.

I looked straight at him. 'Sophie hated masks,' I said. 'She hated them. She hated people wearing them. It really freaked her out.'

He persisted. 'But do you recognise this one? Any idea where it might have come from?'

'No idea.' I lifted my face to the sky, grey and overcast, heavy with clouds, and the rain mixed with the tears on my face. I thought that, forever onwards, nothing much was going to matter. I didn't care how I answered or what he might think; I didn't even care what I looked like. I counted to ten and then I took Mum's arm again, and dug my hands into my pockets.

'What does it matter?' I said. 'It's not important, is it? You don't die because you're scared of masks.'

'Sorry to have bothered you.' He touched his cap again and turned to go, but my mother was staring at those bedraggled bunches of flowers hanging wet and limp, or battered into the grass by the rising wind.

'She hated roses,' she said.

'Pardon?' The policeman looked back. What was he? A constable... sergeant... inspector?

Was it even significant?

My mother was pointing at the single stem roses, and awkward spiky clusters of rosebuds – the sort of flowers you'd give at the last minute on Valentine's Day, or lay on a coffin. 'They've been flown in from somewhere,' Mum told him. 'Or forced. Forced to grow. It's unnatural, Sophie thought. She always said... well, she just didn't like them. She liked proper roses – garden roses.'

Roses from Kenya! Why would you do that? What's wrong with our own flowers, I'd like to know! I'd give them back, well, no, actually I'd throw them. If some bloke gave me roses like that,

I'd throw them right back at him, and if the thorns got him, then so be it.

He looked uncertain now, shifting uncomfortably from foot to foot, unsure of a reply, or if one was needed.

My mother sighed. 'So it's silly, isn't it, really? That people have wasted their money and she doesn't even like them.'

I closed my eyes. Didn't. She didn't like them. In forty-eight hours Sophie had become a past tense. How often would we all forget?

The policeman lifted the mask in a farewell gesture. 'Well, I'll just be getting back now. Sorry again to have bothered you, Mrs Mortimer, Jess.'

As we left I glanced back one last time. I tried not to think about what had happened to Sophie, what quirk of fate had chosen her to be the one who died first, and much, much too soon. And then I realised that Lucas was standing there, on the far side of the cordoned-off area, behind the tape. Standing, watching us. When he saw me look across, he turned and jogged away quickly, down the other side of the building.

*

I scramble to my feet with reluctance. I know that I can't hide in the loo for the rest of the day, and I open the door to find my mother on the other side. She's wearing her holding-it-all-together face, and I'm suddenly frightened that she may not be able to. In the space of a few days, a barrier has sprung up between us, and I'm not sure that either of us has the strength any more to dismantle it. A cold dread worms its way into the pit of my stomach. We stare at each other for a minute, until she drops her gaze.

'Jessie,' she whispers. 'Jess. I'm so sorry, lovey, I never meant...'

I start to say, 'Never meant what...' but she's already wrapped her arms round me, and that feeling of being safe overwhelms me, and we both say nothing and we don't even cry. A small, detached part of me is surprised by this, but it's become too big, we've gone past that, and now the impenetrable wall is slowly crumbling. It's too early to build a bridge yet, but the plans are there, the rough outline. To cross a bridge, you need trust, and neither of us can admit to that yet. We both know it's up to Mum to put the first post in position, ready to hold the planks in place. It won't be safe, that bridge, until it's got a handrail to hang onto when it starts to wobble.

Just as she always has, Mum makes the first move. She lets me go, gently, and says, 'Cup of tea first?' We walk back into the kitchen.

Sophie is sitting in there on her own, leaning on the table while she studies the crossword in the paper that's been left there. She's twiddling a lock of hair round her fingers as she reads. When we appear, she glances up and tucks her hair behind her ears.

'Nobody's done it!' she exclaims. 'What's up with you guys? What are you doing with your time? Such easy clues today!'

I frown at her and wait for Mum to say something, to respond, to react in some way, but she's walked over to the sink to fill the kettle and she hasn't even looked at Sophie. I glare pointedly, and nod my head with a tiny movement towards Mum. Sophie grins at me and shrugs her shoulders.

'I had to choose,' she says, 'and you won. Lucky you, Jess.'

'So no one else...' I start to say, and Mum peeks over her shoulder at me.

'What's that, lovey? Did you say something?'

I shake my head. 'No, it's OK. Nothing.' I want to know so much, but it will all have to wait until Sophie comes to see me again when I'm on my own. I'm not sure why I've kept her visits to me secret from the rest of the family. I wondered, when I spoke to Alex the other evening, whether she goes to see him too, but now I think not. I'm sure it was just his hopeful imagination, as I said to him at the time. Why did she wait so long? Why come for the first time a few nights ago, just as we seem to be setting ourselves on an even path after her death? It doesn't make sense.

Now Sophie clasps her hands together with a gleeful expression on her face. 'This is going to be *so* interesting,' she exclaims. 'Just had to be here. Can't wait to find out all the sordid details! Remember to ask all the right questions, Jessie.'

The icy thread of fear that had lodged itself deep inside me earlier dissolves into a rising wave of nausea. I close my eyes and start to count, silently, and when I open them again, Mum is sitting on the chair where Sophie had been, and my sister has vanished.

*

'Buried or cremated?'

We were taking a break under the trees at the edge of the sports field after our first A-level exam – English Literature. Sophie was lying on her back, eyes closed, and the rest of us – Karen, Em, Polly and me – were sprawled around her in a group. We were putting off the inevitable need to go home and continue revising for our next exams.

'What?' Polly exclaimed. 'You are *so* weird sometimes, Sophie.'

Sophie sat up, brushing tiny blades of new mown grass off her legs and arms and trying to reach round to see whether they clung to her back. 'Seriously,' she said. 'Don't tell me you none of you think about it?'

'Never,' said Karen, our practical, no-nonsense, say-it-how-it-is friend. 'Why would I want to waste time thinking about what's going to happen to me once I'm dead? I won't know anyway.'

'I agree,' said Em. She usually did. 'Someone else is going to make those decisions. Right?'

I propped my arms behind me and leant back on them, my legs straight out in front, and I closed my eyes.

'So, which is it, Sophie?' asked Polly. The way she spoke, her drawling voice, always made it seem like she didn't really care about the answer. The drawl concealed a mind like a steel trap.

'Buried,' Sophie replied. 'Of course. Under the green ground.' Her voice became dreamy. 'Among all those lovely trees and flowers. Definitely buried. Why would I want to be burnt to ashes? Yuk.'

'Jess?' said Em. 'What about you? Do you think about it too?'

I had reached forty-one.

'Jessie?'

I opened my eyes. 'Sometimes.'

'So you both have these weird ideas. Must be in your genes then.' Polly lay down on the grass, and stretched out like a lazy cat. 'You probably have the same kind of thought patterns. Now, was it nature or nurture that forced you *both* to have these crazy ideas?'

We all laughed, and then Sophie said, 'It's probably Per, don't you think, Jess? Maybe we get it from him.'

'What are you talking about?' asked Karen. 'Who's Per?'

Sophie stared at her. 'Are you serious? "Who's Per?" Shall we tell her, Jess?'

We chimed together, 'Our biological father!'

'Remember,' Sophie attempted an imitation of our mother's voice, 'anyone can be a biological father. It takes... What is it, Jessie?'

'Not everyone can be a real father,' I muttered, with reluctance. It seemed a betrayal of Dad somehow. 'That takes a...'

Sophie joined in. '... Special sort of person!'

'Oh my God,' Karen sounded bewildered. 'How come I never knew? So, Mike's not your actual father? Why is no one else surprised?' She looked around our group.

'Because we already knew.' It sounded as if Polly was drifting off to sleep, her voice slow and drowsy.

I reached out and touched Karen's arm. 'I think we just assumed you knew, because everyone else does. I guess we forget you've only known us since we started college.' I smile at her. 'It seems like forever. Haven't you ever wondered why we ask you all those questions about Denmark? I can't believe we've never explained why. Per was Danish. Our biological father. He was an overseas student for a year at Sussex, with Mum. She got pregnant just as she finished uni.'

Sophie shuffled across the grass to sit on the other side of Karen. 'So we'll be needing your expert help, you know. When we go to find him.'

'We could all go?' suggested Em. 'Nice trip after college. Or uni.'

'Emily,' Sophie said, with an uncharacteristic tenderness. 'I think *two* of us turning up is going to be quite enough. Five *might* be a step too far. Remember, he doesn't know we exist.'

'So *I've* got a Danish mother and you two a Danish father!' Karen exclaimed. 'I can't wait to tell Mum. Amazing! All three of us half Danish!'

'And we all have our next exam the day after tomorrow,' said Polly, standing up, her languor gone.

'Shall we wait for the boys?' asked Em, shading her eyes as she looked down the field. 'They said they'd join us soon.'

'Nah,' Sophie said. 'They must be long gone by now, off having a crafty smoke before they get the train.'

'Even Lucas?' I ventured.

Sophie gave me a sideways look. 'Even Lucas.'

We strolled down the field, homeward bound.

Sometimes I look back on those days, those long warm days of exams and revision and anxiety and friendship, and I remember that, not long afterwards, Sophie first became ill.

CHAPTER EIGHT

'I think I thought,' Mum says slowly, staring at her mug of tea and then blowing the steam away, 'that the right moment would come.'

'The right moment?' I am steadfast in my determination not to let her off this revelation.

'To tell you both the truth...'

'And?'

'And I suppose the right moment never came. Life went on, everything seemed OK, and you two had accepted that Per never knew, so it was...'

She takes a tentative sip of tea, and pushes her hair off her face. I notice in a rush how she's aged over the last few months, and I wonder why I haven't seen this before.

Too busy! Too wrapped up in yourself and how you were feeling.

Mum is one of the youngest among my friends' parents, and Sophie and I were secretly always rather proud of this once we were old enough to realise. Her hair falls a little untidily around her neck, and is still the same dark blonde it's always been, but now there are strands of grey appearing which she hasn't bothered to try to conceal, and there are creases round her eyes and her mouth; her skin looks dull with fatigue and her cheeks hollow. She wears a belt pulled in tight on the last hole to make her jeans stay up, and her sweater hangs, too loose and baggy.

I persist, 'Easier? It was easier just to keep that lie going, you mean?'

She stares at me now. 'Not a lie, Jessie. I never actually *lied* to you.'

'What would you call it?' I take a quick gulp of my tea. 'Being economical with the truth?'

'Jess.' Mum reaches across the table and puts her hands over mine; it's to soften the blow she's about to deliver, I realise. 'We're all economical with the truth sometimes, aren't we? You know that as well as any of us.'

I shift on my chair; the familiar flood of guilt surges over me. 'Yeah,' I mutter. 'OK. You're right, of course. I can't...'

We hear Alex in the hall yell, 'Going out! Yeah, back in time to eat, before you ask.'

And Dad's answering shout from his studio: 'OK! Got your...?' but the door has slammed before he finishes.

'Jess.' Mum takes away her hands to pull her chair closer to the table. 'You have to believe... I never meant to upset you both, or hurt you. It was all for the best, I thought. At the time.'

'So...?' I retrieve my hands and, with my elbows on the table, I prop my chin on my fists.

'So.' She takes a faltering breath. 'When I realised... when I found out I was pregnant, I... I didn't know what to do. It wasn't supposed to have happened, obviously.' She's tracing her finger over the dents and smears and crumbs on the table, and her voice has become difficult to hear. I have to concentrate. I watch her as she stumbles on. 'Per was back in Copenhagen. We'd agreed... he'd said... we thought, well, that we had our whole lives to sort out, and that it was too early – too young – to commit to anything... more long-term. So that was how it was. We'd had...' She fixes me with one of her fierce gazes, the sort Sophie and I had always known better than to challenge. '... Very, very strong feelings for each other. You must always, always remember that, Jessie.'

'Yeah, I do.' Now I fold my arms and lean back in my chair. 'Go on.'

'When I realised I was pregnant – but not that it was two of you at that point – I wanted to tell Per before anybody.'

'Not Gran and Grampy?'

'No! Especially not them.'

I'm having to readjust my previous conceptions concerning the whole event all those years ago. 'OK,' I say, hesitantly.

'But he was spending the summer somewhere else in Denmark – I can't remember where now, I don't know anything about Denmark, but it was in a sort of holiday place, I think, and it was really, really difficult to get hold of him.'

'No mobiles.' I proffer my limited knowledge of life back then.

'Exactly. Anyway, eventually I wrote, hoping the letter would be forwarded to him, and somehow it was. By then of course, a couple more weeks had gone by.'

I wrap my arms around myself as if, by holding my body close, I'll banish that coldness, that rising sickness, that buzzing in my head. I'm sure I've guessed what my mother is going to tell me – I can hardly bear to hear the words, to discover I'm right.

'I think he replied very quickly,' Mum continues, 'but to me it was a lifetime. And he said...'

Now I have my hands pressed tight over my ears. 'I know what you're going to say. I don't want to know. I don't want to hear it. Don't tell me, don't...'

My mother shifts her chair round the corner of the table so that she's beside me, and she puts an arm round my shaking shoulders. I can't see her face because I can't bear to look, but I can imagine the anxiety and guilt and fear scored into it, and even so, I know that she's crying, wordlessly. If I hadn't decided to go and find Per, none of this would be happening. We would be getting on with our lives, grieving for Sophie, trying to adjust to the Sophie-sized hole left in our lives, slowly finding ways of coping.

This is something else, something too great for me to manage on my own. Sophie needs to be here. I need her; I really need her. Sophie who liked red, but not pink, who hated reality TV shows, and who'd always wanted a cat, but definitely not a dog; she should be sharing this with me, saying, *It's no big deal, Jess, it's cool, it makes it more interesting.'* Her absence twists like a knife in my heart.

Mum moves my hands away from my ears very gently, and says, 'No, you don't understand, Jess. It was... partly my fault. A misunderstanding. In his letter he asked, wasn't an abortion best? Wasn't that best for both of us, he said. He would send money if I agreed. He wasn't ready, he said, to be a father, but it was to be my decision.'

We're both crying now, properly crying. It had never been about needing another father; Sophie and I had always been happy with the one we'd got – or as happy as any teenager ever is with a parent. It was about finding that missing jigsaw piece, trying to discover who we were and what made us who we were. In a few sentences the dreams have crashed in a landslide of broken hopes. This fantasy man of our plans, this unwitting catalyst for our journey of discovery, had wanted us aborted.

'I knew it... I guessed.' It's difficult to speak coherently. 'But what do you mean it was partly your fault? How can that be true?'

'Because.' Mum takes my hands again and holds them between hers, firmly this time. 'And you must listen now, Jessie, listen to what I'm saying.' She stops for a minute to fish a tissue out of her pocket and blot her eyes. 'Sorry,' she says, sniffing, and then the tears start to run again unchecked down her cheeks. 'Sorry, Jess, I didn't mean... I didn't want to upset...'

'It's OK,' I say, because it is.

Between us, over the last few months, we've shed more tears than I would have supposed humanly possible. I'd never seen my father cry, not properly, before that night when he found Sophie, and the boys – how Toby's face drained of colour, as the awful reality sank in, how his eyes filled, and the way he began to sob, and Alex, who just kept shouting, screaming, 'No! No, it's not true! Let me see her! Let me...' Now all of us, the whole family, weep openly and often completely randomly. We're past caring who sees us, because when something like this happens, your priorities shift and your values change, and all those things that had been so important such a short time ago cease to matter any longer.

Mum says, 'Per and I, on our last day together, before my graduation, we had a wonderful day, an amazing day. I still remember it – all of it.'

She tells me about that final day, how hot it had been, and how they had spent it on the beach in Brighton, near the pier, and then, after a few hours, had started to head back to Per's place. It wasn't a night for staying in – there were fevered rumours of student parties all over the campus and town: people celebrating the end of being students before their impending graduation ceremonies. She and Per wanted to spend their last night together, but they wanted to share the excitement too. So she had decided to go back to her shared flat, start to pack up a bit before Gran and Grampy arrived the next day, and have a bath, before getting ready for a fun evening out. They had planned to join a big group of their friends down by the beach.

She stops and picks up her mug. The tea must be cold by now, but she tips it back and drinks the last dregs like they're some sort of elixir, a magical protection against the darkness gathering around us as the day ticks slowly by.

'Great,' I say, and I can taste the bitterness in my words. 'Not sure I...'

'We agreed to meet by the pier again,' Mum continued.

That's where their friends were gathering, but she got delayed; the packing, and tidying, and bath all took longer – in typical Mum fashion – than she'd imagined. Later than she'd planned, she had caught a bus down to the sea front, and just as she was about to get off, she saw Per, but he was standing with a girl my mother had never seen before. They were talking – she could see they were – and it looked like... well, it looked very intimate, she said. Per seemed very serious and she saw him hold the girl's face between his hands, and then they hugged. Mum said she couldn't see any more because she'd started crying. In that split second it had felt as if her whole world had crumbled. Everything she had thought they meant to each other dissolved into a pool of deceits.

I stare at her. 'What did you do?'

'I didn't know what to do. I felt... foolish, and blind, and... well, I stayed on the bus, and then I went and gate-crashed another party that I knew about.'

There's something missing. It's like the elusive answer in a crossword that's going to fill in all the lost letters for the other clues if only you can find it.

'That's when I was a bit stupid,' my mother adds, almost as if this realisation has just occurred to her. As if she has only now woken up, like Sleeping Beauty, from the longest sleep, but instead of a prince giving her a kiss, real life has punched her in the face.

'What?' It's hard to imagine Mum ever making a bad decision. 'What did you do?'

She had drifted into a noisy, wild party, mostly full of people she hardly knew, and had started drinking glass after glass of cheap wine. There was a boy there who she'd had a bit of a thing about, when they were in their first year. She couldn't even remember his name now.

'Did you...?' I can hardly bring myself to voice the question. It's not one you'd usually expect to ask your mother; I feel my heart hammering at the thought of her answer.

'No. No, I... Per thought... well, first, he found me. He said he was worried when I didn't arrive at the pier, and he came looking. He went all over... all over to different places, other parties, and then I heard him shouting...'

Mum's voice is almost inaudible. Our roles of parent and child change, and I put my hands over hers where they lie, trembling, on the table.

He had had to stumble up the dark stairs, shouting her name, 'Laura? Laura!' stepping over other people who were lying there in varying states of drunkenness and disarray, and then he had found them half asleep, sprawled together in someone's half-packed-up bedroom.

Nothing had happened, Mum said. They didn't have sex, this unremembered boy and her, because he was too drunk, and she, despite her rage after seeing Per, too unwilling.

'But Per thought...' I say, and it's like a blackout blind being wound up a window, bright daylight streaming through, hurting your eyes. And all the streaks and smears become visible. That clean glass was an illusion after all.

Per didn't believe her, wouldn't listen to her slurred account. No more words had been spoken, no further explanations on either side. Mum, feeling sick and unwell, tried to enjoy her graduation ceremony the next day with Gran and Grampy, so proud and happy, unaware of any drama. Per, as far as she knew, flew back to Copenhagen.

'And he thought...' I prompted again.

'Yes.' Mum makes a brief nod of agreement. 'So, when I told him I was pregnant, and didn't know what to do, he still thought it... you... might not be his, and I agreed with him. I mean,' she adds hastily, 'that I agreed that I should... maybe have an abortion. It seemed the easiest thing. I even thought... perhaps we'd see each other again – I don't know.' She gives me an apologetic half smile. 'He sent me money, but when it came to it, I couldn't do it, Jess. I just couldn't... So I used it for the baby stuff I needed. He never knew you'd been born. I never told him.'

Something else occurs to me, remembering my grandfather's face yesterday. 'Grampy?' I say. 'And Gran? They didn't...?'

Mum allows the ghost of a smile, and lifts her gaze to meet mine. 'He's a scumbag, as far as they're concerned. They just thought he didn't want to support me, wanted nothing to do with me, or a baby, and I couldn't tell them...'

'About the other guy, and what might or might not have happened?'

Mum's look is level. She has never been anything other than honest. 'Didn't happen, Jess, definitely didn't. I wasn't that drunk... I would remember.'

'And this other girl?' I have to know the full story now. I've waited all my life without knowing I needed to.

Mum shrugs. 'I never found out. We never spoke again, so I don't know.' Just before her face crumples again she whispers, 'All you need to know, Jessie, all you ever needed to know, is that Per Jacobsen is your father. That's the truth. That's... well, that's it.' She twists the soggy tissue into a crumpled ball with her fingers, pushes back her chair, and goes to put the remnants in the bin.

CHAPTER NINE

Lucas Fleming. From the moment he arrived at school in our final year, Sophie was captivated. His family had moved from another part of the country, and now lived in a neighbouring village to us. He boarded the school bus the first day of that autumn term, and everything about him spoke of an alternative life, of possibilities, and escape, and a different way of doing just about anything. He managed to wear his school uniform in a way that followed the rules but still allowed him to make a statement. Soon, most of the boys in our year who liked to be cool were copying the look: blazer sleeves rolled up just a couple of inches, mismatched socks, tie knotted intriguingly and a little loose.

By the time we started at Sixth Form College, he had perfected his own unique style: he sauntered down corridors and into classes wearing green velvet jeans, a black T-shirt and brocade waistcoat, with a fedora tipped forward almost over his eyes. Sophie was enchanted. Under the hat – and occasionally he changed the fedora for a bowler, worn far back on his head, or a bucket-style Harris tweed – he watched the world through weary, narrowed eyes, and when he spoke it was as if he were unable to prevent a creeping edge of boredom. He worried me a little. I was never sure how to take him, what he was thinking, but Sophie was enthralled. For her, he represented everything that was unusual, exciting and dangerous. She made very sure he became a part of our group.

'Oh my God, Jessie,' she confided in me. 'Love at first sight or what? I adore him, I absolutely adore him. I'm sure I'm right for him. I'd do anything, Jess, anything... He'd only have to say...'

Dad had watched him strolling away down our driveway, after he'd come home with us one afternoon. 'He's certainly... different,' he observed.

Polly was standing in our hall, putting on her jacket. She glanced sideways at Mum.

'What do you think, Laura?' she asked, a deceptive innocence in her tone. Polly found Lucas rather tiresome. She could see right through him, she said, and it wasn't a pretty sight.

'Oh, different is good, in my book,' Mum declared. 'But I'm not sure how far I'd trust him.'

Polly raised her eyebrows at me, because Sophie wasn't listening. She already had that faraway look in her eyes.

*

When I open my bedroom door I half-expect to find Sophie sitting there, but the room is empty. My head is reeling with

Mum's revelations. Confused thoughts roll around like tumbleweeds.

I drag my chair over to the cupboard and stand on it, on tiptoe, to feel for the tin right at the back of the top shelf. My fingers grasp the ridged rim, and I'm able to pull it towards me. I clamber down and take it over to my desk. I use my fingernails to lever off the lid – it's decorated with an old-fashioned sentimental Christmas picture of cottages in a village street, their low roofs heavily laden with snow – and remove it to find Sophie's diary inside.

I hoist myself onto my windowsill, and teeter on the edge as I reach carefully above the curtain pole. The key is lodged on the top of the left-hand bracket, stuck on with a blob of Blu-Tack and, as I pull it off, I lose my balance and land heavily on the floor. I wait. Nothing happens. Nobody calls out to see whether I've fallen. The thud can't have been as loud as I thought.

I sit on the bed and open the diary with shaking hands. The last time I looked through it was just after Sophie died. It felt then as if nothing in the diary could be as devastating as that. Now it's Mum's disclosures that have spun me off my normal axis. For the first time since I decided to go and find Per on my own, my resolution is wavering. I crave the comfort of seeing Sophie's thoughts and written words. I think I'm searching for a sign as I leaf through the pages with my thumb. I know already that there are no entries at all for the summer after our A-levels, and the months – many months – afterwards are blank too. Then a gradual emergence of odd words and phrases, scattered throughout the weeks after the following spring: "Jess home" was one, and later, "Jess gone". In the June it began to sound more encouraging. "Walk" on one day, and "Sun shining" the next, and then a few days later, "Jess phoned". When I see Sophie's handwriting again, I feel a jolt of despair. It's so familiar – the sprawling untidiness, the distinct irrepressible joy of it that she never quite lost.

I keep my finger in place and close the diary over it, to stop my tears smudging the sparse words. I breathe in and out with learned measure and slowness, making a determined effort to calm my thoughts and, while I breathe, I watch the rooks through the window, soaring and gliding above the lacy cobweb of bare trees. We never guessed the depth and breadth of Sophie's illness at that time. Nobody did. We could only offer to listen; ask, encourage and support. But I know that very often that wasn't enough. Not nearly enough. She needed something more from us, but she was never able to put the something into words. Maybe she herself didn't really know.

For the first time in our whole existence, our paths wound in different directions: mine from choice, and hers by unpredictable chance. All the while, my life was moving forward, hers was only standing still. I was at university living the student life, doing all the things that we'd both talked about and imagined for so long. I loved it. I enjoyed my course; I made new friends. I missed Sophie with a desperation and intensity that sometimes made me cry at night, but equally it gave me a breathing space, a space where Sophie and her illness were too far away for me to worry about and fret. For her...

well, my parents never told me, but now I'm guessing that at first it could only have deepened her depression, and added to the gut-tearing misery she existed with at that period.

I'm in control again; the slow breathing has worked. I feel a tiny sense of triumph. I brush my wet face with the heel of my hand, quickly, and flick through the diary page by page until I reach last Christmas. The entries are getting longer again, more detailed. There is a clear uplift in the way she was writing "Looking at universities".

Each day was getting filled now, partly with the minutiae of her life at that time, but also with details and phrases that sounded, at last, like the old Sophie. Our Sophie. My twin. Then, halfway through February, with her place at university confirmed for the autumn, the writing spikes with irrepressible excitement.

"Met Lucas in Brighton! OMG!! He's home from uni. Meeting tonight!! CAN'T WAIT! He suggested it. Think we'll def. get back together now. For ALWAYS."

I close the diary. Oh Sophie, Sophie. I clasp it tight to my chest and rock slowly forward and back on the edge of the bed. By the time I'd come home for my Easter holiday, Lucas had her wound round his little finger again, and I knew only too well how he could do that, the control he could hold over someone's life. Only now she was so much more vulnerable. We knew the slightest setback could tip her off balance again. She was still on medication – greatly reduced, but necessary nevertheless – and a few days after I got home, we five girls met up for an evening in Brighton, a pizza and a film, and our favourite bar.

If I squeeze my eyes tight shut, I think I can obliterate those last few hours of Sophie's life, I can make it more bearable, but then that trivialises those hours too, and I don't want to do that. I want to remember everything, but it's still so painful. However hard I try, I can't conjure up the title of the film we saw, or where we had pizza, or what most of us drank in the bar. Karen was driving; she would have had something soft, and Sophie still had to be careful, because of the drugs. I get small snapshots in my head, like fuzzy stills from a film.

My bedroom door bursts open, and Toby's standing there, staring at me.

'Jess? You all right?'

I'm instantly on my feet, the diary pushed behind me on the bed.

'Yes! Why? Don't you know about privacy, Toby? Have you never thought about knocking before you gate-crash someone's room?'

'Yeah... OK... sorry. Mum just said she thought she heard a thump or something.'

Still holding the door handle, he turned his head and roared, 'She's OK!'

I heard a faint response from my mother, somewhere downstairs.

Toby has let go of the door, and is gazing with unconcealed curiosity.

'Jess? What's that? What've you got on the bed? What were you holding?' He takes a step over the threshold.

I scream, 'Get lost! Get lost, you little shit! Get out of my room! Now!' and I'm across the room in two strides, pushing him out, and slamming the door shut.

I know I'll have to make it up to him later. The expression on his face will haunt me for too long otherwise. It's not his fault. He's thirteen, and his whole life has been upended by tragedy too. It's nobody's fault, but we're still too fragile. It's easy for the slightest thing to make us unravel, to take two steps back from the tremulous one we may have taken going forward. Sometimes it feels as if we're getting there, and then something happens, and I know there's still a long hill to climb and that I've hardly moved any distance up the slope.

*

We had been relaxed and carefree as we'd driven back from our night out in Brighton. Karen was completely sober. She had stoically refused to have even a small lager ('I'm being heroic here, ladies. Hope you're all going to remember this'), knowing she had to drive us all home safely, and Sophie had been reassuringly sensible, making a small glass of vodka and cranberry last the longest time, and then having a tall glass of diet coke.

Never used to drink this, but it does help me stay awake. I even quite like it now.

I felt uncomfortable about this. I felt I should show solidarity and behave the same way, but the other side of me thought, what the hell? I'm her twin sister, not her carer, and it wasn't as if Polly and Em and I were getting plastered: just a little merry.

In any case, we left the bar sooner than we had expected. A loud group of foreign students were sitting at the table next to us. They had bought bags of peanuts, and were having some sort of competition to see who was quickest at ripping open a packet and finishing all the contents first. Peanuts spilled on their table and around them on the floor close to where we sat. Both Sophie and I began to cough, and our eyes started to stream. By mutual consent we all fought our way out, on to the pavement, and the two of us began to breathe easier.

Squashed in the back of Karen's mother's tiny Fiat, I could see nevertheless that Sophie's eyes were glittering, in that familiar way that made me feel uneasy. I reached across Em and touched Sophie's arm. 'Sophie? You OK?'

She turned her head slowly, unhurried, to look at me. I worried that her words sounded slurred. Maybe even that one small drink was too much.

'Just thinking about that film,' she said.

'Good, wasn't it?' Em responded. 'I loved that twist at the end. Really clever.'

'A bit schmaltzy though.' Polly turned round from the front seat. 'I mean, I love a good romance as much as anyone, but...'

'There's no such thing, anyway,' Sophie cut in. 'No such thing as a happy ending. They only happen in books. Or films.'

'Really?' said Em, a note of disbelief creeping into her voice. 'Do you really think that, Sophie?'

Sophie sighed. 'Yeah. I do. Not sure why you all think that's not true.'

'Because we know you, Sophie,' I said, and I kept my voice light and casual with a deliberation born of guilt. 'You've always been the great romantic. Love at first sight and all that. Doesn't it last, then?'

Sophie shrugged and moved her head away to stare out through the window at the other cars, at the flash and dazzle of headlamps as they streamed past. 'Maybe for other people. I don't know.' She rested her head against the glass. 'But there is never going to be a happy ever after. It's obvious.' She closed her eyes until we turned off the main road and into the village.

That stone of treachery dropped in my stomach. Its weight made me flinch, and I felt sick, too, sick with the fear of discovery. What did Sophie mean? Could she have found out something? Or just guessed?

As we drove along the High Street, we noticed a lone figure sitting at the bus stop just past the church crossroads. When he saw us coming, he stepped into the road in a leisurely, indolent fashion, a carrier bag hanging from one hand, and waved his other arm at the car, and we realised it was Lucas. Karen braked sharply, and we all jerked forward.

Karen wound down her window as Lucas strolled over to her side.

'Christ, Lucas,' she said, crossly. 'What the bloody hell do you think you're doing? I could've killed you.'

Lucas tipped back his hat a little, and leant in the window.

'No such luck, I'm afraid,' he said, his eyes roving round the inside of the car.

Sophie was wide awake now, and her whole mood changed.

'Lucas!' she exclaimed. 'You're back again! Hey, I've missed you!'

'Missed you too, baby,' he drawled, and I shivered. 'In fact, was hoping... very much... you'd be in here.'

Sophie started to fumble with the door handle.

'Can we talk?' she said. 'I really, really need to talk to you, Lucas.'

'Sophie,' I said, 'can't it wait? It's so late. You can see him tomorrow.'

Lucas transferred his gaze to me, and let a slow smile drift across his face. 'Still playing spoilsport, are we, Jessica? Still want to spoil your sister's fun? Still the old buttoned-up...'

'Shut up, Lucas.' I glared at him. 'You know perfectly well...'

Sophie was thrusting her bag – the old tattered patchwork one she'd made a few years ago from Gran's collection of scraps – onto my lap. 'Here, take this, Jess. I won't be long. I'll only be a minute. Don't wait! Just need to tell Lucas something.' Then she was half out of the door.

'Sophie!' I could feel a bewildering sense of panic rising in me. 'Sophie, wait! I'll come with you! How will you get...?'

Lucas had started to move, a little unsteadily, round the end of the car, but he came back to the window and grinned in at me. 'Calm down, Mummy,' he said, in that belittling way of his. 'She'll be fine. I'll get her home, don't worry.'

Karen swivelled round so she could see me. 'Jess? What do you want to do?'

'For Christ's sake!' Polly exclaimed. 'She's not a child! She's only ten minutes' walk from home, after all, and she's with Lucas! What the fuck do you think is going to happen?'

I hugged Sophie's bag close to me. 'Yeah, you're right. I'm over-reacting. It's just...'

Em leaned over and gave me an awkward one-sided hug. 'No, you're not,' she whispered, 'it's OK, it's perfectly natural after... everything, but Polly's right.' Then she added with a rueful lop-sided smile, 'She usually is.'

Yet Lucas's words stayed imprinted in my brain. Was that how others saw me now as well, as a fussy, over-anxious spoilsport? For as long as I could remember I'd always been a tiny bit in awe of Sophie; for her joie de vivre, her take on life, her absolute belief in her rightness. I'd always longed to be as feisty as she was, to take risks and not care. Sophie was forever plunging headfirst into a challenge, while I sometimes simply found life itself enough of a challenge. All that had changed with Sophie's illness. Now that she seemed to have started to recover so completely, did I still need to be protective, alert, afraid for her? Maybe it was time to go back to being unsure and afraid for myself, and not worry about Sophie. Maybe she was strong enough to look after herself. But I longed, and feared, to know what could be so important to tell Lucas that it couldn't wait until the next day.

CHAPTER TEN

The year struggles to an end.

Each date, each festival, each significant happening has to be the first without Sophie. We try to ignore Bonfire Night.

What isn't to like about fireworks? I love them! Love the entire thing! Not the Guys though, too creepy. It's the mask thing again.

In the end Mum and I stay at home, curled up on the sofa watching a favourite film, while Dad and Alex and Toby go to the village bonfire as usual.

Christmas, though – that's a different story. It was always going to be difficult, this first Christmas without Sophie. It's a time so rooted in tradition and custom, so full of family conventions. The boys and I make a unanimous decision to stop the whole Advent calendar affair. We have two large fabric calendars, one shared by Sophie and me since we were tiny, and then one for Alex and Toby. Every year Mum extricates them from the attic in November, and hangs them on hooks in the kitchen, ours behind the door and the boys' one next to the dresser. And every year, as we've grown older, she's grumbled a little more about the time it's taken her to find cheap and small enough gifts to pop in all the twenty-four pockets.

Well, this year she doesn't need to grumble, because we agree between us that this particular custom should end. I feel sorry for Toby, though. It seems as if he's missing out on one of his last childhood rituals; he's obliged to grow up too soon, just because it's so painful for me to have a calendar to myself, each pocket containing only one gift, not two.

My father suggests we should all go away somewhere, because that's something we've never done before. There would be no memories of happier times attached to a Christmas spent swimming in a warm sea somewhere, and a festive dinner that contained no turkey. But Sophie had loved Christmas, and we agree that however sad we might feel, we'd rather keep the memories intact and spend Christmas in our usual way.

It seems impossible to imagine a pile of presents under the tree that are not each going to be lifted out, prodded and shaken.

Quite heavy, this one, Jess! From Gran and Grampy... What do you think? Have you got one the same? Go on! Have a look!

I always refused to join in Sophie's addictive present-guessing moments.

No one will know!

If I guessed, I thought, then how would I seem when I opened it? How could I be surprised, and pleased? But Sophie – who loved surprises, but liked trying to guess even more, who left clues littered around in the days before Christmas to try to tempt others into guessing their unopened presents – had no problem appearing both amazed and delighted.

We drag ourselves through the week, spending Christmas Day at my grandparents' house and persuading them to join us for a long, windy walk by the sea on Boxing Day. In truth, it's not too bad, because we keep busy. My parents try to keep introspection to a minimum, while still recalling out loud how much Sophie would have enjoyed Grampy's unsuccessful attempts to win Jenga, and Gran's optimistic but hopeless balancing on a skateboard along the sea front. It's still a relief when the whole period is behind us. I feel as if another hurdle has been leaped. Next year, surely, it will be better. Won't we be adjusted by then to Sophie's absence? Or will it lurk forever, just round the corner, waiting, always waiting, for the chance to pounce from the shadows, shake me from side to side and toss me in the air so that when I land, with a jolt, I remember only: Sophie's dead.

Sometimes I mutter it like a mantra: 'Sophie's dead, Sophie's dead, Sophie's dead.' I still hope it's a nightmare. I want to wake up, and count to twenty, and there she will be, alive after all.

*

My mother and I had stayed sitting, squashed on the third from the bottom stair, for several minutes after my father left to look for Sophie. I had counted to fifty silently, in my head, and then started again in French. I had only reached *"neuf"* when I began to shake uncontrollably, and I put my hands on my throat. I felt as if I couldn't breathe.

'Jessie, Jess.' Mum stood up, and pulled me up too. 'It's OK. When has your dad never been able to sort out a problem?' Her words were strong, but her voice was thin and wavered with worry and fear. I was struggling and gasping to take in gulps of air. It was terrifying.

'It's a panic attack, Jess,' my mother said soothingly. 'You'll be all right. Drop your shoulders, take a breath. Just one. That's right, and another. You're doing fine, lovey, and another.'

We stood together in the hall, and she inhaled gently with me, and finally my heart rate slowed and I could feel my lungs expanding and then the air leaving them, and my breathing returned to normal. Still there was no news from Dad, and Sophie hadn't phoned either.

Then it came to me. I eased myself away from my mother, and turned round to reach the chair where I'd flung Sophie's bag when I'd got home. How long ago? Two hours? Three? I knew what I'd find as I reached into the bag and fumbled through its contents. I could feel her purse, some balled-up tissues, a lip-gloss, her EpiPen, a brush, three biros, a half-used tube of mints, and right at the bottom, slipped down under everything else, Sophie's phone. I drew it out, and held it up to Mum.

'It's on silent,' I said. 'She must have done that when we were in the cinema. So when I was ringing her…'

A surge of hope swelled up inside me, and I could see it on Mum's face too.

'That explains why she's not answered,' she said, with a smile of relief. 'I knew it! I knew there'd be some perfectly simple...' She took the bag from me and hugged it to her as she sank down on the chair.

But as quickly as the hope had appeared it vanished, kicked and trampled underfoot by a wholly unexpected feeling of dread, which seeped through my entire body. My legs gave way. I sat curled in a ball on the floor, and rocked myself. Something like an interminable blackness was shrouding my vision, and my hearing, and my brain.

'Jess?' said Mum. She stood up and came over to me. 'What is it? Jessie. Lovey. What? Tell me.' She knelt beside me, and put her arm round my shoulders.

'I don't know,' I whispered. 'I don't know.'

When Dad came in, however much later, with two police officers behind him, we were still sitting there together on the cold, hard hall floor.

*

I use the flat, aimless days after Christmas to start planning my trip to Denmark. I'm filled with a sudden and renewed enthusiasm, as if Mum's revelations and my grandparents' misgivings are spurring me forwards instead of holding me back.

I have a wonderfully clear picture in my head of the moment I meet Per and tell him who I am, of the delight in his face at discovering he has a daughter, and his eagerness to include me in a new, Danish family. However, the actual logistics of getting over there, and where I'll stay, and how I'll find him, are hazy and a little elusive.

I'm lying on the sofa one afternoon, savouring the silence while the rest of the family are out. I drain the last drop of coffee from my mug as I ponder the best way to organise my proposed trip, and I realise Sophie is sitting on the chair opposite, her feet tucked under her. I set the mug on the floor with unusual care.

'You could ask Karen,' she says. 'Don't you remember? How she always said she could help us, explain stuff to us? Honestly, Jess, can't believe you've not thought about that. I bet she'd love to help.'

She straightens up, planting her feet on the floor and tucking her hair behind her ears. One of her earrings is a large metallic hoop, the other one a trail of three hearts linked together. The ones she was wearing that fateful evening. Her silver rings glint on her fingers. 'You'd better get a move on,' she adds, 'because, aren't you going to go back to uni in the autumn? There's only so long they're going to hold your place for you, you know.'

'I'm not sure...' I begin, but she cuts in as if I haven't spoken.

'Plus, if you don't go back this year, you're just going to be so *old*!'

'Sophie.' I'm transfixed by her feet. 'Sophie. Your toenails. They're still...'

She glances down at them briefly. 'Still what?'

'Still just the same,' I mutter. 'Still chipped. Still blue and purple. Still... the same. The same as... before.'

'Stop changing the subject, Jessie. Concentrate. Speak to Karen, one. Two, get on to... whoever it is you have to get on to, about going back to Warwick. How difficult can that be? Two very simple things to do. Believe me, you'll feel so much better.'

We look at each other without speaking. I'm thinking how bossy she sounds, as if somehow she's trying to stay in control of my life. A hundred questions tumble into my mind – things I want to ask her, things I need to know. Where is she coming from, for a start, and where does she go? I swing my legs off the sofa, and reach down to pick my mug up off the floor.

'Sophie,' I say as I raise my head again, but there's no one there. The chair where she was sitting is empty, and the cushion is smooth and undented.

I speak to Karen, and she's thrilled by the idea of being my chaperone, as she calls it, my guide, in Denmark. I can't believe that during these last few weeks the thought hadn't ever occurred to me. I'm even a little irritated by the fact that it should have been Sophie who suggested it, but of course I can't tell Karen that. I haven't told anyone. Sophie's random visits to me are my secret.

I don't, however, get in touch with my university. After Sophie died, I had returned there eventually to complete the rest of my second year, but I'd found it difficult beyond belief, and done badly in my end of year exams. I couldn't concentrate, and all the will to study hard and succeed and move on had been crushed. I had felt as if I were floating in a glass tank, aimless and untethered, with no clear idea of what I should or could do, and no inclination to make any decisions anyway.

So the university had agreed to keep my place open for a year. I know that means I need to make a decision soon about what I should do, but right now seems wrong. I need to get to Denmark and then, I feel, everything will fall into place. It will become obvious to me where my life is leading. Some sort of beacon will light up the path I need to follow, on my own, without Sophie. This year would have been her first year at uni after her struggle back to normal life, and it would have been my third, but still we would have been pursuing similar goals, our lives nearly parallel again.

Karen has been studying some sort of degree that I'm unclear about. I know she's explained it all to me in depth, but even so I find it too much of an effort to really understand what's involved. It means she's been spending her third year out in the "big wide world", as she describes it, working for a manufacturing firm, and getting lots of practical experience. For some reason, she will finish there in April.

'I *should* spend the whole summer studying,' she explains. 'But that's OK. We won't, like, go to Denmark for months, exactly, will we? I can fit the studying in around it, and any opportunity to practise my Danish is good. I'm probably going to be looking for work over there when I graduate.'

Listening to her on the phone makes me realise how disconnected I've become from the real world. The thought of graduating, and then having a career of some sort, feels an impossible achievement to me. So my next decision, with no help from Sophie, is to find myself a job in the meantime to help with funding my trip. I can't believe I've spent so long doing absolutely nothing at home, drifting around, wallowing in my own self-absorption and sadness.

Nobody is more surprised than I am when I'm offered a job in our local garden centre.

Even the manager of the centre seems a bit baffled when he interviews me.

'So – no experience then?' he queries. 'No hidden green-fingered ambitions, either? You've not...' he seems to be searching for the right terminology, the appropriate way of phrasing the question, '...dabbled in your parents' gardening schemes, for example?'

Even with my limited experience of job interviews, he appears to be ill-matched to his position. I find myself imagining a career that might suit him better, one where he could plant words, not seeds, and watch their effect on the world as they blossomed and grew and reseeded themselves in someone's life.

I bring myself back to the present, and shift slightly on the uncomfortable folding chair he's dragged out of a stockroom into his tiny, stuffy office, presumably just for interviewing purposes.

'None at all,' I admit, and I can't help inwardly admiring my frankness. 'I did grow a sunflower once, and a bean, for a competition at school, but it didn't win, it wasn't nearly tall enough.' It occurs to me that I may be the only candidate for this humble position. January is unlikely to be a peak time for people to want to work in a garden centre.

He sifts through some papers on the jumbled table in front of him. A couple of catalogues float to the floor as he does so, and the mug from which he's taken a few furtive sips while I've been with him teeters near the edge. He moves it away from the danger zone, and fixes me with an earnest expression, clasping his hands together. As I try not to stare at his nicotine-stained fingers, and the earthy line of dirt lodged under each nail, I catch a glimpse of Sophie. She's standing in the cluttered shadow just behind his shoulder. How have I not seen her earlier? She's peering down at the papers, and when she catches my eye she grins, and gives me a thumbs up sign.

'I think we'd like to offer you this position, Miss... er...' The manager glances down at the papers again. 'Miss...'

'Mortimer,' I say, helpfully.

'Yes, Miss Mortimer. Well, we don't go much for formality here, so shall we just say...' He looks down again, and behind him Sophie raises her eyebrows and rolls her eyes.

'Jessica,' I say. 'But I'm usually Jess.'

He clears his throat. 'Yes. As I was saying, I think you'll fit in very well. I'm sure you'll pick things up as you go along. Soon become part of our team. We usually find students are, you know, quite... quick at that sort of thing. You'll be a bit of a Jack of all trades, I'm afraid.'

There is a small silence. 'Or rather I should say Jill, I suppose, equality and all that. We're very pro that here, very, very pro, you know, equal rights, and so on.' He coughs again, raising his hand with those brown-stained fingers to his mouth.

I take a deep breath and decide to cut in. It seems otherwise we might never reach a conclusion. 'Thank you very much. When do I start?'

In the silent depths of the dark corner of the little room, Sophie lifts her hands to applaud.

CHAPTER ELEVEN

My first day at the garden centre is raw and icy. I had planned to cycle there each day, but I quickly ditch that idea in favour of using Mum's little car instead. It's still dark when I leave in the early morning of that first day. I'm filled with apprehension.

'The garden centre?' Mum had exclaimed, her voice teetering with disbelief when I'd told her about the job. 'What? You hate gardening, Jessie!'

'Hate's a bit strong.'

'Well... never shown much interest, then.'

She was right, of course, annoyingly right as usual, but it was more to do with age, I think, than choice. When we were younger, we'd played in the garden all the time. It had been a tangle of long grass and overgrown shrubs and bushes when we'd moved in – fantastic for hide-and-seek and making dens – but over the years Dad, mainly, had tamed the area into submission, creating a big grassy area and putting up a swing and climbing frame. We had missed that wilderness, though.

There are no wilderness areas at Flowers' Garden Centre. Flowers... I thought at first that it had been named by someone with a great lack of originality, but I discover on my first day that in fact it's the name of the family who own it. I imagine Sophie's joy on hearing that: *How bizarre! That is so weird! Do you think you'd feel you had to be into gardening, with a name like that?*

Now I drive into the customer-only car park, and try to remember where Andy, the manager, had told me the staff should park. I'm too early – there are no other cars here yet – and I sit, gripping the steering wheel and trying to control a rising wave of panic. Here I am, waiting to start a job I know nothing about, for which I'll get paid not very much money, when I could be still at home in bed, where my life is safe and comfortable. Why have I chosen to take this unknown step? What am I trying to prove?

I close my eyes and start to count, but before I reach twenty, I hear a tentative rapping on my window.

'You must be Jess,' says the woman standing next to my car when I wind down the window. 'Andy told us to look out for you. Come on in with me and I'll show you where we need to go.' She's wearing a stripy knitted hat, bright pink woolly gloves and a long purple scarf wound several times round her neck.

'My name's Paula,' she says, as we walk to the entrance. 'This door, Jess. This is the one we use. Us workers.' She laughs.

It turns out that Paula laughs quite a lot. Once she's removed her layers of knitwear, I can see the crinkles at the edges of her eyes – 'Laughter lines, Jess,' Gran would say, 'the best kind to have' – and her mouth looks as if she's constantly trying to control a giggle from escaping.

Paula is the person appointed by Andy, as it happens, to "show me the ropes" (everybody seems to speak in clichés here – I press my lips together to suppress my grin at the thought of Sue Everly, my old English A-level teacher, and her expression of horror if she could hear them).

I spend the first day being shown the different areas, and what happens in each. I will indeed be a "Jill of all trades" as Andy the manager had so carefully explained but, cliché or not, it means I'm never bored which, if I'm honest, had been one of my worries. It seems strange to have this behind-the-scenes experience when I can so clearly remember visiting with Mum and Dad, trailing around behind them as they chose plants to put in pots, and shrubs to replace ones that had died, and giant bags of compost.

I meet other members of staff: Bernard, Chloe, Sally, Freda and Eric. How will I ever remember all these names? There are more, too. People who work in the café, and someone who does deliveries – whatever that means – and a cheery assurance from Paula that I'll meet others as the week goes on. 'Lots of us are part-timers,' she explains. 'Well, not me, of course. Not since That-Bugger-Who-Shall-Remain-Nameless had his mid-life crisis and went off into the sunset with Little-Miss-Trollop. I'm going to have one of those,' she adds. 'A mid-life crisis. Just as soon as I find the time.' She laughs, but this time the laugh sounds not so much merry as hollow.

Meeting so many new people all at once makes me wonder how I'll ever recognise who's who, never mind remember their names. It reminds me of my first few weeks at uni, and for a minute I feel a stab of regret that I'm not back there in Warwick instead of here in an empty, echoing building full of Christmas decorations and snowmen and lanterns and cards. Here is all the paraphernalia you could possibly have needed to make your home ready for the festive period. Now they're just looking shoddy and dejected: unhappy rejects way past their selling date.

Somebody's saying something about having a coffee before we get going properly.

'We all pull our weight here,' the bald-headed man with the very red nose says to me; I think he's Eric. Outside it's barely light yet, and a thin drizzle of snow has given the piled up left-over Christmas trees a brief white coating, which would be pretty except it melts almost straight away.

I follow Paula and the others into the café area, and we sit together with mugs of coffee or tea brought over by someone called Nicole. She's tall and willowy with a frizz of bright red hair, and looks about my age. She gives me a tentative smile.

Andy appears and pulls out a chair which he sits astride, back to front, leaning his arms on the wooden back. It makes me feel uncomfortable just watching him. He says things like, 'Well, it's back to the grindstone now, folks,' and 'No rest for the wicked.' And everyone laughs. It's difficult to tell if they're just being polite, but in spite of all the worn phrases, and the strangely assorted collection of people who make up the day's quota of staff, there's an indefinable sense of something good that I can't quite name. I imagine telling Sophie about it, and then I change my mind because I can already hear her finding it too funny for words and, against all the odds, that makes me feel uncomfortable.

I come back to the present with a jolt as I realise everyone is looking at me and smiling, and it registers that Andy has just welcomed me to "The Team". I smile back and I think how well I'm doing, and how much easier life is when I don't have to cope with constant reminders of Sophie.

*

'Look here, girls.' Grampy opened the little packet and tipped some stripy seeds into his hand. 'Now, can you imagine what might grow from this tiny seed?'

We'd gone to the garden centre with Gran and Grampy that day. We loved spending time with them: it still made us feel special, particularly now that Alex and Toby took so much of Mum and Dad's attention. Our grandparents' garden was a riot of colour and confusion in the summer, full of plants and flowers that appeared, quite haphazardly, all year round. There was always something interesting to look at, and that meant that Gran and Grampy spent a lot of time going to local plant sales or visiting the garden centre.

Sophie and I had each filled a small flowerpot with compost, poking seeds down into the soft flaky blackness with our fingers and covering over the holes. We used a little metal watering can to spray them carefully afterwards.

'Remember, young ladies,' Grampy added, 'you'll need to check them every day and see if they need watering. They have to drink, just like us. They can get very thirsty.'

The sunflowers had grown taller and taller with satisfying compliance. Then, we had gone on holiday to Cornwall for two weeks and forgotten to give them to Grampy for safe keeping. Sophie had sobbed and sobbed when we returned home and saw the limp, browning stems and curling leaves. You could just see where the flowers would have started to open, the yellow petals stuck forever inside the buds, never to emerge.

'Now they won't!' Sophie wept even more. 'They've died, they've died!' She had taken a shuddering gasp. 'And it's all our fault, Jess! They needed us to look after them and we didn't.'

'We should have given them to Grampy while we were away.' Mum had picked up the pots, and prodded the dry soil with her fingers. 'They've dried out completely – it's just been too hot while we were away. Never mind. You can grow some more. Maybe next year.'

Sophie covered her face with her hands, and wailed, 'I wanted those!'

'I wanted those too,' I said, and knelt beside Sophie, and put my arm round her. 'But they're dead, Sophie. So... we can't bring them back to life, but we can plant some again, can't we, Mum?'

'They won't be the same! They won't be at all the same!'

'They'll be better,' Mum said. 'Because you'll be so careful looking after them next time, won't you? You'll remember what's happened.' Then she turned towards the house and called my father.

Dad came outside with his smallest camera, and crouched down and took a photo of the sad, shrivelled sunflowers. 'There,' he said. 'Evidence! We've got it on record, girls. Now... anyone for ice cream?'

Just like that, the dying sunflowers were forgotten.

*

Paula takes good care of me. She makes sure I know where everything is, and what happens when, but it isn't very difficult, this first month, as what we mostly do is count and pack away every single item of left-over Christmas goods. We wrap items when necessary, pack them into one of the dozens of boxes, label each with its contents and quantity, and tape them shut. It's bitterly cold outside, and inside is not much better. The building is tall with high steel raftered ceilings. As we empty the shelves and display areas, it becomes gradually bleaker and echoing, and whenever anyone goes in or out the doors open automatically and let in huge draughts of icy air.

We see very few customers.

'This time of year they're all snug at home,' Paula laughs. 'And who can blame them?'

'Not much gardening gets done in January,' says Bernard, coming in from outside where he's been pressure washing the display benches, ready for them to be treated. 'Gordon Bennett! It's a bit nippy out there! Gets worse every year does this job.'

A few older people come to sit in the café for a hot drink or lunch. It's the cosiest area in the building, with heaters blasting out hot air all day long, and I sometimes glance over with envy at Nicole and the other café workers – Tina and Jane – warm and comfy behind their counter.

I'm finding that I'm enjoying each day, against all expectations. It's hard, physical work. Everyone joins in and does whatever needs doing, apart from the café staff – 'Health and safety,' Paula says. 'Of course.' She grins.

So sometimes I'm outside, helping to move shelves and display benches around, or cleaning different areas; then I might be inside, still packing away the never-ending detritus of Christmas.

'How is it then, Jess? Come on! Tell us all!' says Gran, when I call in to see them at the end of my first week.

I move a basket of material scraps and slump down on a chair. 'I'm shattered!'

I feel as if I could stay in their kitchen and sleep for a whole night and day.

'Not much to do this time of year, I shouldn't have thought,' says Grampy, and I take some pride in explaining exactly what there is to do, at which they are gratifyingly amazed. I tell them a little about some of the other staff, things I know they'll find funny: Andy and his fondness for trusted sayings, Eric who thinks that what's wrong with the world is that people don't know their place anymore, and Paula and her capacity to find something amusing in almost every situation.

'Is there anyone your age, Jess? Anyone you've got things in common with?' Gran asks.

'Well, there's Chloe – she's a bit older. Although... she's got two children, so I guess quite a bit... but she's nice.'

I stop and picture myself at work for a minute. Nicole nudges herself into my head. She came and sat with me on my second day, during my break. There were only two customers in the café and I guess she had nothing to do.

'You OK?'

'Fine, thanks.'

'It can be *so* boring here?' She twiddled with her hair, twisting curls round her fingers.

I took a sip of hot chocolate. 'I bet it can, but at the moment it seems there's a load to do, so I've not got bored.' I grinned at her, to show solidarity. 'Yet.'

'You look, like, I don't know, like, I feel I've really seen you before?' Her voice rose up at the end of each sentence.

Mum's eyebrows would be raised too by now, and she'd be muttering about the terrible influence of Australian TV soaps on our generation. I couldn't meet Nicole's gaze. I stared with concentration at my mug, and cupped my hands round it to warm them up.

'Probably just, when I've been in before, maybe.' Although I had no idea when that would have been. Long before Nicole started working here, for sure. I asked her where she'd gone to school, and which Sixth Form. Perhaps we'd been at college together, doing different subjects, I suggested.

'Oh, you have to be joking! I like, left as soon as I could?' she said. 'I mean, it was *so* boring. Is that what you did, then? Fuck me, I'd have, like, died or something if I'd had to stay on after sixteen? You're pretty clever, then, right?'

Tell her, Jess, four fucking A's. Remember? Pretty clever, yeah.

'Not really,' I said, 'but I did work quite hard. I wanted to get to uni.'

Nicole stared at me. 'Right,' she said, 'but still... still, like, think I know you from somewhere?'

Those pictures in the local paper and even, briefly, in some of the national press – what a lot they have to answer for. I felt like Judas as I shrugged and said, 'Search me, Nicole, don't think we've ever met before. Maybe you've just seen me around.'

'Whatever.' Nicole stood up, her chair scraping along the vinyl. 'But – really like your hair, by the way. Like, it really, really suits you? I'd love to be able to have my hair like that. Really, really short? What do they call it, pixie cut? Something like that.'

I stood up too. 'Thanks, Nicole.'

I explain about Nicole in the café to Gran. 'We get on quite well,' I say, avoiding a description of Nicole's habit of punctuating nearly every sentence with "like" and "so". It seems pretentious when Nicole's been nothing but kind and open with me. 'But they're all nice, Gran. Really lovely. Friendly, and helpful.'

'So do you think you might change your mind, then? Stay here, after all?' Grampy asks.

I can't miss the optimism in his question, and I feel I'm bursting his little balloon of hope, but still I have to say, 'You *know* this is just to get me over there, Grampy. This is my way of earning some money to get me to Denmark, and keep me going once I'm there. I am absolutely not going to stay here, working in the garden centre for the rest of the year.'

He is undeterred. 'Well, who knows? Never know what's round the corner. You just never can tell.'

CHAPTER TWELVE

Karen and I arrange to meet in Brighton. My work at the garden centre means I have to be there every other weekend, but I do get a couple of days off during the week instead. Karen has taken an extra week's holiday after the New Year to study, she tells me, although it seems to involve a number of shopping trips and general socialising. She's always been such a hard worker, though, and so focused; she must surely be fitting in lots of reading and preparation too.

We go to a café in the North Laine, and we're glad to get inside and order food and drinks. It's bitterly cold outside, the wind cutting straight off the sea. I pick up the two mugs from the counter and follow Karen over to a table in the window: peppermint tea for her, a cappuccino for me. We sit in silence for a while. Karen lifts out the tea bag from her mug, squeezing it against the side before discarding it, and I stir the froth into my coffee and watch the man at a table near us as he makes extravagant gestures to the woman opposite. He's flicking his fingers, raising his hands, pointing and gesticulating, and wiping invisible crumbs off the surface in front of him, again and again, with the flat of one hand.

'I'd quite like to go to New Zealand,' his companion's words float over to us. 'But until they do some sort of, you know, "Beam me up Scottie", then I'm afraid it's just too long. Too long in a confined space.' She loosens her scarf from around her neck as she speaks, and shakes back a mane of bright blonde hair, lightly streaked on top with pink.

Karen's taking small experimental sips of her tea. The steam from it hovers in front of her face, and then cowers and dissolves in the draught from the café door as two women come in.

'I rang her,' one is saying as they pass us, 'and, no reply! Well, I thought, she'll be in the bath. Tea, dear? Or hot chocolate? Yes, it is a hot chocolate type of day. What was I saying? Oh, yes, then her neighbour rang, and she's died! Just like that, from a brain...' Her voice grows fainter as she approaches the counter, until I can't hear any more.

'So,' Karen begins. 'When did you think we'd leave?' She ventures another sip of tea. 'May would be good. Or June, because of the weather, really. Did you get my text the other day?'

My coffee's hot, but not scalding. I pick up the mug. 'Text?' I begin to drink.

'You know, about staying at my Mormor's?'

The waitress, who is wearing a large black T-shirt with the words "Café Coco" in red strained tight across her front, runs up to our table in little, plodding, heavy steps: 'Two more minutes! OK? Panini, wasn't it, and a brown rice salad? Sorry for the wait.' Then she runs back across the room to another couple, with the same message, 'Just two minutes. So, so sorry for the wait.' She returns, breathless, to her position behind the counter.

'Well, I'm going to have pudding, I'm afraid,' the pink-streaked hair lady is saying now, avoiding her partner's gaze, her words loud and strident. 'I never do. Well, hardly ever. But today I've been to a funeral so, I'm sorry, I'm having a dessert, and that's that.' She picks up the menu card and studies it with unwavering determination, while Gesticulating Man shakes his head slightly, and raises his eyebrows.

I force my attention back to our table. 'Oh yes, yes I did get it,' I answer. 'Are you sure she won't mind?'

I drain the last drop of liquid from my mug, and then use a teaspoon to scoop out the remaining froth. The waitress appears with our plates, carrying them with care, her steps slower and more measured. 'There you go! Anything else I can get you?'

'We're fine, thanks,' says Karen.

'No problem! Enjoy your meal.'

We grin at each other, and begin to eat quickly. Behind us a woman is hunching a mobile close to her ear with one shoulder, while she pinches tiny pieces off a croissant. 'But if I could get a T.A. job... brilliant!' she's declaring. 'No planning or marking, just go in and help a few children...' There's a pause during which Karen and I give each other meaningful glances. 'Oh yes, still have the care job. I'd do that as well.'

Karen's forking up a third small mouthful of rice and peas and peppers, and she pauses with it halfway to her mouth. 'Mind?' she repeats. 'Mormor? She'd love it! She's always saying she doesn't see me enough. And she'd love to practise her English on you.'

I take another bite of my hot sandwich. 'Well, if you're sure... it would make it easier to start with, wouldn't it? Until, you know...'

'I'll email her,' Karen announces. 'Tonight. Or, maybe I'll phone. No, I will. I'll phone, she'd like that. Trouble is, I always feel I have to speak Danish, and it's really, really difficult on the phone.'

'So, what will you say?'

'What? In Danish?'

'No! No, I meant, when will you say we'll go?'

Before Karen can reply, I become aware that the elderly lady on the table next to us is still sitting on her own. She's been there for several minutes, waiting. Now her face brightens as another woman of a similar age joins her, balancing a tray which she puts down with a tiny sigh.

'Well, the thing is,' the woman with the tray says, 'I wouldn't have had the soup if she'd told me. But she rang it all up and then she said there'll be a fifteen-minute wait! Well, I'd have chosen something different, I felt like saying. Funny thing is, I would have had an egg sandwich like you, but they only had the one, so I got that quick, for you, before someone else took it.'

She sits down opposite her friend and eases off her coat with careful unhurried shrugs and tugs. It collapses over the back of her chair like a shorn fleece.

The lady who has been waiting begins to pour a cup of tea. Thin splashes spatter the saucer and surrounding surface, but I don't think she notices. 'Oh!' she's saying. 'Oh well, I suppose I didn't really have to have the egg. You could have had it after all. No, because we're having lamb tonight. So I didn't really need the egg.'

My shoulders start to shake. I put down my panini, and press my fingers into my eyes. Then in my head I start to count.

'Jess?' Karen sounds concerned. 'Jessie? You OK?'

I take away my hands and fold them between my knees. I smile at her. Karen, my friend. Our friend.

'Just missing Sophie,' I say. 'That's all.'

'Do you want to wait?' Karen says, and her voice softens. 'Would you rather be having this conversation another time?' She's giving me one of her special, concerned expressions.

'No. No, it's fine. It's... good. It's only that Sophie...' I lower my voice a little. 'We just used to listen in, all the time, to other people's conversations.' We'd make things up about them, I'm thinking, invent entire scenarios, intimate dramas. Sophie was especially good at it. But it's not just that. Today my eavesdropping, funny though Sophie would have found it, seems to have been centred in a peculiar way on significant themes. Or am I simply more sensitive to those themes – a funeral, and travel, and the trivial but important details that make up our lives, the triggers for pathos?

I can hear her voice.

That weird couple over there... must be having an affair! How sad are those two old ladies? Why can't you have egg if you're having lamb later? What's that all about?

I expect to see her, somewhere in the café, watching, but when I glance around she's not there.

'She always wanted to be able to see people,' I add. 'Liked to get the whole picture. Don't you remember how she had to sit back to the wall so she could see the rest of the room?'

Karen's propped her elbows on the table now, smiling at me. 'Yes, I do,' she says. 'I do remember.' Then she sighs. 'I miss her, I really do, but it always seems... kind of inappropriate? I feel like I have no right, that none of us do, when it's all so terrible for you – your Mum, and your family, all of you. That the rest of us should just have... coped.'

It's never occurred to me. I know how upset our friends had been by Sophie's death. I've never realised they might still carry those emotions, still miss Sophie after all these months, just as I do. I'm not sure what to say, so it's lucky that Karen continues.

'When you talk about her,' she says, 'it sort of brings her back, for a bit. It's part of the reason I want to help you find Per. Why I want to go to Denmark with you, because that's what you both wanted to do, wasn't it?'

When I nod, she carries on, 'So me going there with you is my way of keeping Sophie's memory alive. It feels like I'm doing it for both of you. I'm so glad you asked me, Jess.' Then she stops and looks across at me with an uncertain expression and I know I must reassure her, and make her realise I understand.

'I'm really glad I asked you, too. It was Sophie's idea... in a way, so you're doing us both a favour.'

'And now,' Karen becomes her brisk, practical self again, 'you were asking what I'd tell Mormor about when we'll go. What shall we say? May? That seems a long time away but I can't really go before that.'

'And I need to save up as much as I can.'

'May it is, then.'

We exchange relieved looks of triumph at having agreed on something so momentous, before Karen gets up to pay the bill and I squeeze my eyes shut, count to ten and quell the rising wave of nausea at anticipation of our plans. When Karen comes back, we decide to go shopping together and find a travel guide for Denmark. I buy a phrase book as well – 'But you won't need it, they all speak English, more or less,' Karen assures me – and a slim book called "Copenhagen the Easy Way". It feels as if, at last, finding Per is actually going to happen.

*

Sophie often said she was going to write a book one day. It would be called, she announced, "The Final Denouement". There was a provocative look in her eye as she declared this, as if daring anyone to challenge her on the pros and cons of the success of such a manuscript.

'Isn't that what denouement means?' I ventured once. 'Final?'

She lifted her eyes skyward. 'You are *so* pedantic, Jessica Mortimer. So... literal!'

Had I never heard of irony, she asked, never considered how it's possible to be quirky and risqué and to make people – readers in this case – think outside the box? She had been very keen, around this time, about thinking "outside the box", about having unusual ideas. In particular it was Lucas's thing; he was fond of throwing outrageous and controversial suggestions into the air and watching where they would land. I often suspected that the whole "Final Denouement" thing was his idea in the first place.

Sophie liked to be different; she enjoyed confronting what she called bourgeois ways of thinking. Lucas lit the match and watched the fire smouldering, and sometimes the flames grew out of control.

We'd cycled up on to the Downs, escaping the tedium of revision for a few hours, and were sitting right on top of Wolstonbury, a steep hill not far from our village. It's ancient, an old Iron Age fort, although sitting up there you wouldn't guess that. Alex and Toby, when they were younger, were always sure they were going to discover an arrowhead, or a flint spear, or some previously unexcavated and valuable Iron Age implement or dwelling, and often thought they had.

Now we sprawled on the close-cropped turf, taking care to avoid touching anything that looked a bit prickly. You could hear the drone of bees around the gorse and clover, and the monotonous swish of traffic far below on the Brighton road. Otherwise, there was an absolute silence around us and that dry, dusty smell of hot grass and warm earth. We both lay and contemplated the Final Denouement and what it might reveal. I envied Sophie's complete faith in her ability to write something that seemed so vague. Her vision of the book was not mine.

There was a brisk breeze, but the sun shone with a fierce intensity, and soon Sophie sat up and began to roll up her jeans before lifting up her arms to remove her top and rolling onto her front.

'I'm keeping my bra on,' her voice was muffled by her arms, 'because of prickly stuff.'

'And creepy-crawlies,' I added, because both of us had a fear of anonymous insects. Alex and Toby loved catching bugs when they were little and then tormenting us with them. We'd run away screaming.

'Ignore them,' Mum would say. 'You know that's why they do it. It just encourages them.'

Now it felt comforting to know that among what felt like an increasing number of hidden thistles and brambles in our relationship, we still had so much that we shared. There was so much we never needed to explain to each other.

I reached over to pull a bottle of water out of my bag, and nudged Sophie with it.

'Want some?'

'Got some.' She moved her head to the side to speak, and then stretched out an arm to reach inside her rucksack.

'Hey, water's water,' I said, but already I could feel that familiar thread of anxiety curling round inside me.

'Yeah. Right.' Sophie grinned and tipped back her head to swallow a few gulps from her bottle. Then she held it out to me.

I wrinkled my nose with disgust when I smelt it and realised. 'Vodka? God, Sophie. Are you mad?'

'Just gets me through, baby, just gets me through.'

'Through what? It's the middle of the day! We're in the middle of revising. Our next exam is the day after tomorrow. What do you mean, gets you through?' I could hear my voice rising in a sort of panic, and then I added, 'And don't call me "baby". That's such a Lucas thing. I hate it.'

Sophie was stowing the bottle back in her bag. 'It doesn't mean, like, "*baby*". It's a term of affection, dumbo.'

'I know that,' I muttered. 'But I still don't like it.'

'Yeah, well.' Sophie had turned onto her back, and was arranging her head on her bag with her eyes closed. She fumbled with the button of her jeans and loosened the zip a little, easing the jeans down to expose more of her stomach. 'Anyway, a tiny amount of vodka is not going to have some terrible effect, and it just makes me feel more... on top of things. More able to cope.'

I'd stopped listening, and was staring instead at her bare skin, the part she had just exposed above the skimpy line of her knickers. A small blue and green dragonfly was lying, perfectly etched, across under her hip bone. 'Sophie?'

She knew, of course, what I'd seen, and what I meant in that one single question of her name.

She propped herself up to peer down at it with a grin. 'Beautiful, isn't it?' she said. 'It was a kind of eighteenth birthday and anniversary present all in one from Lucas.'

'Anniversary?' It was all I could think of saying immediately, and then, 'You know what they'll say? Mum and Dad? They'll go ballistic! A tattoo? Shit, Sophie, what were you thinking?'

'Why didn't I tell you?' She knew me too well.

'That too.'

'Because... it was just between me and Lucas. I knew what you'd say, Jessie, so it was easier just to...' Sophie stretched out along the ground again, and winced as her arm touched a bramble. 'And since you ask, the anniversary of us. Lucas and me. Getting together. *You* know.'

She gave me a look under her eyelashes that was almost coy. Of course I knew. I knew she had first slept with Lucas on her sixteenth birthday because she couldn't wait to tell me.

How many other secrets were there now, buried in the gap widening between us? How would I ever know? When she and Lucas first started spending time together – 'Going out,' as Mum liked to say – Sophie had told me everything. She'd ask my advice, just as both of us had always done, she'd shared how she felt, told me what he said, asked me what I thought. But gradually, as time went on, I had realised she was choosing with care what she told me. I was being excluded. I knew that, under the surface euphoria, she was beginning to have her own doubts. There was a confusion in her mind. Suspicions were festering.

But Lucas was like a drug. She couldn't get enough of him.

CHAPTER THIRTEEN

After a week of being chaperoned by Paula, I'm allowed to work on my own. This has the potential to be quite scary but I wake up on my second Monday knowing I'll be unsupervised and feeling only positive and excited.

'Have to get you trained on the tills, Jess, sometime this week,' Andy announces during the early morning staff meeting. 'Freda? Are you able to sort that out?'

'Ooh, you'll have the right person there,' Paula giggles. 'She's a dab hand is our Freda on the tills. Aren't you, love?'

I like Freda. I think she's probably about the same age as Gran, which seems odd. She has numerous grandchildren who are all still quite little. She's always sharing their latest antics with Paula, and anyone else who'll listen.

It makes me realise how relatively young my own grandparents must have been when Sophie and I were born. I'd always assumed that they were simply delighted to find out we were on the way; for as long as I can remember that's what they've said. But perhaps it was more of a shock for them than Sophie and I had ever appreciated. Grampy was still working at his solicitor's practice; Gran had her own busy, independent life as an artist. When Mum moved back to live with them and we were born, Gran, especially, gave up a lot of that independence to help look after us both.

Learning to use the tills is more complicated than I expect, but I soon find that I'm enjoying using my brain again. Plus, it makes a change from the interminable wrapping and packing of Christmas stuff.

'Well, never mind me,' Freda says towards the end of the week. 'It's you that's the dab hand at this, I think. I'll have to make sure Paula knows.'

There are still very few customers around, so I'm allowed to work on my own and see how I get on. My first few transactions go well; there's a limit to what people want to buy in the middle of January. Most people choose greetings cards, or house plants, or something from the gift or kitchen accessory section, and I have a real sense of satisfaction at registering the purchase and giving change, or using the card machine. Freda busies herself within earshot of the tills, so that I can call on her if necessary.

It's Thursday and nearly time for my lunch break. I recite the Flowers' goodbye mantra – 'Thank you for shopping here. We hope to see you again very soon' – to an elderly couple who've just bought a reduced and rather sorry-looking fern in a pot. I'm aware of another customer – a woman – waiting to be served next. I glance at her, ready to give my welcoming smile, and my stomach knots and my heart flips. At almost the same time she recognises me, too. It's Lucas's mother.

She plonks her basket on the counter: inside it lies a large pair of extra-thick gardening gloves, some garden twine, and what looks like a flowery birthday card.

'You've got a nerve,' she mutters, all the while staring down at the items.

I think I've misheard. 'Sorry?'

'A nerve. Working here. Thought you'd have taken yourself well away after... all that trouble.'

She won't meet my eye. I swallow, blink hard, and pick up the gardening gloves to scan them. 'I'm not sure I know...'

'Oh, you don't fool me. Not for one moment.'

For a second – only a second – I think that the last months must all have been a dream. It's Lucas who died, and Sophie is still alive and somehow responsible. Then I breathe in carefully, and take the garden string.

'Do you have any idea,' Mrs Fleming continues, and each word erupts violently from her mouth, tiny globules of spit landing in front of me, 'any idea at all what it's been like for us?'

I can only shake my head. I don't trust myself to speak. Silently I start to count, backwards from twenty, in the hope that by the time I reach zero she will have gone.

'Your sister,' she hisses. 'Your precious sister. Little Miss Fascinating, wasn't she? Ruined my son's life, that's what she did. Ruined it.'

I have to stop scanning the twine to brush the heel of each hand under my eyes. The tears flow, unchecked. I peer over my shoulder in the hope of catching Freda's attention. Then I take a deep breath. I've already reached zero.

'Mrs Fleming, shall I... would you... prefer someone else?'

She's moved down to stand at the other end of the counter now, and is putting the gloves into a carrier bag. She still hasn't met my gaze, and she ignores what I've said. Now she holds out her hand, waiting for me to give her the string and the card. Everything looks blurred but I can see that the words looping across the flowers on the front of the card read "In Deepest Sympathy".

'I'll have those now, thank you,' she says, continuing to hold out her hand.

I lean forward, gripping the edge of the counter. My heart is pounding, and my mouth has gone dry. Grief and fear, in equal measure, wash over me in hot and cold waves.

'Did you hear me?' she says, raising her voice. 'Shouldn't be doing this job if you can't cope. You're no better than her. Spoilt little madam. Wrapped him round her little finger, she did. Took us all in. Well, never took me in.' She comes back to stand in front of me.

She's breathing heavily, and she pushes her face right in front of mine: 'Not. For. One. Minute.'

Another couple have arrived; I'm aware of them in the corner of my vision. I pick up the card with trembling fingers and scan it, and then I hand over both items.

'Unfortunate.' Mrs Fleming puts them in her bag. 'Very unfortunate that she died. Nobody would have wanted...'

Her voice is dropping. I stare with grim determination at the ceiling and, with all my strength, will her to leave. Behind me the other couple are shifting their feet, and one of them coughs.

I look over my shoulder, searching with a forlorn hope for someone to arrive and relieve me. 'Mrs Fleming, I don't...'

She moves back to stand right in front of me, and hisses, 'Don't imagine, for one minute, that I don't know what *you* got up to. My Lucas, that poor boy, taken in, he was, by the pair of you!' She shakes her head, slowly. 'Unbelievable. Her. And you. Unbelievable.'

I breathe in and out with jagged, desperate breaths, and start to count in tens.

'Telling him she was pregnant! Oldest trick in the book. Little bitch. Well, as I say, I was never taken in, but Lucas, now, he's got to live with this for the rest of his life. Nobody ever thought about that, did they? Oh no. It was all about,' she makes her voice simper, '... poor Sophie. Poor Sophie's family. So brave. Such a tragedy.'

'Jess? Everything all right?'

I slump with relief. I hear Freda's voice behind me and now she appears like my guardian angel. She takes one look at me, and then at Mrs Fleming, and she says, 'Time for your break, isn't it? Off you go. I'll take over now.'

As I move away I hear her say, 'Now, is there some sort of a problem, madam? Can I help?'

If there is a reply, it's too low for me to hear. I stumble to the tiny staff room, next to Andy's even smaller office, and I shut the door, sink onto a chair, and start to shake.

*

Sophie was lying on the waste ground behind the old telephone exchange when Dad found her. He had walked down our lane and into the High Street, his jacket collar turned up against the chill of that early spring night, his hands dug deep in his pockets. It was very late, over an hour since Sophie had jumped out of Karen's car, and the village was silent: the windows of the houses and cottages along the street all unlit, a deep blackness shrouding everything. A figure was stumbling through the darkness up the middle of the road towards him. It was Lucas. His face was bleached of colour, Dad said later, gleaming pale in the shadows. When he saw my father, he became incoherent, sobbing and shuddering and unable to articulate any words that made sense.

Dad had grabbed him by the shoulders. 'Lucas? Lucas! Where's Sophie? Where is she? Is she OK?'

Lucas was shaking, his breath coming in juddering gasps. 'Over...' he shook off Dad's grip on him, and pointed, his arm trembling, across the street, where Furnace Lane turned down, '... there. The... the... She's behind the... She's lying...' He broke down.

Dad had left him then. He'd raced down the road to the old, disused exchange, and fumbled his way round the side, through the weeds and brambles, tripping and nearly falling in his panic to find Sophie. It was too late; he knew when he saw her that it was already too late. He'd tried to lift her, had held her limp upper body close and rocked her, backwards and forwards, as if somehow, being close, she'd come back to life.

What? You didn't think you could get rid of me that easily, did you?

But it was much, much too late.

He'd stayed sitting there, holding her, my sister, my beloved twin. He'd heard the police sirens and the ambulance as they screeched through the village. When they appeared, those people in uniform who'd come to help, called at last by Lucas, Dad had looked at them with disbelief. They'd moved him away from Sophie's body and he'd waited while they tried to resuscitate her, knowing all the time it was much too late. Then he'd been brought home, and held us both, Mum and me, and told us that Sophie had died. Sophie – who had blue eyes like me, and blonde hair; who tipped her head to one side when she was listening to you; who was ten minutes older than me, and said being a twin was the best thing ever.

Really it is, Jessie, don't you think? You do, don't you? It'll always be us against the world, we'll always have each other. That's what's so great.

Sophie had died.

*

Sophie's voice comes from nowhere. 'Nobody knows,' she says. '*You* thought "nobody knows", and now see what's happened.'

She's sitting on the floor, fingering her odd earrings, and then she tucks her hair behind her ears and says, in that quick, fierce way she has of challenging a difficult situation, 'You should have got a job somewhere else. Brighton, for example. If you didn't want anyone to recognise you. The girl with the dead twin sister.'

I take a look over my shoulder, scared of someone walking in and finding Sophie, and then I realise how ridiculous that is. It's become obvious that nobody else can see her. Still, I wouldn't want anyone thinking I'm talking to myself.

So I keep my voice low when I reply. 'Nobody's said anything. I don't think anyone does know. People forget, Sophie. It's news, and then things move on and there's different news.' I press my hands between my knees because they're still trembling. More than anything I need Sophie to come over and give me a hug.

But she's twiddling the rings on her fingers now, concentrating on turning them round and round, and then she says, 'That cow.'

'Mrs Fleming?' I rock on my chair, and try to stop my legs from jittering.

'Yeah. Lucas hated her, you know.'

'His own mother?' It seemed unlikely.

'Well, you see what she's like. Who could blame him? I always thought she'd got some sort of problem. She never liked me, anyway.' Sophie lays her hands in her lap, and fixes me with an earnest stare.

'You never said.' I can't keep the accusation out of my tone. 'You never told me she was funny. Odd.'

I know how difficult Sophie would have found that to cope with. Sophie was used to being adored. Sophie who had watched The Sound of Music so many times she could sing all the words off by heart, but always slightly off-key; who took three goes to pass her driving test, and had a list of all the jobs she'd never want to do – 'However much they paid me!' Since she was a little girl, everyone who had ever met her was won over. I can't think of anyone who hadn't eventually fallen under her spell, and I suppose that included Lucas, of course. But not, I now realise, his mother.

'Yeah, well. You know,' Sophie says, with a sigh. 'Hey, time to leave, Jessie – things to do!'

I want to answer, 'Places to go? People to meet?' like we always have, but instead I glance at her wrist, and then around the tiny room, and I wonder how she knows what time it is when she's not wearing a watch and there's no clock in sight. What possible things could she have to do, in any case?

'Places to go, Sophie?' I say. 'What places? Where do you go? Who else do you meet? Why can't you just stay here?' Then I add, 'With me.' As I say it, I think how pathetic I sound.

I don't know if she was going to answer because, before she can, I hear the door behind me being opened very slowly, and Paula's voice says, 'Jess? Oh, good, you're here. Freda said you seemed a bit...' I turn to see Paula, and then remember I need to watch Sophie, but it's too late. When I glance back, she's gone.

*

Polly and Em come to visit me. I have never been more pleased to see them. They arrive just as I'm about to have my lunch break on Friday, so we choose sandwiches and soup at the counter and sit together in the café. It's one of Nicole's days, and she watches us with open curiosity until other customers arrive and she has to serve them.

'This is nice,' Polly says, looking around, and with a barely concealed sarcasm in her voice.

For once I'm unafraid to face up to her. 'Yes. It is actually. It's just the loveliest place to...'

She interrupts, 'We really don't understand why you'd want to work here when you could be temping in Brighton or somewhere. Earning a lot more...'

'A lot,' Em agrees, taking a bite of her sandwich.

Polly ignores her: '... In much better conditions, and not having to wear that hideous sweatshirt.'

I fold my arms across the front of my green Flowers' staff sweatshirt, and wonder how I can stop Polly noticing my name badge – "I'M JESS! HAPPY TO HELP!" I'm not sure I can be bothered to argue all the relative merits of the best places to work, and as I'm here, and happy with my decision, I say, 'So, when do you both go back to uni?' We veer off the subject of my working environment.

I don't have much time, and I want to tell them about my confrontation with Mrs Fleming. I relate it all, in between trying to take mouthfuls of hot soup.

Em whistles. 'Yikes! Poor, poor you, Jess. Just what you didn't need. How brave, just to stay there. I'd have run a mile.'

'That wouldn't have helped much,' says Polly. 'You definitely did the right thing, Jess, staying there. What a cow.'

'I know.' I put down my spoon. 'That's what Sophie says... said.'

'I always thought she seemed a bit odd,' Polly agreed, 'Lucas's mum, but then, we didn't have much to do with her, did we?' She crumbles her bread roll, and scatters some of the bits over her soup, before picking up her spoon.

'What *did* Sophie say?' asks Em. 'Did she tell you much about her?'

I hesitate. 'Not a lot,' I say, after a pause.

'But maybe it explains something about Lucas,' says Em. 'Don't you think? If his mum was a bit... you know, loopy, it's bound to have an effect on how he behaves. How he is as a person, even.'

We are all three quiet as we think about this, by Em's standards, quite profound statement.

'All that alternative stuff,' says Polly. 'All that needing to be different.'

'Do you ever see him, Jess?' asks Em, as she puts her empty sandwich packet on the plate, and pushes it into the middle of the table.

I can't help the tiny pause before I shake my head. 'I've no idea where he is, or what he's doing. What about you?'

They exchange glances. Then Polly says, 'He's doing a Masters at Sussex after he finishes this year, I think.'

Em adds quickly, 'But we don't see him, do we, Poll? None of our crowd does, really...' Her voice tails off, and she concentrates on brushing crumbs off the table, and then her jeans.

There's more, of course there's more, but they're not going to tell me, and I'm not sure I want to know. For weeks and weeks after Sophie died, I was obsessed with thoughts of Lucas; where he was and what he was doing. My anger towards him verged on the uncontrollable, especially after he was released by the police, and later after the coroner's verdict. I would never have imagined it possible to feel so much hate for one person. It didn't bring Sophie back, though, no matter how hard I wished the same fate on him. Now I know I'll have to battle with this new picture of Lucas, strolling through his charmed life at Sussex, gaining qualifications and a career and plaudits and commendations while Sophie rots in her coffin underground.

'That's where Mum went,' I say, almost to myself. 'Sussex. It's where she met... where she and Per... and now, God! It seems like he's still trying to punish us somehow.'

Polly sees my face. She says, 'Jess, don't. Don't think about him. Don't waste another precious minute, not even a second. He's not worth it.' She reaches across the table to squeeze my hands with hers.

We hug each other goodbye, and as I walk away from them across the café, I can see Sally and Chloe working on the tills. I'm counting in French and before I reach 'vingt-cinq' I say to Chloe, 'I'm back! It's OK. I've had my break.' It's her turn for lunch.

I stop counting, and think only how simple life would be if I could stay here, working in Flowers' for the rest of my life. But as I squeeze past Chloe to take her place at a till, what I know is that more than ever it's important to go and find Per.

I need those missing pieces of my jigsaw.

CHAPTER FOURTEEN

The weeks speed by. The bleak dark days of January give way to a sharp, cold, but brighter February. I feel I've never been as aware of the weather and seasons as now, working here. I'm almost an old hand these days, checking the rota each day for my duties, grumbling with the others if I'm down for unpacking and sorting deliveries. Despite the incident with Mrs Fleming, my favourite role is still behind a till. The pre-season orders start to arrive – pots, canes, baskets. They all have to be put out on display somewhere.

'Always a month ahead here,' Eric with the red nose explains in a quiet moment while we open boxes and take out packets of seeds and bulbs. 'Always a month ahead of when a gardener is going to want it. Even your very organised gardener type.'

'They don't catch us out,' Bernard chuckles, as he goes past, rubbing his hands. 'Never been caught out yet, has Flowers'.'

'Your dad a gardener, is he?' Eric is fitting small sachets of seeds into tall racks after I've organised them into alphabetical order.

'Well... sort of.' That seems the kindest way to describe what has always been my parents' rather carefree attitude to our garden. Mum likes pottering – planting up tubs, often at the last minute, to flower in the spring and summer, organising herbs, clipping straggly shrubs. Dad does what he calls the hacking and hewing, and that includes mowing the grass. 'My grandparents love gardening, though.'

'You know you get a staff discount, don't you? Andy's told you that, I expect. So anything you want, you get twenty-five per cent off. Might be nice for your grandparents – you could get whatever they want. Big saving that. One of the perks.'

I've started using my bike to get to and from work. As long as I wear thick gloves and a beanie pulled down over my ears it's not too bad. I cycle past Gran and Grampy's on my way home that day. I find them in the kitchen, enjoying a glass of wine – 'Before dinner, Jessie. Just a small one. As it's Tuesday,' – and explain Eric's suggestion.

'Now that does sound like a plan,' says Grampy. 'Let's see. What's best? Shall we make a list, Frances? For Jess to buy.'

Gran pushes her specs up onto her head, and turns round from where she's leafing through some sheets of illustrations. She leans back against the worktop and picks up her wine. 'And how will she carry stuff home, John?' she asks, ever the practical one.

'Good point,' Grampy nods. 'I wondered if you'd spot that deliberate mistake.' He gives me a wink.

I tell them that I can still use Mum's car some days, although part of the reason I'm cycling is because she says she needs it more during the day. I'm unclear about why that is, other than supermarket shopping and things like that. However, Gran thinks they would like to call in at the garden centre and see me one day, and wonders if they could find some things they need then, and I could put them through the till and get the discount there and then.

'How's it going, Jessie?' she asks, after we've decided on that course of action.

I'm full of enthusiasm. 'I love it! Not the cold, obviously, or the really boring bits, but I... it's good. I'm... thinking less. About things.'

Gran takes a sip of wine. 'Good. I'm sure it must help – being busy. But... I didn't actually mean your job, Jessie. I meant your plans, for going away, and home too. How are things at home?'

Sophie's voice arrives, uncalled, just her voice – I hear it from the past.

What is it about Gran? How does she pick up on stuff? I'd love to be like that! Wouldn't you, Jess? Maybe when we're older...

I realise that I don't know exactly how things are at home. I imagine life is going on as it has for the last few months, because I'm not aware of anything changing, but these days I'm either at work or in my room trying to sort out ideas for my journey. I only really see my family in the evenings, or if I happen to be home at the weekend on a day off. Before too much longer I'll be leaving them, probably only for a couple of months, but I've become immersed in my own time capsule, oblivious to how they're all continuing to cope. Dad has his work, the boys have school, and now I'm at work too. But Mum? What's she doing, these long winter days? I have no idea. I haven't bothered to ask, let alone think about it.

My grandparents both look at me with a studied innocence. If there's an ulterior motive in Gran's question, she's not about to tell me.

'I'd better go now,' I say. 'I need to get home. Nearly time to eat.' As I glance at my watch I remember Sophie in the Flowers' staffroom, and her comment about time, and her bare wrist. That familiar sick feeling, absent for so many weeks now, begins to reappear. As I go outside into the dark to find my bike, propped against the wall of the cottage, and wheel it down my grandparents' path, I start to count. I think that if I can reach home before I've got to fifty, then everything will be all right, and the next time Sophie visits she'll tell me where she is, and what happens to her all the time I can't see her. And why her toenails look exactly the same as they did when she died, ten months ago.

*

I spread out the map of Copenhagen on the kitchen table. It's where we'd always planned to start our search for Per. Mum had said he came from there, his family were all in the city, and that's where he was returning to after his year in England. He was going back to university in Copenhagen, and he wanted to be a journalist.

Alex arrives in the kitchen and whistles when he sees the map. 'Shouldn't be too difficult then, Jess,' he says. 'Not exactly a massive search area, is it?' He wanders over to the dresser and picks up the biscuit tin, then puts it down and goes over to the fridge instead. He's peering inside it when Mum comes in.

'Nearly dinner time!' she exclaims when she notices Alex. 'No snacking! Close that door right now, Alex Mortimer.'

Alex takes no notice and reaches inside to take out a plate consisting of three cold roast potatoes and a chicken leg.

'Alex!' Mum says with the sort of threat in her voice that we all know better than to ignore.

He turns to her with a wounded and starving puppy dog expression on his face. 'You cannot be serious? I am so hungry – you have no idea. I could report you for wilful neglect, you know. Where's the Childline number? It's virtually child abuse – letting your growing son collapse because he's not allowed one tiny mouthful of...'

'Ooh! Cold roasties! *Love* them.' Toby bounds into the kitchen.

'Hands off!' yells Alex, and holds the plate above his head, and we all watch as Toby tries his best to grab it, only it's too high for him to reach and they're scuffling, making mock punches at each other. Before long the plate will get dropped, but I realise we're smiling, Mum and me. She's given up on any kind of pretence of being in control of the situation, and we're laughing and shaking our heads at their silliness and raising mock-resigned eyebrows at each other. It seems like a normal day.

Any minute now Sophie will wander in and say, 'Oh, mine, I think!' and somehow extricate the plate of food before either Alex or Toby can do anything, and they'll be outraged: 'Hey! What the fuck...' and Mum will say, 'Language! Language, Alex! Unnecessary. Anyway, it's your own fault.'

Sophie will be crowing with delight, twirling out of the kitchen with food she doesn't want – a little war-dance of triumph – and we'll all be collapsing with giggles, Alex despite himself, and Toby still aggrieved.

But of course, that doesn't happen.

*

If Dad was an excellent photographer, and we knew he was, my mother was an amazing teacher of history. I'm not sure we appreciated that fact for years and years. Because what she did, in a completely brilliant way, was make history come alive. It never felt like history to us; it was exciting and real and happening.

At our secondary school, Sophie and I could never understand what people meant when they said history was boring, all about dead people and things that didn't matter anymore: 'Who cares, anyway?'

We'd look at them in amazement. Had they never stood at Battle, and watched as William of Normandy and his men began their steady climb up Senlac Hill towards them?

'Here they come,' Mum would shout. 'How are you going to manage to fight them? You're exhausted, after that long

148

march down south, and what else? Have you had anything to eat lately?'

'No! We're starving!' we'd shout back, aged ten.

'King Harold wants you to stay exactly where you are. Don't break rank!'

We had stood there stiff as iron railings, having positioned Alex and Toby in front of us for extra protection.

At Hadrian's Wall, we were Roman sentries on look-out for those northern barbarians, alert to the smallest noise: a rustle of grass, a movement in the distance. Or we were camp followers: women who were fed up with this wet, cold, hostile land, trying to make the best of it but longing to get back to the warmth and luxury of their Roman homes. Or cooks making futile attempts to produce something edible from a few very uninteresting ingredients; or the children outside playing tag or rolling hoops, shivering and blue with cold as the snow piled up around the garrison.

'What are you going to do? It's so boring here, stuck inside.' We'd have to think of our own entertainment. Endless games, Mum said, of jacks maybe, or marbles.

We never questioned Mum's apparently all-encompassing knowledge of just about any period in history. Wherever we were, whatever we were exploring or visiting, it would be preserved on film by Dad, but made real by Mum. I understand now how she must have been a wonderful teacher, but that part of her life didn't last long. She never returned to teaching after the boys were born, and she never showed the slightest hankering for it, either.

All that knowledge and enthusiasm was transmitted to us, instead. Except I don't believe we ever felt we were being taught anything specific, as we stood on the battlements at Lewes Castle, or at the dockyard in Portsmouth, or as we ran around between all the buildings at Singleton Open Air Museum. Even now they're like films in my head. I sat in a damp brick cell, listening to the lap of water below the window, waiting for my trial in the Tower of London, already aware of its inevitable outcome. I was on the Titanic, frantically scrabbling to get up onto the top deck from my humble position down in the belly of the ship. Gasping for air, terrified for my children, my dreams of a new and better life in America drowning as we waited, hopelessly, for a lifeboat.

'Everybody is living their own bit of history,' Mum explained. 'Everybody.'

'Not now!' Sophie said, unable to keep disbelief out of her voice. 'We're living now, not in history!'

'But what we do now, what we experience, will be history one day.'

'Only if we're famous,' Sophie said. 'Not just for doing... nothing much.'

'Even that.' Mum was adamant. 'Your history started right here, in Sussex, and moved to Manchester, and came back down again. If you have children one day, you'll pass that history on. You two have got another, separate, piece of history that you don't share with anyone else in our family. Part of your own history is over in Denmark.'

She was good at reminding us about that, in a subtly deliberate way, bringing the fact of our birth into our lives without making it a big deal. It was simply unfortunate that for so long we had believed her original version, and not been aware of the one that emerged later.

'Well, anyway,' Sophie said, 'it doesn't matter because, one way or another, I am going to be famous. So's Jessie, aren't you? I just haven't quite decided how...'

*

The map of Copenhagen, as it turns out, is the catalyst.

I fold it up so we can eat, but then later I spread it out again, and we all crowd round the table to peer at it.

'I'll get the address I had for him,' Mum says.

It's gone, that awkwardness, that denial. It's as if some light has been switched on, as if she's suddenly, for no reason, remembered all that discussion we used to have about making history. As if she's accepted that it's inevitable, me going to find Per, and her best course of action will be to help all she can.

'He won't still be there, surely?' Dad says. 'We're talking – what...?' and he gives me a considering gaze, 'over twenty-one years ago!'

'Just go online, Jess,' Alex urges me. He's fascinated, almost obsessed, with computers, and the world they open up.

I explain that I have already searched on the web, but there seem to be several Per Jacobsens in Denmark, and it's difficult to find more details. The best option seems to be starting with the address Mum has and trying to get a lead from there.

'You'll be like private detectives!' Toby says, his face alive with the excitement of it. 'You and Karen – private eyes! Cool! It's *so* cool... I really wish I could come too.' His voice drops with disappointment.

'He'll obviously have moved on, but I suppose if that was his parents' address it's quite possible that they still live there,' Dad agrees.

Mum comes back with a scrap of paper in her hand. 'It's his phone number too,' she says, scrutinising the unfamiliar writing. A small flurry of anticipation stirs in my stomach.

I hold out my hand: 'Let's see.' I take the piece of paper, and study my birth father's writing for the first time. Strong, confident letters, numbers, dots and dashes spell out foreign, nearly undecipherable words.

'Like I said,' says Alex, who appears to have become some sort of authority on the whole enterprise, 'it's not exactly a megacity, is it? You compare that map to London – you'd be able to fit several Copenhagens into London. You're not going to be tramping the streets for weeks, are you?'

I'm looking for the street name, but it's tricky on this big, spread-out plan, and I decide to go upstairs and bring down the "Copenhagen the Easy Way" book, which has an index and smaller, pull-out maps.

'Assuming he's still alive, of course,' Alex adds, and as he says the words they plummet, one by one. They fall and bounce and whirl around, and as they drop into the silence and shatter into a thousand tiny pieces I can see them in my head, but I can't process them. They keep breaking up into smaller and smaller pieces of choking debris.

'What? What?' Alex is saying, and I can see Dad frowning at him and shaking his head. Toby is staring from one parent to the other, uncertain of whether any response is needed, but it's Mum who gathers up the words, bundles them together and douses them with disbelief until they shrivel away.

'You're right, Alex,' she says. 'Maybe a bit brutal but still... better said than not. Yes, he could be dead, but unless Jess goes to find him, she'll never know, will she? And isn't it better that she does, one way or another?'

I hear a slow hand clap from Dad, and Toby gives Mum a hug, then looks embarrassed and shoves his hands in his pockets again, while she ruffles his hair and gives him a quick squeeze in return, and I say, 'Anyway, I was just going to get...'

'Sorry, Jessie,' Alex's voice is gruff, and he doesn't look up. 'Didn't mean...' Then he does meet my eye, and lifts his shoulders with that rueful, puppy dog expression we know so well.

I'm halfway out of the door. 'Yeah, well, you never were very good at thinking first, speaking later. I guess it's a teenage boy thing... hormones or something, all that testoster—' and then I dodge quickly into the hall so that when he hurls the kitchen chair cushion at me it thuds against the door and falls to the ground.

Upstairs I sit at my desk, in front of my laptop, and bury my head in my hands for a minute, until my heart stops pounding.

He's not dead. He can't be dead. I'm sure he's not dead. Of the many Per Jacobsens who have appeared on my screen over the last few weeks, one is a journalist living in Copenhagen. The site features an extract of an article he wrote last year, comparing life in Denmark with other countries in the E.U. but specifically Britain. He's a perfect fit.

I reach for the travel book, flick through to the back for the street index and run my finger down until I find the one I'm searching for. I open my notebook, the one with the marbled hard cover and a stretchy band you can use to mark the page you need, and I add all this extra information: the address and phone number from Mum, and the details of the Per Jacobsen I've found: his latest article, and which publication it's in. Then I go downstairs with the travel book, and Alex and Toby help me locate the street name of my father's family.

CHAPTER FIFTEEN

There is no good way to commemorate the anniversary of the day someone's died.

Our twenty-first birthday has come and gone. *My* twenty-first birthday. Mum and I took flowers to Sophie's grave, but of course she wasn't there. I did spend some time feeling glad we'd had such a great eighteenth birthday celebration together three years earlier, just after the millennium, and also how lucky that Grampy had given us the money then. I'm using my share to help with the cost of the Denmark project, just as Sophie and I had always planned.

As the first anniversary of Sophie's death approaches, it hovers over us all, unspoken, unmentioned. It's Gran who raises the matter. It's Easter, and my grandparents have come to lunch. I have to work on the Saturday and Monday, but Easter Sunday is free.

'A year!' says Gran, helping herself to roast potatoes. Easter's always a special occasion in our family – despite our lack of formalised religious belief – and special occasions always merit

155

tablecloths, and flowers, and vegetables in dishes on the table, and a proper pudding. 'It's hard to believe.'

There's no need for her to expand further; we all know what she's talking about.

'Thanks for that,' says Mum. I look over at her, frowning at the sharp bitterness in her voice, and I see her eyes have filled and she's pushing her lamb round and round on her plate without actually eating it.

'Laura.' Gran puts down her knife and fork. 'Darling. I didn't mean... Of course we all know it's next week, but isn't it better to talk about it?'

Grampy clears his throat. 'Your mother and I thought it would be... good... helpful, even, to do something. Just to mark the occasion. You know...' He's looking uncomfortable, and he picks up his glass and takes a large gulp of red wine.

'What?' says Toby. 'What were you thinking, Grampy? A party?'

There's a strangled gasp from my mother, and Dad intervenes quickly. 'Just be a bit careful what you're saying, Tobe. Is that going to be appropriate, do you think? A party for Sophie?'

'You're such a div, Toby,' Alex mutters.

I kick him under the table, and he shoots me a furious glare which I answer with what I hope is a meaningful widening of my eyes and raising of eyebrows. 'Actually,' I say, 'Sophie loved parties.'

Mum lays down her knife and fork with great precision, side by side on her plate of untouched roast dinner. 'Shall we change the subject?' she says. 'Are you all seriously suggesting that we are going to celebrate my daughter dying in the way she did, barely a year ago, with...' she hisses the last words, '... a *party*?'

'Not a party, no,' Gran persists, 'but we all have to do these things in the way we think is best. Don't we?' She looks around the table for some support.

'But do you really imagine,' says Mum, speaking very slowly and carefully, as if we're all unable to grasp what she's saying, 'that I don't still think about Sophie every single day? Every hour? Every minute, sometimes. She's lodged in here,' she taps the side of her head, 'and whatever I do, wherever I go, she's still there. All the time.' She uses the back of her hand to wipe across her eyes, and then picks up her cutlery again, holding them poised above her food.

'Laura,' says Dad, 'we all do. We all think about Sophie, and we talk about her, don't we, all the time? That's important. But Frances is right. Sometimes we need to do things our own way, and maybe there isn't a right or wrong way for that, just whatever works for each of us.'

Grampy clears his throat, a sure sign that he's about to make some momentous announcement, but before he can, there's the sound of a phone ringing. Dad looks furious.

'Alex! How many times... not when we're all eating!'

Alex is trying to pull his mobile out of his pocket. 'Yeah, yeah, sorry,' he mumbles, turning it off, but not before he's glanced down at it to check the number. A slow grin drifts across his face.

'As I was about to suggest,' Grampy says, 'it's perhaps not... fitting... to actually mark the dreaded day itself, but Frances and I *had* wondered whether some sort of fund-raising event, in the summer, might be a nice way of putting some good back into what's happened. Holding the event as a sort of... tribute to Sophie's memory, and doing some charity fundraising at the same time.' He stops and looks around the table for our reactions.

'Nice one, Grampy,' Toby beams. 'Cool idea!'

One by one the rest of us agree, even Mum, and we spend the rest of the meal discussing which charity, and what to do – 'Some sort of garden party, we thought,' Gran says, clearly thrilled that we're all united in this – and when to hold it.

'But can you wait till I get back?' I ask. 'I don't want to miss out!'

I've been struggling throughout this whole conversation. I want to blurt out the fact that Sophie is not only in *my* head, but has also been appearing to me, randomly and without warning, for what is now several months. But I manage to keep this to myself; I can imagine my family's reaction only too well. There would be a mixture of pity and condescension. My parents, and my grandparents, would so clearly have an opinion of the truth of her visits. It's all in my head, they would say, I'm simply seeing what I want to see. So I know I can never share these encounters. They're between Sophie and me. It's precisely like it always was, before she became so mesmerised by Lucas, before she became ill, before I went away to university. Before I became someone I wasn't – just for a while, but long enough to cause such unforgiveable hurt – when it was simply the two of us. Yin and yang, peas in a pod, the same but different, and with Sophie always leading the way. Sophie was the force. I was her follower.

*

Karen and I book our flights to Denmark for early May. I tell Andy that I'll be leaving at the end of April, and he looks crestfallen.

'I had hoped you'd stay,' he says, the sincere disappointment in his voice making his words genuine and heartfelt. 'You've got on so well, you've become such a part of our team. No chance I can plant some seeds of doubt, I suppose?'

I assure him that there's no way I'll change my mind – my ticket's booked, and Karen's grandmother is full of plans for our stay with her. And my motive for going to Denmark is stronger than ever.

The rest of the team respond to the news of my departure with gratifying regret. At my final staff meeting Paula makes a short but lovely goodbye speech, and even though it's a bit early in the day, we have cake with our teas and coffees. There's been a collection. Freda gives me a small parcel, wrapped in tissue paper, and inside is a card they've all signed, and an envelope with the results of a collection they've made. It has some Danish krone inside, and a packet of sunflower seeds.

I tell them how much I've loved working at Flowers', and how much I'm going to miss it, and them. I tell them it's the nicest place I've ever worked and I think back to other, part-time, jobs I've done when I was studying for my A-levels, and in my uni holidays, and I know it's true. I could never explain how important a part they have all played in my recent life, my post-Sophie life, and they could never imagine.

I am so touched by their thoughtfulness, and I say what a brilliant idea it is to give me the krone – because it is. I hold up the seeds with a questioning expression.

Bernard rubs his hands together with a look of glee. 'Ah!' he exclaims. 'That's my brainwave! You see, I thought – if you plant those seeds now, before you go, they'll be all grown, tall and lovely by the time you get back. A nice welcome back, plus a small memory of us here.'

As long as someone waters them, I think, but out loud I say that it's the most wonderful idea, and that I'll leave them with my grandfather because I know he'll take care of them for me. Bernard looks delighted beyond belief.

At the end of the day, everyone who's been on shift comes to say goodbye and good luck. I find it all rather emotional, in a totally unexpected way.

'So,' says Nicole, 'you didn't, like, last very long.' It's a flat statement. 'Look at you? Going off travelling and I'm still here? S'pect I'll, like, still be here when you get back.'

For a moment I feel the lucky one. My family and I grieve still, every day, for Sophie. The hole her death carved in my life hasn't got any smaller. And I know too that deep down, none of my family wants me to leave and go searching for Per. But I am going, and that gives me a lift, and when I look at

Nicole – stuck in a job that she enjoys after a fashion, but going nowhere – it makes me want to cringe with sadness.

'Well, I hope so,' I say. 'Because then I can drop by and say hello, and tell you about my trip.'

That seems to cheer her up, and she smiles, gives me an unexpected hug, and says she'll miss me.

As I cycle home along the lanes that now smell sweetly of new growth and greenness, I start to count in my head, but this time I'm not just reciting numbers. I'm counting all the people I've met who never knew Sophie; people who only know me, on my own. People never even known by Sophie.

*

There are only a few days left before I leave, and I spend the time making last-minute alterations to what I've planned to pack, and then changing my mind again. I study the map and the travel book with the zeal of a born-again evangelist, as if I need to memorise the details; as if I won't have the information with me once I arrive. My stomach curls with apprehension and that fear of the unknown I've always had.

Excitement, Jessie. That's all. Why do you always worry about these things? Just chill.

I check my passport and ticket several times each day, and I double check my marbled notebook with the few scanty details of Per that I have.

I fetch Sophie's patchwork bag, and begin to fill it with some of things I'll be taking: the documents, my purse, things

I want with me on the journey. It makes me feel warm and comforted, like I'm taking a part of Sophie with me, and also that I'm more complete somehow. 'You're not with me, Sophie,' I whisper to myself, 'but here's your bag, the one you made, the scraps of material chosen by you.'

I turn it over in my hands; it's looking a bit old and tatty now. I have a sudden image in my head of the afternoon when Sophie had started making it, in Gran's kitchen. I can see her, so clearly, choosing the different pieces she wanted for it.

When I can't think of anything more to do or check, I play mindless computer games with Alex and Toby and the three of us go over to our grandparents' home to eat, a few evenings before my last day.

'It's kind of the Last Supper?' says Toby, whose voice is not only beginning to crackle and change pitch with startling frequency, but who has also developed a tendency to make every statement a question. Somehow, I find this less irritating than when Nicole spoke like that. 'Oh no!' he adds. 'Duh! That'll be the day after tomorrow, won't it?'

Grampy is unable to hide a wide smile before he answers. He has always found Toby amusing beyond words. 'Well,' he says now, 'let's hope it's not Jessie's last supper, shall we?'

Then, of course, there's one of those uncomfortable silences we still get in our family whenever someone accidentally says something too near the mark – too close for comfort, I think, wondering if pondering in clichés is an inevitable result of working at Flowers'.

'Before she leaves, I meant?' Toby adds.

'Yeah,' Alex growls. 'I think we all knew what you meant, div.'

Gran is spooning out Bolognese sauce onto bowls of pasta, and handing them out. 'Jessie. You know Grampy and I have been a bit...'

I take my bowl from her. 'A bit negative, Gran? About me going to find Per, you mean?'

'Not negative, Jess,' Grampy interrupts. 'Worried. Concerned.'

'Yes. OK. It's all right, Gran, I do know, but you don't need to worry. I'm not planning to stay out there. And I don't have any wild expectations of what's going to happen, either.'

'If you do find him, Jessie, he may just be very different from what you...' Gran's peering over at me now, with a gaze I find unsettling.

Alex is shovelling pasta into his mouth as if it is truly going to be his last supper; as if he hasn't eaten for days. Toby has put down his fork and is turning from one to the other, watching our reactions.

I try and keep my voice steady. 'Yes, I know that, Gran, I know all that, and I've talked to Mum. You honestly don't need to worry.'

'But really we just wanted to tell you...' Grampy's voice falters and he makes a visible effort to carry on. 'What we wanted to say is how proud we are.' He looks round the table. 'Proud of all of you. Such a difficult time...' I watch his hand clench his spoon, and the back of it, freckled with brown

spots, goes pale, and the thick veins stand out even more. '...
For all of us.'

He reaches out to touch both Alex, on one side of him,
and Toby on the other. They nod at him and I can see the
acute embarrassment they feel, but the affection too. Both my
grandparents can often say things to us that we might not be
able to tolerate from our parents.

'Some families fall apart,' says Gran, sitting down at last
and taking a sip of wine. 'You can understand why. I think
we're very lucky that – well, that we're still surviving.'

'Still propping each other up?' I suggest.

'Exactly,' says Grampy. 'And that's why we're anxious,
Jessie. Thinking that you going off – whether it's going to rock
the boat.'

'She's flying,' Alex says, with a small grin at his own wit.

Everyone ignores him.

'I think it's exciting,' says Toby, and I feel a rush of affection
for him, and his honesty and openness. 'I don't think any boats
will get rocked. I think...' He pauses as if trying to scoop his
thoughts together and shape them into a coherent mass. 'I
think it's amazing, and really brave. I'd like to go too, but I
can't... it's Jessie's father, Jess and Sophie's. I... I think it's her
birthright to go. To find him – Per. Just to know, once and for
all.'

He looks pleased with himself for having this sensitive
insight, and so he should. How he's grown up, I think, how
he's changed over this last year. We all have, in different ways.
We've hauled ourselves up from that quicksand of misery that

threatened, again and again, to suck us under, but we've started to drag ourselves out, in whatever way we can, and we're not there yet, not on that firm, grassy field of normality, but it's not as far away as it was. It's not as unattainable.

'Good on you, Tobe,' Alex says, and he gives him a look that's close to respect.

Gran's inspecting our bowls. 'Now,' she says, 'who can manage some more?'

As both Alex and Toby open their mouths to reply, the phone rings.

Grampy pushes back his chair, saying, 'Now, who can that be?' as if expecting one of us to actually know, and he goes over to pick the phone off the wall behind us. After he's answered it, he hands it to me with a raise of his eyebrows.

It's Karen. She's tried my mobile, and she's phoned my home. She's fallen and twisted her ankle – quite badly – and it's all strapped up. She's got to rest it, for at least a few days, maybe longer, and she can't fly out with me after all. I can hear how upset she is. She was longing to show me the Copenhagen she's visited so often with her parents; she was desperate to be the one who helped to track down Per. All I can think is: what will I do?

Since January I've imagined my trip to Denmark, and, in the picture, Karen is there too, safe and dependable, knowing what to do. I guess she had almost replaced Sophie – certainly in my mind she was taking over Sophie's role – if only because of her confidence in this foreign country we'd be exploring. I have to put out a hand to hold the wall, because it feels like the room is spinning. I feel dizzy. My mouth has gone dry. I've never been abroad on my own before. I close my eyes and start to count.

When I open them, everyone is staring at me. I replace the receiver without a sound.

'Jess? What's happened? Is everything all right?' asks Gran.

I have to explain, even though I'm still trying to process all that Karen told me, and I'm not really sure how the accident happened. I can see by their expressions that they're horrified – my grandparents and even my brothers. They look shocked, but their concern is for Karen, and how she is, and what will happen. Whereas all I can think is I must go home and tell Mum, tell both my parents in fact. Tell them that now I'm not sure if I can go to Denmark.

CHAPTER SIXTEEN

Sophie is sitting halfway down the stairs when I let myself into the house. Alex and Toby have decided to stay with my grandparents for a while; there's football on television tonight, and Grampy always likes what he calls a bit of moral support ('Just in case'). Her elbows rest on her knees and her chin is propped on her fists. She looks exactly the same as the last time I saw her.

'So now what?' she says as I push the door shut behind me. 'Denmark's off, then! Poor Karen.' She pushes her mouth down at the corners to emphasise the sadness. 'You could be a little sympathetic, Jessie, it's not her fault. Back to the garden centre after all?'

I frown when I see her, because I'm not sure where my parents are, and I call out, 'Hi! I'm home!' There is a muffled answer from somewhere upstairs. Are they both up there?

'What are you doing?' I shout.

Mum's face appears over the banister on the landing above me. 'Just... sorting stuff out,' she says. She looks flushed, and for a heart-sinking moment I wonder if I've interrupted something. They don't still do *that*, do they, I think – surely not?

Sophie is leaning back on her elbows against the step above her, wearing an expression of patient aloofness; it says she has all the time in the world.

'What?' I start to go upstairs. 'What are you sorting out?' and I push past Sophie, only she's not there. She's gone. For a second, I hesitate, and place my hand on the carpet where she was sitting, but even before I feel it I know there will be no warmth; and I lean down and inhale, but there's no lingering scent of her, either.

When I reach the landing, Sophie's bedroom door is wide open. We had left her room just as it was after she died, except Gran went in the following day and took away the half-drunk mug of tea and the dried-up sandwich, and picked up the discarded clothes from the floor and put them away. She must have washed a few clothes as well; I don't remember. She made the bed straight and tidy. Now there are open drawers, and piles of clothes on the bed, and her wardrobe door is ajar and her secret boxes, filled with mementos and souvenirs, are lying on the floor in front of it. I close my eyes and take a breath and start to count, but before I reach ten, I hear Dad's voice.

'Jessie! We weren't expecting you home just yet...'

'Yeah, I can see! So... what? You thought I wouldn't find out what you've been doing?'

Eyes wide open, I push past my father, who's standing in Sophie's doorway, and then I falter on the threshold and try to register what's happening in the room.

Mum comes back in behind me, and I feel her hand reaching for me, and she says, 'Jessie. Lovey. It's not what you...'

I whirl round, all thoughts of Karen, and Per, and Denmark lost, annihilated by this single violation.

'It's not what I... what? What are you *doing*? Jesus, what were you *thinking*? How can you even begin to explain? I thought...' My legs give way, and I kneel on the floor and start to sob. 'I don't understand.'

*

All through the last weeks of the long winter, Mum has been having counselling, she tells me. Bereavement counselling. Not only that, but she's also been doing a course on returning to work, and applying for jobs. She has an interview next week to work in the education department of a local museum. How can this be? When did my family start keeping secrets? Was it after Sophie died, when we were all trying to get through the best we could? Or are there more secrets, more half-covered facts, more economies of truth?

As a family we had all been offered counselling after Sophie's death, but at the time we had each agreed that we'd rather find our own ways through. We'd support each other, we thought, and only use the services offered if we really felt the need.

'And when were you going to tell me about the job?' I say now, curled in a corner of the armchair, and staring blindly at the detritus on the coffee table. A browning apple core, last

Saturday's paper folded half open with the supplements piled beneath, a couple of pens, a school tie – knotted and twisted – and an odd football sock lie scattered on it. Random objects abandoned at some point by different people in our house, waiting for someone to come along and restore order, put them all back in the right place. My parents are sitting together on the sofa, opposite me.

'On the way to the airport? Or when I was safely in Denmark? Not that I *mind*. Of course I don't. I think it's a great idea. I just don't understand why you haven't told us.' Then another thought occurs to me. 'Or have you told the boys already? Please, please don't tell me they know and I don't.'

'Of course not, Jessie.' My father interrupts brusquely. 'Don't be ridiculous. And your mother is allowed some privacy, you know. What is it about this family that everyone seems to think that everything has to be shared all the time?' He reaches out to pull Mum closer, and inside the curve of his arm. 'Well, more specifically, that we – the parents – need to share, and the rest of you can be as secretive and mysterious as you like.'

Then he adds, 'As we found out, Jess. As you yourself well know.' It's not said unkindly, but it's very deliberate.

It's an unusual outburst from Dad, and I lift my head to look at him directly. He's always been the peacemaker in our family, the one to smooth the jagged edges of conflict, and hearing him speak like this is far more upsetting than if it were Mum. How protective he is of her, I think as I watch them, and I feel a sharp jolt of something like envy, that they still have each other to lean on. Gran was right. Our family tragedy hasn't pushed them apart, only bound them tighter.

And yet that's not been enough for Mum. She's still felt the need, apparently, for more help, for professional support. A wave of anger surges through me. I can almost physically sense it rushing through my veins, and for a moment I'm too numb with fury to speak, and I'm too frightened of what I might say, and then regret. How dare she, I think, how dare she have Dad, and all of us, and still think she can't cope. What about me? How do they think I manage? She's now reached a stage in her "healing process", she tells me – the very term makes me feel sick – when she needs to deal with the aftermath, the memories. And that involves sorting out Sophie's room.

'Didn't you think I might want to do this?' I say, pressing my hands between my knees to stop them shaking, and speaking the words cautiously, a tiny pause linking each one to the next, in an effort to stay in control. There's been too much breaking down, I think, too much reliance on emotion.

Mum stands up and comes over to perch next to me on the arm of the chair. I edge further back into the corner. 'Yes, I did, Jessie. I did. We weren't expecting you home just yet, and in my head... I only wanted to make a start, and then at least I'd have done something, and then... I don't know, wait until you're home again. From Denmark. So we could do the rest together.' She adds, 'If you feel like it, of course.'

An idea swims up with sluggish resolve through the swirling undercurrents of my brain, and surfaces with limp but determined triumph. It's the realisation that I can be the grown-up here. I have two choices, and one of those will blacken and sully my last days at home; that's the one where I refuse to acknowledge my mother's point of view, and whether I consider what she's done is right or not.

The other choice is gracious, and forgiving, and will take a supreme effort. It involves me cramming all the hurt and emotion, and the disbelief that both my parents should seem to have such scant regard for my feelings, into a large dustbin, and banging the lid down, tight. I could stick a label on the front saying: "To be opened at a future date", but right now I can't visualise when that future date could possibly be. The trouble with the second choice is the festering, the possibility of the gnawing sense of loss, of unresolved issues. Left to rot somewhere together they could multiply and sprout and send up new shoots from the decaying mass, new shoots of bitterness.

Then I notice Sophie. She's sprawled next to Dad on the sofa, and she's turning her head from one to another between the three of us, a look of gleeful expectation on her face. In a second, I've leapt that canyon of uncertainty and reached the other side, and I'm clinging on somehow with my fingertips, hauling myself onto firmer ground, finding a foothold on the loose scree of maturity.

'Well, who knows?' I say, pushing myself up and off the chair, and walking with slow, careful steps over to the door. Sophie watches my every move, her eyes narrowed.

'Who knows what I'll feel like when I'm back,' I continue. 'Karen's not flying with me, by the way. She's hurt her ankle. I'm going on my own.'

There's a united gasp of concern, and then, 'On your own?' my father repeats. 'What... Is she OK? Will she be able to fly out later?'

I keep my voice deliberately airy. 'Oh yes, I'm sure she will. She really wants to, but by then I may have found him, of course. Per. I may not need Karen after all. Be good if she can come though, eventually. More fun.'

My hand's on the door, and I run my fingers lightly up and down the worn uneven surface of its edge. My parents' voices lift and fall with a rush of exclamations and questions.

'Think I'll get off to bed now,' I say. 'I'll pop over to see Karen tomorrow, and you can tell me all about this job, Mum. Sounds good. You do need to use your brain now. It's about time.' I half turn to give her a fleeting smile. 'But I'm a bit tired, so...'

Sophie's voice rises over us all; it's clear and firm and exultant. 'Go for it, Jessie! Yeah! I knew you could do it! I always knew it! Denmark – here we come!'

But nobody seems to hear.

CHAPTER SEVENTEEN

I fly to Denmark on a day of heart-breaking loveliness. As I drink a mug of tea first thing in the morning, standing in the kitchen, I watch the sun side-stepping its way across the wet grass, dappling the lawn as it slides through the branches of the trees. I'm full of hope and expectation and fear.

About what? Get a grip, Jessie. What is there to be frightened of?

We'd planned this journey together, Sophie and I, but so long ago now. Long ago, when life really was full of hope and expectation.

Imagine. Imagine his face. And TWO of us! Poor guy. I almost feel sorry for him.

We'd intended to travel up through Europe.

Easy, so easy. Ferry. Or through the tunnel maybe, on a train? We need a map. Where is it – Denmark? Shit! Miles and miles and MILES away! Still... France, Belgium, Holland...

Our fingers traced the route, Sophie's silver rings clinking as she drew her hands further up the map, and turned page after page of the Europe road atlas following the interminable route north.

Before Sophie died, when she was still with us, I sometimes used to imagine my life if I had been born alone. If I had been my mother's only daughter and Dad had adopted just me. Snapshots of how it would be ran through my mind: taking the bus to school on my own, enjoying television in peaceful silence, going shopping and making my own choices about what clothes to buy. There I'd be reading a book, and all I'd hear were the pages, turning. Here I am at a party, on my own, and I'm chatting and giggling and being fascinating and amusing all by myself. I'm dancing all night. But after a while I would have to shut out the images, push them into a dark corner, and pull down the blind. They seemed like an ultimate betrayal, a death-wish. As soon as they crept into my head, I wanted them crushed.

It was a fantasy, back then, to think I could ever survive on my own. I relied too much on Sophie: Sophie who liked dance but not gymnastics, who loved comedy shows but hated reality TV, and who could read maps but still forgot which way to turn out of a shop. Sophie was the survivor, and my own survival, I'd always thought, depended on her existence.

*

Even with my limited experience of planes, this one – small and blue – is disappointing, outstripped on the runway by other much larger aircraft waiting to carry holidaymakers to warmer,

175

more exciting destinations. Still, what it lacks in size it makes up for in the friendliness of the crew and other passengers. Tall blond smiling cabin staff greet us as we board. I have a window seat and, after storing my hand luggage above me, I settle down with my "Copenhagen the Easy Way" book and pretend to read with absorption. But I'm fascinated by my fellow passengers. My eyes keep straying, watching these people whose space I'll be sharing until we land. Families, business men and women, students – I can identify them all.

This being Friday, it's clear that the largest group of people are flying because of work, but there are parents with small children too, and English and Danish words flow comfortably between them with ease and fluency. I have a sudden vision of how my life – our lives – might have been as the daughters of parents who shared two cultures and languages with us, and how we wouldn't have known anything different.

I feel, with a brief stab, my own potential loss of identity, but while I'm mourning it inwardly, a young guy, my age or maybe a little older, swings easily into the seat beside me with an engaging, '*Hej.*'

I nod. 'Hi.'

'English?'

I nod again, and then, 'I'm sorry, but I think... I don't think that's your seat.'

'No?' He sounds amazed.

'Well, no, you see... my friend, she should have been travelling with me but she couldn't, she's not well, and I think – well, that would have been her seat.'

176

Words fail me, Jess! What are you like? And such a lovely guy!

But I'm also thinking that if Sophie appeared, she could sit there, next to me. We could still share the journey. This, however, is not a thought I can share with anyone else, particularly not a total stranger.

He stays sitting where he is. 'So, no one is here then? If your friend, you say, cannot come, so this seat must be...' He shifts a little to look at it. '... Empty?' He smiles again. 'Oh, except of course, perhaps you mean you don't want anyone to be here, instead. So, I can change, maybe.' He makes no attempt to move next to the aisle. There's something reassuring about his confident assumption that I'll be happy with his close company. I remain silent, and pretend to study my travel guide again.

He seems to be travelling light. With some difficulty he tucks away his boarding card and passport in the back pocket of his jeans, keeping only a tattered copy of "To Kill A Mockingbird" on his lap, as he clips his seat belt together.

I venture, 'They'll get creased.'

'What?'

'Your passport and ticket. Won't they get creased if you're sitting on them?'

'I don't know.' He laughs. 'Perhaps. I'll find out when we land. I'm sure they'll be fine. So, have you family or friends in Copenhagen?'

And then we chat. He's very relaxed. Even in the restricted space of his seat, with such cramped leg room, he seems to sprawl, unconcerned. I tell him how I'm going to stay with my friend's grandmother, how my friend, Karen, would fly out as soon as she's fit enough, and how I hope to look up an old friend of my mother's.

We introduce ourselves.

At last, at last! This is good, Jess. You're doing really well. Proud of you, in fact. And wow! Is he sexy or what? Hot, hot, hot.

His name is Kasper. He's been visiting a friend for a couple of days, an old school friend who is doing some work experience in England – 'In Bry-ton. Do you know Bry-ton?' – and now he's flying back home. His parents are divorced, and he lives at home with his mother in her flat while he's at Copenhagen University.

He's easy to talk to, and he speaks English with only a trace of an accent; a few odd inflexions and stresses on some words, and a stumbling over a couple of sounds. The pre-flight instructions and demonstration provide a background hum to our conversation, and I hardly notice as the plane taxies along the runway and surges upwards to finally move effortlessly over a patchwork landscape and through clouds and then over, far below, the sea. We only pause when the trolley of drinks arrives. He stuffs his paperback into the webbing in front of him.

'We studied that at school,' I tell him. 'We loved it.'

I mean Sophie and me, of course. Sophie, whose favourite book was "To Kill a Mockingbird", who loved poems about war, and Mike Leigh plays, but hated Jane Austen.

Too prissy, I just don't get it.

'For you and your friends, perhaps,' says Kasper. 'It could be a little easier to read. Some of it is... quite hard for me to understand, but I can see it is a great book.'

Good taste this guy, Jess. It was my absolute fave. You could tell him that.

Time passes in more idle chat. I turn to gaze out of the window. We're losing height now, dropping down. The seat belt signs have come on. Below us is flat land scored by straight lined belts of green and grey. Ordered areas of buildings appear, dark and light anonymous structures, and curved tongues of land licking a smooth blue sea. What am I doing? What have I been thinking? I'm nearly overwhelmed by the longing to stay where I am, cocooned in this flying suitcase of passengers, forever voyaging though the sky. How can I even begin to search a strange unfamiliar city on my own? I close my eyes and begin to count, slowly.

I've already decided to book an immediate return flight home the minute we've landed and gone through passport control, when Kasper speaks again. 'Here is my mother's telephone number.'

When I look, he's handing me a torn piece of squared paper. 'You can call some time, if you want. Maybe if you want to see some parts of København not in your book.' He looks down at my unopened travel guide with a grin. 'In Danmark, we do not say "Copenhagen". That is your English name. For us, it is København.'

We're bumping along the runway, small juddering skids before the plane settles into a rapid whiny braking as we approach the airport building. I take the proffered scrap from his hand, and push it deep in my pocket. Perhaps I can do this after all. Perhaps. Or I could try. It seems a shame to have come this far and go no further.

'Thanks.'

Kasper leans back, stretching, and as soon as the plane stops, he unfastens his seat belt, ready to stand up. I manage not to point out that the seat belt signs are still on. We leave the plane together and I'm glad to have someone who knows what to do, in the absence of Karen. The airport is shiny and slick, the signs easy to follow in English as well as unfamiliar Danish. We travel as far as baggage collection together, and then Kasper holds out his hand.

'So, goodbye, Jess. I hope you like Denmark. I hope you find who it is you look for.'

I shake his hand. It seems an odd, formal thing to do.

'I hope so too,' I say. 'But anyway, I'll try to remember Denmark is Danmark. Copenhagen is...' I stumble, 'Kerbenhown.'

We both laugh, and he starts to walk away.

Then he turns and lifts his hand. 'And don't forget. You have the number. Anytime.'

I watch him lope away with long easy strides, his small bag hooked over one shoulder, and then I wait for my enormous backpack – the one my parents fretted would be far too heavy for me to carry on my back – to come round on the conveyor belt.

*

'I always think,' mused Gran, 'that a piece of patchwork is like a family.'

We were sitting in her kitchen one dark winter's afternoon. It was warm with the smell of scones, and a faint scent of scorching where Gran had left the iron too long on a piece of material.

I was drawing at the table, quick, scribbly sketches of things around me: the stripy jug that had always held custard on apple crumble days, a brown pottery bowl full of oranges, Grampy's jacket flung over the back of a chair. Sophie was hunched over an assortment of fabrics opposite me, choosing some to go in a pile next to her, and discarding others.

'I remember this!' she exclaimed, holding up a gauzy scrap shot through with shimmering threads. 'We had fairy costumes made with this! Remember, Jess?'

I glanced up briefly and nodded. 'Too thin for patchwork though, isn't it? Especially a bag.'

Sophie sighed. 'Yep, you're right. Shame though, it's so pretty.' She put it on the reject heap.

'What did you mean, Gran?' I looked over at her, crouched in front of the open oven, scrutinising her scones. 'About the patchwork?'

My grandmother straightened up, closing the oven door as she did so.

'You mean about the family?' she said, as she walked across the kitchen and picked up the piece of patchwork which

Sophie was working on. 'Well, look at this. This bit that Sophie's already sewn is made of quite a few different squares, isn't it, and all put together like this, it's strong enough that when she's finished both sides, she can make a bag. Which needs to be quite sturdy, after all, to hold all the stuff you'll no doubt cram in there, Sophie.'

Sophie's head was bent over the table, her fingers busy with smoothing out some material, and pinning on a template. She shrugged a response. 'I guess so.'

Gran raised her eyebrows just a little, and then turned to me. 'I always think,' she continued, 'that in a family, each person is like one little square, or hexagon, or whatever, of fabric, and that one small bit on its own isn't much good, but when they're all sewn together, they suddenly become much stronger.'

'Love your ideas, Gran.' Sophie was watching her now, grinning. 'Your little... homilies – is that the word? Love it!' Then she pulled back her sleeve to peer at her watch, and jumped up with a gasp. 'No! Is that the time? Got to go, got to rush! Meeting Lucas in ten minutes!'

'He can't wait?' Gran asked. 'While you have a scone?'

Sophie was scooping all her patchwork bits together, and stuffing them in a carrier bag. 'No, he can't.' She pointed at the bag. 'Can you take that home for me, Jess? Only... don't want to be late.' She grabbed her coat off her chair, and wound a bright red scarf round her neck. It only took a few seconds, but with a couple of flicks and tucks she had straightaway achieved her own effortless style. She gave Gran a quick peck on her cheek. 'Thanks, Gran. You're a gem. Can't wait to finish the bag now. It's going to be so cool.' She grinned suddenly. 'So unique – don't you think?'

Then she was gone. The draught, as she banged the door behind her, lifted and blew a couple of fallen scraps across the floor. An unnatural quiet seeped round the corners and into the edges of the kitchen.

'Well,' said Gran, 'the scones are ready now. You'll have one anyway, won't you, Jessie?'

*

As I walk out of the safe, official area of the airport, past Customs and into the main concourse, I am met by a bewildering mass of people. They're waiting, I suppose, to greet other travellers. Some people seem to be holding flags on sticks, small paper ones, or others made of cloth, each one red with an off-centre white cross. There is a lot of waving going on, especially of flags, as different people emerge with their cases or bags. I wonder whether it's some sort of special Danish festival today. All around me there's that roar and hubbub of an unfamiliar foreign language being spoken very fast.

I move to the side, out of the way of the throng, and I'm wondering if I can remember what Karen's grandmother looks like, from her description and a photo, when there is a tap on my shoulder.

'Yess?' says a voice behind me, and I turn to find a tall, very slender woman with an astonishing shock of very short, spiky white hair smiling at me. She holds out her hand. 'My name is Anne,' she says, shaking my hand. 'And you are Yess, I think?'

I smile back at her with relief. 'Jess, of course, that's right.'

'Welcome to Denmark,' she says, and then, 'Velkommen til Danmark. So, your first liddle Danish sentence, yes?'

I'm so relieved, after all Karen's warnings, that Anne is speaking English and in a way that I can understand, that I decide not to tell her about my pronunciation lesson on the plane, and simply agree. For some reason, I had built a picture in my head of someone austere, and formal, and even a little frightening. Anne is so welcoming that, as we walk out of the terminal together, I feel myself starting to relax. I'm even composing an amusing postcard to send home, describing my safe arrival on Danish soil. Until I realise that the picture in my head, of my family passing round the card and even chuckling a little, includes Sophie. There she is, standing on tiptoe, trying to peer over Alex's shoulder. I shiver, and the image shrivels and curls and withers away to nothing.

'You are cold?' Anne sounds concerned as she unlocks the boot of a small blue car. We seem to have reached the car park very quickly. I heave my backpack into the boot and go round to the side to wait to get in.

'Oh no. No, I'm fine,' I reassure her.

She reaches round me to unlock the door, because of course it's the driver's side. I'm waiting the wrong side of the car. I'm in a foreign country, where they speak a language I don't understand, and drive on the other side of the road, and wave flags. Tomorrow, perhaps, or the day after, I'm going to look for my father – my birth father – who lives in this country, and has always understood all the things I'm already finding strange, and who doesn't know I exist.

And your problem is? Chill, Jessie! Stop fretting. He'll love you. Of course he will. What's not to love? It's going to be so amazing. Really amazing. Just don't count. I mean, honestly. People will just think you're... weird, and you're not, Jess. You really aren't. You're just you.

CHAPTER EIGHTEEN

Anne parks in a small side road, and together we go in through the wide entrance door of a tall building just round the corner. I carry my huge backpack, with some difficulty, up to the second floor. There's no lift. The apartment is lovely, all wooden floors and white walls and a calm uncluttered atmosphere. It's mid-afternoon now, and the sun, low in the sky over the buildings opposite, floods the living area with light.

'So,' Anne says briskly. 'I show you your room, and then maybe we have a liddle *kaffe*?'

'Coffee, you mean?' I check, and then, 'that would be great. Thank you.'

She gives me a quick tour of the flat, and lastly opens a door from the tiny hall into a small room with two single beds, a bright rug between them on the floor, and a round table with a lamp on it. There's a huge window, with a deep sill running underneath it, which looks out on a sort of large yard. Anne follows my gaze, and walks over to the window.

'That is where we put our...' she's searching for a word, '... old stuff.'

'Rubbish?' I suggest.

'Yes. Rubbish. Also things which you can use another time...'

'Recycling.'

'So. My bicycle also is there. We all can keep them in that place.' She points to a long, low building, open down one side and filled with cycle racks, and several bikes.

Anne demonstrates the blind that I can use at night, and shows me a small wardrobe with shelves and baskets inside as well as hanging space. 'For your things, Yess, and my Karen also when she arrive. I hope soon.' She doesn't say the "r" in the middle of the name as we do: "Karn", it sounds like, all running together.

I agree, and I tell her that Karen was in less pain when I saw her just before I left England, and as soon as she could take weight on her foot she hoped to fly out.

We sit on a low black sofa in the big square living room, and Anne pours coffee from some sort of smart stainless steel thermos jug into small white cups. 'We drink it like this,' she tells me, 'but you like milk, perhaps? I know Karen like...' She passes me a little jug.

On the long, high coffee table in front of the sofa is an array of food: bread, some thin slices of pale cheese and rings of red pepper, pieces of melon, a cake which looks home-made – carrot cake, Anne tells me – and a plate of small biscuits. I'm hungry, I realise, and everything I try is delicious, but then I hesitate, my hand hovering, over some small, unfamiliar cakes.

'Kransekager,' Anne says, noticing my uncertainty. 'Karen loves them. They're very good.'

'I was just wondering...' I'm positive Karen had explained about this to her grandmother before I'd arrived; now I'm unsure what to say. 'I wondered what they're made of? What's in them... the ingredients?'

It's Anne's turn to look uncertain. 'I fetch...' She waves a hand, before standing up and walking over to the long, low shelf unit that runs along one side of the living room, pulling out a large old battered red book and bringing it back to the table. She holds it up so I can see the title "DANSK/ ENGELSK. ENGELSK/DANSK" and starts to leaf through it. 'I know this word,' she mutters. 'I have learn it many times, but never can I... ah! That is why I forget. Always I forget this. It is the same word. Nearly the same word. *Marcipan.*' She leans across to pass me the dictionary, with her finger under the word: marzipan. 'You know this? You like it I hope?'

I hand the dictionary back to her and she puts it down on the floor.

'I'm sure marzipan is delicious,' I say, choosing my words with much more care than I would at home. I'm worried about seeming rude, or difficult. I'm also wishing fervently that Karen could be here. 'It's just that... I have an allergy. I can't eat nuts. They make me... very ill. Karen said she'd explained to you. I'm so sorry.'

For a brief moment Anne's expression is pure bewilderment, as she struggles to understand my long explanation, and grasp what I'm trying to tell her. 'Nuts,' she says at last. 'You do not like them. Ah yes, so now I remember what Karen tell me. But marzipan...' She makes a small dismissive gesture, and shrugs her shoulders. 'It is just almonds, but so small...' She rubs her hands together in a grinding motion. 'Made in a – what do you call? – *dej*?'

It's my turn to shrug, and shake my head. I've no idea how marzipan is made, only that it's mostly all ground almonds. 'I don't know, I'm sorry, but it's not that I don't like nuts. I just mustn't eat them. Not at all.' I feel panic rising at the thought of ensuring that Karen's grandmother completely understands how important this is; vital, in fact. 'Even if I only touch nuts, I can be affected. If they go in my mouth I could... stop breathing.'

The language barrier seems immense suddenly. This is just another European country, I'm thinking, and yet I could be in Tibet, or Outer Mongolia, or somewhere else remote and far from civilisation as I know it. I can't believe that Karen has failed to explain the importance of my nut allergy to Anne. I reach over to pick up the dictionary again, and flick with desperation through the beginning of the English section.

Allegiance... Allegory... Allergy. I look up, my hand on the page: 'It's the same word – almost. *Allergi*?' Now it's my turn to show her the word, and I listen to her say it, but quite differently from my pronunciation.

'*Allergi!* Ah, yes. This I did not understand. I think only that you do not like the taste perhaps. In Denmark – we love marzipan! We eat it a lot.' She makes a regretful face.

I'm relieved to have solved the whole nut allergy issue, and anxious to make everything all right again. I think to myself how I must show Anne my EpiPen, and explain how to use it, but for now I just say, 'Sorry. Sorry about the marzipan. I'm sure it's lovely, but luckily,' I reach forward to pick up a piece of melon, 'I do love fruit! And I'm definitely not allergic to it!'

So then we can smile at each other, and I even feel quite proud to have jumped the barrier, and restored Anglo-Danish relations.

Clever you, Jessie. Well done. That could have been a tricky moment. Imagine!

While we carry on eating and drinking coffee, Anne tells me how pleased she is to practise her English with me, and how I must be patient with her. After we've talked about Karen, and Karen's mother, and the apartment, and how long Anne has lived there, and how she spends her days (very busily, it seems), and where the flat is in Copenhagen, she asks me about my family, then looks at me with great concern and says, 'I am sorry, yes, very, very sorry about your sister. Karen tell me. I hope you do not mind that I say this.'

I find I don't mind at all, in fact, I'm relieved. The spectre of Sophie would be hovering with unspoken constancy otherwise round every corner, and how could I then have suddenly introduced her into conversation? So much better like this. I feel a smile begin to spread as I shake my head and say, 'I'm glad you've said it. Truly. Do you know why I've come here? To Denmark? It's to try and find our father. My sister's and mine.'

'Karen tell me. Of course.' Anne makes a small nod. 'Why you come now, is it because your sister die?'

The words are direct, but there's no shred of callousness. I choose my words carefully; simple words, short sentences. I use gestures as if I'm in some ridiculous comedy sketch on television and I explain the story of Sophie and me, and how Per has no idea about us. Karen was going to help me, I say, but now I'm on my own I don't want to wait. I'd like to make a start, before she arrives.

Anne is intrigued. She asks more questions. I go and fetch my bag – Sophie's bag – from my room, and pull out the scant information I possess. I show her the old photo of Per, and she studies it thoughtfully. I explain about the Per Jacobsen I've found on the internet, and I show the address Mum gave me.

'So,' she announces, putting down the photo, 'you do not have Karen with you, but I can help. I can do this. If you like?'

I feel almost overwhelmed with gratitude. Before I arrived today, I'd had no idea how Karen's grandmother would be. I'd worried that I might find it awkward being alone with her, sharing her living space: this unknown older person in a strange foreign city. But now I can see that having her with me is a far happier alternative than setting out on my own.

'I would love you to help.' I take a deep breath. 'Can we start soon?'

'Tomorrow,' Anne says with a determination in her voice that I recognise from Karen. 'But you must know that there are many, many people in Denmark with this name, I think. So it can be difficult for you to find the one you want.'

'Maybe if we start with the two I know about,' I say. 'The one I found on the internet, and the address my mother gave me... well, that's a start.'

'The soon is the best, is that how you say?'

'The sooner.' I give her my happiest smile. 'The sooner the better.'

*

I wake in the morning with sunlight filtering through the blind, and a smell of coffee. Now I feel a little awkward, not knowing when to get up, or use the bathroom. I lie still for a few minutes, my head resting on the thin square pillow that I'd found uncomfortable to sleep on, and start to count with my eyes closed. The night before I'd lain awake for a long time. It wasn't just the pillow. The day's events had raced through my head, like stills from a familiar film. You know what you'll see next, but then you find an odd expression, or pose, or random activity, and you hit the pause button, and you realise you'd forgotten that particular moment.

I'd seen myself, barely fourteen hours before, driving off to Gatwick with Mum, while Dad, Alex and Toby waved goodbye. Toby had run after us, down the drive and out into the lane, both arms windmilling up and down, until we disappeared round the bend. 'Alex will be back in bed by now,' I'd said to Mum as we drove down the High Street and she had smiled, her eyes on the road.

'Probably.'

I must have checked my passport and ticket several times on the journey to the airport.

'Jessie,' said Mum. 'They were there last time you looked.'

'I know, I know.' I leant back in the seat, and clutched my bag to me. Sophie's bag. The thing that had belonged to her that I was taking to Denmark. It was an awkward bag for finding things in, though, and I was almost beginning to regret my decision.

Mum stopped the car in the lay-by at Passenger Drop-Off. We'd already agreed that she didn't need to park and come in with me. I wasn't a child. I knew what to do. She leaned over after she'd pulled on the hand brake, and gave me a hug. 'Take care,' she said. 'I hope you find...' Her voice wavered and she stopped and then added, 'And be strong.'

I moved back in my seat and looked straight into her eyes. 'And you,' I whispered, and then I was out of the car and extricating my backpack from the boot. As I walked away into the terminal, I turned because I knew she'd still be waiting there, and at exactly the same time we each lifted a hand, and blew a kiss.

In the rush and flurry of my last day, all the hurt and difficult feelings had slipped away, and I think we both hoped they would stay lost for ever. Somebody had closed the door on Sophie's room, and it felt like that whole episode had been shut away too. I couldn't cope with it now, in any case. I had too many other thoughts and anxieties in my head.

It's such an odd thing, grief. I don't suppose it ever disappears. What I think is that it walks alongside you every day, always there, but not like that first overwhelming torrent. The one that engulfs you straight after someone dies like Sophie did. I'd crawled through each day then like a tortoise, carrying the grief on my back, bent over with the pain of it. I'm upright now and the grief is packed away in a suitcase. I have to carry it everywhere, and mostly it stays locked inside, but sometimes, if there's a trigger, the locks burst open and out it rushes – all that pain and misery – just when I'd thought I was in control again.

I can close my eyes then, and count, and when I open them the sadness has been sucked back into the suitcase, and I can press the locks down, haul up my luggage again and stagger on towards some kind of normality. I like to imagine that one day I can let the grief out of the suitcase and allow it to flutter free. I'd like to think I can cope with that. But not yet.

In a flash, my next image was Kasper on the plane, the easy confidence of him, that impression as we talked that we had known each other much longer. I could feel the firm pressure of his arm against mine on the arm rest, and I could see the back of his hand, scattered with tiny blond hairs, and his wrist as it emerged from his sleeve, broad, strong, capable. I wanted to meet him again, very much, I realised; I could imagine no one I would rather have to show me around Copenhagen. But Anne had offered.

By the time we'd had dinner last night my eyes were getting heavy. Tiredness inched its way through my whole body. The day had been long, and emotional, and dense with expectation and apprehension. I'd phoned home and Toby, who'd answered the phone first, wanted to know every detail so far before I had a brief reassuring chat with Mum.

'Turns out that looking for a Per Jacobsen over here is nearly like looking for a John Smith in England,' I'd told her, and the relief of sharing that and knowing she understood was immense.

'Let's hope you're lucky first time then.' I could sense her smiling all those miles away, the phone sandwiched between her ear and shoulder as she prepared the evening meal.

We'd eaten at a table by the lofty curved window in the living area, looking down at the street below. Two tall candles flickered on the sill, and on the table a group of tea lights shone in small delicate glass holders. A lamp hung down from a hook on the high ceiling, its white metal dome low over the table. I had no idea whether this meal was how most Danish people ate. Nor whether they all lit candles and tea lights in the evening, and left their windows clear of blinds or curtains.

'Remember, girls,' Dad had always said, on holiday in France, and Italy, and a Greek island I've forgotten the name of, 'whatever you do, and however you behave, that's what the people who live here are going to think is typical of all of us Brits.'

'Yeah, OK, whatever.'

He was right, of course. He usually was.

Now I was going to find out how these other people lived. Perhaps it was not so different from us. Only with candles and flags.

My concerns about getting up are solved by a gentle tap on the door.

'Yess? *Sov godt*? You sleep well? Are you awake? There is breakfast for when you want it.'

I stop counting and open my eyes.

'Thank you,' I call back, and I'm out of bed, my bare feet on the warm wood of the floor, and I think I could do anything today, anything. That resolve I'd had back in the autumn, the first time Sophie came to see me, has returned. The excitement sparks like an electric current through my veins.

You're here, Jessie. You've made it. Now you're going to find Per. Yay!

*

One morning, a few weeks after we'd finished our exams and left college...

Forever, Jessie. That's it. End of an era, and all that. Kind of scary, isn't it?

Sophie didn't get up.

It wasn't that she didn't get up in an "I'm having a lie-in" sort of way, more that she didn't get up at all, the whole day. We'd started working in a local pub, and I had left to be there for a mid-day slot, so when Sophie was still in bed, I'd thought nothing of it. She was due to do the next shift, replacing me. It was confusing for the customers, the regular ones. Some of them would be there at lunchtime, and then come back in the evening for a quick pint. The more observant would notice what we were wearing and comment on how we'd changed our clothes during the day. Or they'd allude to something they'd said earlier, or that had happened on the other one's shift, and wonder why we looked puzzled. Or call us by each other's names.

On this particular day, the first I knew of Sophie's extravagant lie-in was when Carl, the pub manager, called over to me and said, 'You didn't tell me your sister's ill. What's all that about?'

Carl's eyes were small and sharp and cold in his pudgy face. He was a stocky, bull-necked, aggressive-looking man, and I never felt entirely comfortable around him. He was full of jokes and joviality with the customers, but with us the jokes were often awkward innuendos, and he was renowned as well for his short temper. He wasn't the sort of person you'd want to upset in any way. Sophie and I had already discussed whether we wanted to stay working there the whole summer, but jobs weren't that easy to find unless we decided to travel into Brighton every day.

I shook my head and said, 'Search me. I don't know. I didn't know she was ill when I left.'

He eyed me with suspicion. 'Well, your Mum's just rung in. So – what am I supposed to do? One member of staff down, just like that. Not really on, is it?'

I made a non-committal noise and gave a half shrug. I was too busy wondering what could be the matter with Sophie to care very much about how Carl was going to manage that evening.

I tried to think how she'd been yesterday. 'Have to see if Shirley can come in,' Carl muttered. He turned away, and then added over his shoulder, 'You can tell your sister from me she'd better get her arse in gear before tomorrow. What she have? Hangover, is it? Late night last night, was it? She's got responsibilities working here, you know, just like we all have.'

'I know, Carl, I know,' I said, desperate to finish the conversation. I gathered my thoughts around me like a protective cloak. 'I'm sure it's genuine. It's... it's not like Sophie. I'm sure she'll be back tomorrow. I don't know...'

When I got home, my mother looked more worried than I could ever remember. 'Go up and see if she'll talk to you, Jess. She's just... lying there.'

Sophie was curled on her side in bed, facing the wall. I walked across the room to sit next to her and reached out my hand to touch her arm.

'Sophie? What's up? What's the matter?'

She didn't reply. Her eyes were open but vacant, unseeing; she was staring at the wall, but nothing about her seemed properly awake. When I took her hand, it was floppy and limp. She didn't look at me but she made a small noise, as if the effort to speak was so great as to be impossible.

'Sophie? What's happened?' I was trying to sound calm but inside I felt cold with fear, scared beyond reason by Sophie's behaviour. 'Is it Lucas? Is it something to do with Lucas?'

I tried to remember when she'd last seen him, and how she'd appeared afterwards, but my mind refused to accept any images other than the one in front of me, on the bed.

'Hey, come on.' I forced an unnatural cheerfulness into my voice. 'You can tell me! Can't you?'

Sophie turned her head then, so slowly that it seemed as if it were causing her great pain. She tried to lift her hand, but it fell back on the bed beside her.

'... Nothing,' she whispered after what felt like a lifetime, and she took a great, shuddering breath. I heard quiet footsteps behind me and realised that Mum had tiptoed into the room. I moved enough to give her a quick, almost invisible shake of my head, and a tiny frown. She raised her eyebrows but nodded, and crept out again. I waited, stroking Sophie's hand, helpless in the face of this sudden misery and lethargy. Sophie's behaviour was as far removed as it was possible to imagine from her normal state of being. Where had it come from, this overwhelming unhappiness? I decided it must be something to do with Lucas.

'Have you split up, then?' I was desperate for a response – any response. 'Is that it? Have you and Lucas...?'

Sophie kept her head flat on the bed, and tears flowed down her face, trickled back towards the pillow and down her neck, and she left them.

'No... Jessie. No.' Every word was an effort. 'It's not... It's nothing. Nothing like that. I told you. It's just... there's no point... any more. There's... nothing. I can't... I can't. Explain. I just... want to... stay here. Not ever... get up.'

I was playing a part now. I kept my voice absolutely level in an effort to hide the rising panic inside. Just like that, we'd swapped roles. Just like that, Sophie, who liked Marmite, and the colour blue, and fudge (but not toffee), and always being first... Sophie shifted sideways, and nothing that she could do better than me, or the same, or not so well, mattered any more.

'Count with me, Sophie,' I whispered, as I wiped the tears off her neck and face with a tissue from my pocket. 'Count. It helps. It always helps when you can't cope, or you're a bit... worried. Come on. One. Two. Three...' I paused, but she'd closed her eyes, and even though I carried on counting out loud until I reached twenty, she'd not joined in.

CHAPTER NINETEEN

Anne and I discuss our strategy over breakfast. She doesn't know that word and is delighted to add it to her small store of English vocabulary, once she's checked it in the ancient-looking English-Danish dictionary. In return, I ask her for the names of things on the table, and realise that the phrase book I'd bought with Karen is not going to cover everything I think I need to know ('But everyone speaks English...' – I can still hear the ring of Karen's confident tone). I recite each word Anne tells me, but I have to repeat it nearly every time until she's satisfied. Either she's an incredibly rigorous teacher, or it's a language that's more difficult than I'd imagined.

I sit shaking my head with despair, and she laughs and says that the Danes have been speaking this language all their lives. 'So you must have a little... What you call it – patient?'

I nod. 'Patience. Yes, you're right.'

But I want to know how to speak it. It should be a part of me, surely? Aren't the instruments for learning it already there, polished and shiny, all set up in my brain? Doesn't being half Danish make it somehow easier for you to absorb the language?

We've finished our coffee, drunk from those small thin white cups again, and eaten sliced cheese on dense, dark brown rye bread, and delicious white bread with butter and jam. Anne stands up and starts to clear things onto a tray.

'So we are together going out,' she says. 'And we walk to this street, the one you show me, and what?'

'I'd just like to see his house,' I say. 'Or at least, the house where I think he lives. I'm not sure what to do then.' But I'm sure I'll know when we get there – that surge of confidence from earlier has stayed with me.

We've already located the road in Anne's "Copenhagen Street Finder" book. It's the address I'd found using my laptop for the journalist Per Jacobsen. I still have the phone number that Mum had given me for Per's parents, and their address too, but the likelihood that they still live there seems remote. In my head, his parents must be very old. It all seems so long ago. But the reality, of course, is that they may only be the age of my grandparents in Sussex who, as grandparents go, are no age at all. I try to work through this logically, but the image of an elderly, rather decrepit couple persists. I look over at Anne, and I think she's old, but I couldn't possibly say how old. Certainly she doesn't fit any kind of idea of how "old people" should be or behave. She's bright and lively and energetic and busy, and would probably be horrified to hear my thoughts on her advancing years.

'So,' she says now, with that briskness in her voice which already seems familiar, 'we have a liddle tour, yes? I can show you some of our beautiful København, and we find also this place you look for.'

The early May sunshine slants through the window of her tiny kitchen, but it's deceiving. Anne says that outside is cooler than it looks and we'll need jackets. When I look down into the street from the living room, people are walking along huddled into warm clothes. I check that I have the details Mum gave me, as well as Per Jacobsen the journalist's address scribbled down, and I can't help feeling a little proud at my detective work so far. Finding out any details on the computer hadn't been straightforward, so I'm hoping all that time and effort has paid off.

Anne lives in an area of Copenhagen called Frederiksberg. She points it out on the map at the back of my "Copenhagen the Easy Way" book. Then she traces our route across part of the city to the street where my journalist is supposed to live.

'We walk, I sink,' she announces. 'I have also bicycle for you to use, but I sink maybe this is too difficult for you in strange city? Later, maybe?' I ask about buses and underground trains, and she laughs. 'Buses, yes of course, but today we have no need to use bus. And metro, they make metro now. Already in some parts. Soon, soon it will be finished. There will be place here for it, in Frederiksberg. This is planned for this year, 2003. So... that will be good. We hope.'

I try, and fail, to imagine London without its tube trains or Manchester without its trams, and we walk down all the stairs and out into a sharp, windblown street.

*

I had to go into college on my own to collect our A-level results. It wasn't how we'd planned it.

OK, girls. This is how we'll do it. One. Meet in hall for results. Two. Whoop of joy at our combined brilliance. Three. The pub to celebrate. Make that The Park View, it's nearest.

'We might want to phone home?' I'd suggested.

Oh, yeah.

An airy wave of the hand.

That too. Of course.

In the event, I met up with Karen, Polly and Em, and some of the boys. There was a strange undercurrent of anxiety, inevitability, and suppressed excitement. Lucas was there on the edge of our group, wearing a contrived expression of boredom, his fedora tilted low over his eyes. Crowds of other students stood around together, talking in low voices; an indefinable mood of anticipation hung over the large panelled room. I was called over by different people, all wanting to know about Sophie, and where she was.

'Not very well,' I partly lied, because the truth was too painful to explain. Only our immediate close group knew what was happening. How a good day was when she managed to get dressed. How medication was changing her whole personality. How Sophie, my Sophie – who liked Maltesers, and walking through wet grass barefoot, and knew, just knew, that she and Lucas were destined to spend the rest of their lives together – stayed indoors and pushed her food around her plate until she could find the energy to leave it. How she'd drag herself back to her room, or sit unseeing in front of the flickering television, ignoring everything that was going on around her.

Even Lucas, when he came round, failed to raise any kind of normal response from her.

'Why don't we go out, babe? Huh? That would be good, wouldn't it, Sophe? What do you think?'

Sophie would give a barely perceptible shrug. I could see Lucas forcing himself to swallow the frustration, uncomfortable with the mystery of her condition, completely adrift, as we all were, on an ocean of uncertainty. This wasn't the life he'd imagined. But then, it wasn't the life I'd imagined either.

My life had always had Sophie at the forefront. We'd deliberately selected different universities for our first choices, but they were close enough that we'd still have been able to visit each other whenever we needed to. We'd agreed together on the importance of making new friendships with people who had no idea that somewhere, living in another part of the country, was the other half of each of us.

Sometimes, when faced with the reality of that happening, I'd had to count for a long time. But mostly I'd been excited, if a bit apprehensive, about the idea of a life distinct from Sophie. As long as I knew she was there somewhere – on the end of a phone, on a train coming to see me for the weekend, at home with me sharing stories in the vacations – then I was sure I could cope.

But this was something beyond any reckoning, this illness, this "condition" as my grandmother called it ('I'm sure it's only temporary, Jessie darling. Just some sort of condition. Just something to go along with and then one day – pff! We'll have the old Sophie back again').

Nothing brought the old Sophie back. Certainly not her exam results, which exceeded all her hopes. Certainly not Lucas. She listened to her results with the same dull, uninterested expression she wore the entire time. I could have been relating the shipping forecast. I was aware of Lucas gradually slipping away, easing himself, in that sinewy way of his, out of the whole distasteful situation. Each time he visited, it was for a shorter and shorter time. He held Sophie's hands, but his eyes told a story of growing indifference. Of course they did. Why would he want to spend time with someone who showed no interest in him, who seemed mostly unaware of whether he was there or not? Why waste the end of a good summer stuck indoors with someone who had ceased to be the person he once thought he knew? Lucas had plans of his own. They had never included hours spent with a frail and feeble invalid. He wasn't prepared for the loss of his feisty, bubbly, adoring girlfriend, the one who encouraged his unconventional style and ideas and constantly bolstered his ego.

Gradually the visits from Lucas dwindled away until just before I was due to leave for university, when Mum and I realised it was at least two weeks since we'd last seen him. I mustered all my inner resources to phone him. I felt I owed it to Sophie. I didn't like him. I didn't trust him either, for no particular reason I could name, but he belonged to Sophie, or she had thought he did. She had thought they belonged together.

Love at first sight, remember, Jess? It's the only way. Anything else is boring. And once it's happened, you wouldn't want it any other way. You'll find out one day. Promise.

I'd sat on the old swing at the end of the garden, and dialled his number with shaky hands.

'At least come and say goodbye, Lucas,' I said. 'Don't you owe her that, at any rate?'

There had been a long, long silence.

'Why don't you do it?' he said eventually. His voice was husky and low, and I hunched over my phone, gripping it tight against my ear in an effort to hear him. '*You* can just say that, can't you? Goodbye? She's not bothered, is she? Doesn't care one way or another.'

I'd stayed sitting there for a long time, one toe on the ground, pushing myself backwards and forwards, the phone between my hands, and tears running down my face. It felt as if life as I knew it had changed for ever. I could never have imagined then how things could be even worse.

*

Sophie follows us along the pavement as we walk into the centre of Copenhagen. I can see her out of the corner of my eye. She tiptoes with exaggerated care along the edge of the kerb, dodges in and out of the cyclists on their designated path between the road and walkway, and dances ahead of us, only pausing at junctions to check our direction. I'm trying to listen to Anne as she points out things she thinks might be interesting, moving faster to keep up with her purposeful stride, but I find myself increasingly distracted by Sophie's behaviour. I realise, of course, it's because she doesn't have my undivided attention. She's always wanted to be the centre of my universe. She loves to be in the limelight.

'All these cyclists!' She appears beside me, as we cross at a main intersection. Everyone had waited for the green light before they crossed. No one scurried over on a red light, causing cars to brake or swerve. But the cyclists were something else. You had to watch out for them just as much as, if not more than, the other traffic. 'Crazy or what?' Sophie adds. 'Did you find this out in your research, Jessie? The fact that this city of our birth father actually appears to have more cyclists than are known to man. It's over-run with them! And they're kind of aggressive, aren't they? I mean – I know they've got rights but they seem to take it a bit too... look out!' she screeches, and I jump back as we reach the other side of the road, and another bike hurtles past.

Anne is laughing. 'You must watch for the bikes, Yess. It is their... I don't know... Road?'

'Right of way, I think you mean.' I can see Sophie leaning in a shop doorway. She rolls her eyes.

'Always so bloody polite!' she mutters as we walk past her. 'You could just point out it's not normal. So many bikes, all whizzing along like that. All these poor pedestrians having to watch out the whole time.'

'Stop being ridiculous,' I hiss. 'It's their right of way. It's just how they do...'

'What?' asks Anne, and I think how much easier it would be if Sophie disappeared. I feel disloyal the minute the thought pops into my head, but it's too complicated. I can't deal with her as well as everything else.

I realise we've turned into a different street, lined with tall, gabled buildings on both sides, and Anne points up at the street sign. At street level there is a scatter of shops, a couple of cafés, and a few anonymous commercial premises, but it's obvious as we walk down the road that most of the buildings are flats. By every entrance are bell pushes, each with a number and a little metal holder next to it with names slotted in to show who lives in each one.

It seems we've arrived in the street where Per Jacobsen, my journalist, lives. Or is supposed to live. But now we're here my courage begins to fail me. Is this really a good idea? Should I have tried to phone first? What am I going to say? Anne is marching along, head up, her spiky white crop of hair easy to follow as she weaves in and out of other pedestrians, confident as she is that I'm right beside her, or following close behind. At each doorway she pauses and scans the list of residents, shakes her head, and then strides on. I hurry to keep up.

'I'm not sure...' I start to say, and at the same moment she turns with a triumphant smile and waves at a large blue door at the top of a few wide steps behind her.

'So!' she says. 'So we had no number, Yess, but like good police workers we find your missing person.' She looks noticeably pleased with herself, and I realise how much she is enjoying this whole venture.

I hang back a little. 'Oh yes. OK. But I'm not sure...' I shift Sophie's bag higher onto my shoulder, and wonder if this is a good time to count. That's what I'd like to do. I glance around for a glimpse of Sophie, convinced she must be somewhere very near: leaning on the wall of the next building maybe, or behind one of the refuse bins, or even just inside the door to the apartments, eager to watch me as I make my faltering introductions.

Anne is raising puzzled eyebrows. 'You do not want to call him?' she asks, and I can hear the disappointment in her voice.

I shake my head. 'No. It's not that. It's just that, now I'm here...'

The problem, which is too much of a struggle to explain to Anne, is that this isn't how it should be, not at all. This isn't what we'd planned, for so many months and so many years. It seems all wrong that I should be standing on a bleak windy pavement under a weak Danish sun, outside an anonymous grey nineteenth-century apartment block, with a sprightly but nevertheless much older lady whom I've known for only twenty-four hours. Not having Sophie next to me makes it even worse. Or Karen. I experience a brief flare of anger towards Karen, who was going to be my prop, my guide, my supporter, but who'd allowed herself to trip over and down several concrete steps so carelessly.

This has all happened too quickly. In my intricately plotted imaginings it should have been several days before we tracked down Per's exact address, and by then I'd have been feeling so much more confident, as if I'd started to belong here, in this tiny, unknown city. It would be more familiar, in that way that foreign cities start to fall into place once you're there endlessly wandering around, gradually piecing together the way different streets and places link up. But that hasn't happened yet.

'I haven't even seen the Little Mermaid,' I say, and I can hear how childish that sounds. It's impossible to explain any other way.

'The liddle...?' Anne says, and then, with an emerging understanding, '*Den Lille Havfrue?*'

I shrug my shoulders. 'I guess so...' In spite of my unhappiness and discomfort I can't resist attempting to repeat it: '... Din lilla howfrew?'

I close my eyes just for a moment and count, very quickly, to five, and when I open them again I see Anne is climbing the steps and lifting her finger to press Per Jacobsen's doorbell.

I shout, 'No! Please... No. Not—' I rush to stand next to her, raising my hand to grab her arm, when something catches my eye. Behind Anne, strolling down the street, is my fellow traveller from yesterday, his jacket – hooked on one finger – flung casually over his shoulder.

Against all the odds, Kasper is walking towards us down the road, and he looks up and notices me at almost the same precise minute, and immediately quickens his pace.

CHAPTER TWENTY

'You know that thing about babies?' Sophie said, picking a blade of grass and chewing it briefly before throwing it on the ground with a disgusted expression.

We were sitting together cross-legged on the lawn in the middle of our grandparents' garden. My head was bent over my daisy chain, and the sun was warm on my bare neck. If you squinted up, you could see tiny flecks of white scudding across the blue of the sky, like the sponge prints we made sometimes with Gran's paints in her studio. I remembered the sticks of candyfloss we'd had at our village fair a few weeks ago, and imagined pulling off tiny pieces and throwing them in the air and watching them float away and I thought they'd look like that. Like the clouds.

It was nearly the longest chain I'd ever made, and any minute now Grampy would be coming outside to cut the grass, which would destroy any remaining wildflowers.

'Babies?' I said, shuffling forward a little to reach another couple of daisies with longer stems. 'What about them?'

'About getting a baby in your tummy by sitting on a loo seat, *straight after* your one true love's been sitting there. Like Melanie Tucker told us. *You* know.' Sophie was wearing her special "I know-something-you-don't-know" face, and she could hardly contain her delight at being about to reveal something new and possibly rude.

I was absorbed in joining up the last flowers in the chain. I'd added a few buttercups for luck and variety, painstakingly making a pattern with them: one buttercup, two daisies, one buttercup, three daisies, one buttercup, four daisies, and so on, and I'd nearly made it long enough.

Sophie was gleeful with triumph and importance. 'That's not true *at all!* It's something *completely* different. You'd never guess, Jessie, never in – oh, a million, billion years, so I'll just tell you, OK?'

Listening to Sophie had stopped me being able to count properly, so I started again with a frown of deep concentration. '*One* yellow, *two* white, *one* yellow, *three* white...' I muttered under my breath.

'OK? Jessie? You listening?'

When Sophie was like that, it was always easier to pretend. Easier just to go along with it.

'Mmm,' I said, but I was too busy with counting my pattern and stringing the last flowers. Although I could hear that she was explaining it all at great length, I only caught a few random words, and the rest was an incoherent babble. She always talked very quickly when she was explaining something, as if afraid that she'd never have time to finish what she was saying, as if the words were bubbling up inside her and to stop them spilling out and disappearing, she had to gabble to get them all out in one go. '... Cuddle... hole... stick... egg-but-not-the-sort-you... special hug... spurty stuff... yucky, yucky...' I heard, but they didn't make sense because I kept missing all the bits that joined them together, so I had as much idea what Sophie was telling me when she stopped talking as before she'd started. I became aware of a silence and looked up, thinking *five* white..., to see Sophie staring at me, bright with expectation.

'Polly Henderson told me,' she added. 'And her Mummy told her, so it *must* be true!'

I had to go along with the pretence of having listened to every word. 'But have you asked *our* Mummy?' I said, rather pleased with myself for my careful and cunning reply.

Sophie always ignored what she didn't want to hear: 'This next bit is *very* important, Jessie. You can *only* do it with your one true love, Polly said. Otherwise – it doesn't work!' Then she threw herself back on the ground, and rolled about on her back, her hands clasped over her tummy where her daisies had fallen and kicking her legs in the air and shouting with laughter. 'But it's *so* yucky! Yuk, yuk, yuk!' She bounced herself upright again, holding the few remaining daisies scooped together, and knelt opposite me with serious, narrowed eyes. 'So I'm *never* going to fall in love! Not ever! It's disgusting!'

It was too late now to question her further without making her realise I'd not listened properly at all. I screwed up my face with the effort of remembering some of what she'd said, while still holding tight to the count of my pattern. 'So Mummy's done that... thing what you said – *three* times? It can't be *that* yucky. Can it?' I gazed hopefully at Sophie, willing her to enlighten me further. But she was already moving on, impatient for the next game. She jumped up, all the daisies she'd collected and left abandoned in her lap spilling onto the grass.

'It means,' she said, with great solemnity, 'that she's definitely had *two* true loves. *Two!*' She began to spin round and round on the spot, faster and faster, and when she spoke it came out in little jerky bursts. 'But Polly's Mummy's... only done it twice... and not... with her true love... Polly said... because of her Daddy... going away.... and Polly's Mummy... having a baby... in her tummy... that *died*. When I go fast like this, Jessie, can you still see me?'

'You're all blurry,' I said. 'Like a ghost.'

*

While we're talking – Kasper introducing himself to Anne with his slow, easy smile and a handshake, smoothing over what could be awkward but isn't – something unexpected happens. A man comes down the steps from the building just behind us, gripping the handrail, and taking one step at a time with great care and deliberation. We'd been explaining our whole dilemma to Kasper, in a bewildering mixture of breathless English and indecipherable Danish, but he must have grasped the essentials because as soon as he notices the man he saunters over to where he's standing and speaks to him for a few seconds, waving up at the building, and over towards Anne and me. There is a small mime of more hand gestures, head shakes and nods. Then Kasper turns back to us with the widest grin, and says in English, 'Jess, you won't believe this, but here is Per Jacobsen.'

I put out my hand and clutch Anne's arm, because the pavement's tilting. My heart thuds very fast. Anticipation and surprise and fear tumble and fight for supremacy.

'Per?' My voice sounds hoarse and shaky. I don't care anymore that this is only my first day in Copenhagen and instead of searching for my birth father, following a trail where he would be the prize at the end of the treasure hunt, here he is already, just a few metres away from me. I try to remember the story I've prepared about my search. I don't want to spring the fact of my birth on him immediately.

Anne says, 'Yess. I sink...' When I glance at her she's staring at the man and looking perplexed.

I look at Kasper again, and he repeats, 'This is Per Jacobsen.' Slowly, slowly, I start to walk over to them and I lift my eyes for my first proper look at this man, this mysterious father of mine. His fine silver hair is long and tied back with a black ribbon so that it falls in a tail down his back, but his face... His face is lined and grooved with the creases of old age: two deep lines running down from his nose each side of his mouth, a crinkle of crows' feet at the corner of each eye, and a ploughed field of furrows on his forehead.

He looks back at me with an expression of puzzlement, but there's an amused glint to his eye too.

'*God morgen.* Per Jacobsen.' He holds out his hand. His other hand rests on an elegant silver-topped black stick.

I struggle to regain some composure. I shake his hand with what I hope is dignity. 'Hello, I'm Jessica Mortimer.'

He turns his gaze to Kasper, and lifts his shoulders as if to say, 'What now? Who is this? What have you to say to me?'

We have nothing to say, because this is the wrong Per Jacobsen. Yes, he's a journalist, he's telling Kasper in excellent English. He's lived in England for several months at a time over the years – a country he likes very much, he adds with a grave nod in my direction. He's written extensively about cultural differences, standards of living, education... his voice drones on. In fact, it was in England, he says, that he had an accident which has meant he now must rely on walking with a stick. He taps it on the ground. 'Though fortunately...' and on, and on. I can understand every word, but disappointment and deflation roar in my ears and muffle the sound of his voice, and I stop listening.

He's swept away with a sense of his own importance in our small drama. But he's much, much too old. It can't be the right Per. My father, Mum had told me, was twenty-three that summer – the summer she became pregnant – which would make him, what? Forty-four now? Forty-five, maybe? Whereas this man must be at least sixty-five or seventy.

I'm desperate to get away, but I'm paralysed by politeness. Anne and Kasper rescue me, Anne saying something in Danish to Kasper, and Kasper shaking hands again while explaining to Per that I was searching for an old friend of my parents but we must have made a mistake with the address, and apologising. Everyone parts on the friendliest of terms. I watch Per Jacobsen – the wrong Per Jacobsen – limp away down the street, his stick thudding rhythmically on the pavement, and his silver ponytail blowing sideways in the breeze.

Then Kasper raises his eyebrows at me. 'What do you call this?' he says. 'A happy coincidence? To meet again so soon. I tell you on the plane how small is København. I live not so far from here,' he explains. 'And today I am supposed to be meeting someone.'

I arrange my face before he goes on, hoping my disappointment won't show.

'But,' he continues, 'I'm too early. Very much too early. It seemed like a nice day to walk.' That easy grin appears, familiar already from our short flight together. 'We Danes like to be outdoors. Especially when the sun shines after our long winter. Shall we find somewhere to have a drink maybe? That could be nice. We can see another part of København.' He includes Anne with a casual gesture, but she's quick to shake her head.

'For you two young people that is very fine,' she says. 'So nice for Yess. So lucky. So sad that the man was not right person.'

We arrange a place they both know where we can meet in a couple of hours.

'Come,' Kasper says to me. 'I know a quick route. We're going to Nyhavn – you'll like it.'

And we hurry away.

*

The area by the harbour is busy, teeming with what seems like the entire tourist population of Copenhagen, plus a sizeable number of locals. People have chosen this morning to descend, a swarm of ants, on Nyhavn, seduced by the sunshine. They are strolling along by the edge of the harbour, or sitting outside the restaurants and cafés, eating and drinking. The bleak sun is gathering strength, but it still feels chilly to me. I notice that where people are sitting there are rugs and cosy blankets thrown over the backs of chairs for customers to use, and most of the outside areas have powerful, roaring patio heaters. It seems very civilised. I'm glad when we choose a café where we can watch this molten mass of humanity, this random stream flowing past. Different languages float by, dipping and swaying in the warm salty air. I think I see Sophie in the crowd, passing by, but she's gone, and it could have been anyone. Anyone in this city with a swing of blonde hair, and a certain way of walking.

Kasper is explaining about the area, how Nyhavn means New Harbour, and how once it was an area of, '... I don't know the word, but not a good place to be. Sailors and prostitutes were here, and maybe you would not want to be here on your own. Many people who were...'

'Up to no good?' I suggest, staring around at the brightly painted facades of the buildings, so pretty and colourful in the sunshine. I try to picture the area in the old days, and fail.

Restaurants of all kinds and bars and cafes have replaced the brothels and boarding houses, Kasper says. 'But you can still have a tattoo, if you like.'

I smile. I'd never followed Sophie's lead and allowed myself to get a tattoo. I didn't intend to start now. Across from the café where we're sitting, several old boats bob in the water. I get a real sense of the history of the place, despite all the modern changes, and I think how much Mum would love it. I feel properly abroad.

A blonde waitress wearing a name badge labelled "Mette" takes our order, and we sit watching people walk or cycle past as we wait for her to reappear. She sets down our drinks with exaggerated care, but even so some spills on the table as she says, '*Værsgo.*' Then she staggers back. Her hand waves wildly for the chair behind her, to support herself. It all happens so fast I'm hardly aware of the crisis that's unfolding.

'Mette?' One of the other waitresses is shouting from the doorway. 'Mette!'

Mette's face is the colour of driftwood, and her arms and legs jerk like a marionette.

Kasper has leapt up from his chair, knocking it over as he does, and someone behind him shouts something. I stand up too, but before we can move, a man at the table next to us has gone swiftly to the girl's side, and has folded her onto the pavement. He holds her wrist, leans his face close to her mouth, and then he turns her on her back and starts to pump her chest urgently and rhythmically with his hands.

Passers-by stop and stare, forming a tight half-circle around the man and the girl. Others wander past, apparently oblivious to the events taking place within a metre or so of where they're walking.

I stand transfixed. Kasper and I are silent. I think he yelled out something at the beginning. Maybe it was Danish for "help!"? How would I know? My heart thuds.

We wait and watch and without either of us speaking I know that the waitress, that young, smiley, blonde waitress with the name badge that says "Mette", is dying. I can see her badge as it lies still and unmoving on her chest. The man is still pumping: pumping and then blowing into her mouth, beads of sweat running down his forehead, his face flushed with effort. We hear sirens, and the crowd are muttering and looking over their shoulders and moving aside in a shuffling wave as an ambulance shrieks to a halt on the quayside.

I stumble away, through the congealed mass of bodies, towards the water, and then I vomit in the gutter. Sophie's face bobs and spins in front of me as I lean over, coughing and retching. How can this be happening, I think, when the only person with me is Kasper, and I hardly know him at all? It's beyond embarrassing. I'd like to slip away, and go and find Anne wherever she is, and pretend this hasn't taken place, but I don't know where to go. I'm a stranger in this city. I'm lost without the only two Danish people I know. I don't even have my guidebook with me.

Kasper leaves money on the table, and we go and sit by the water in silence. I find tissues in my bag and wipe my face, and

Kasper fetches me a glass of water from the café. Then I tell him about Sophie. It's like shedding a skin. I'm stripped raw, as if every nerve ending and each of my five senses has been fine-tuned; all my fragility exposed.

Nothing happens. Everything stays the same. The world continues on its path of rotation and people carry on past us, intent on their own pursuits. I'm here in Copenhagen, which I must remember to pronounce properly, and I'm still going to search for Per. Except Kasper moves closer, shifts along the bench and takes my hand loosely in his. It feels like the best thing that's happened to me for a long, long time.

*

A few days after Sophie died, I slipped into her room and retrieved her diary from where she'd hidden it. They hadn't looked for it after all; that never happened because it became clear how she'd died and there was no need of any further evidence.

I sat on the edge of my bed, holding it in my hands, feeling the weight of it, rubbing my thumb over the worn fabric cover of the spine. Then I lifted it to my face and breathed in the scent of her. The essence of Sophie. That would fade first, I thought. Smells don't last in the same way as images. I'd always have photos and those funny little family videos of her. I could always look at her handwriting, and remember her sitting curled up in that deliberately uncontrived way of hers, scribbling frantically as she made late notes for an essay or put furtive entries in her diary. In this book. I could go into her room and sift through all her things, and for now, for a little while, she would always be lingering there, unmistakeable. Everything – clothes, hairbrush, carpet, favourite books, bedclothes – would smell, faintly. But although they'd last, all those solid, material things, her scent on them would wither over time, and then disappear.

I sat quite still. I could hear the rooks in the trees at the end of the garden, screeching and cawing, and then some friendlier birdsong – a blackbird, maybe, or a robin – quite close by. I never could tell which sound was what bird. I could hear my grandparents talking quietly downstairs, their measured voices rising up through the banisters, as they worked together trying to make things better for us. It was a pointless task. Nothing could make things better. But they were unable to sit around feeling dreadful; their way of coping was to help Mum and Dad by taking over all the mundane stuff. They'd been shopping, and the sound of drawers and cupboards being opened and closed drifted up the stairs, followed presently by a clatter of pans as my grandmother decided to cook us all something that I knew already none of us would want to eat.

I opened the diary, with a small shiver of dread at what I might read, and flicked through the days and weeks and months until I reached the last entries, written just a couple of days before we'd gone into Brighton.

There it was.

"Must see Lucas. Must ask him if it's true. Don't want to ask Jess because I'll know if she's lying and if..."

Her scribbly writing was getting too difficult to read.

She had guessed, somehow, she'd known, I realised. Something like a sixth sense – that tight indescribable link that we had, our "twin link" as we'd called it, soppily – had inched its grimy trail into her head, and had refused to disappear. I could imagine the way her pen would have been going faster and faster, and her writing smaller and more and more untidy with the desperation that was forcing her to put down in black and white what she was hoping was just paranoia. Once you've been ill, she'd told me on the phone a few weeks before this entry, and then you're getting better, back to what you hope (but can't really remember) is "normal", it becomes incredibly difficult to separate your thoughts into what you believe to be reality, and what you wonder might be just the result of your medication. Or the last stray dregs of the end of that illness.

The sentence she'd written had stopped in mid-flow, as if she'd been unable to finish what she wanted to say. I have to hold up the diary close to my face, and squint a bit to decode the next part.

"But I know them, don't I? know them both so well and now I'm late. Should have started 2 days ago it's all a mess I can't bear thinking about it got to stop writing got to…"

She'd carried on the next day.

"And think I feel sick this can't be happening. A nightmare a nightmare…"

I read it with an eerie detachment. I could picture her putting all this down, and I could plainly hear her voice as if she were sitting next to me saying the words, fear and despair

spiking the sound of them. Yet because of everything –
everything that had happened since – it seemed unreal. More
like the scribblings of some overwrought, hysterical teenager
than a young twenty-year-old woman with her whole life
before her, waiting for it to happen.

CHAPTER TWENTY-ONE

Karen arrives. Anne and I go to meet her at Kastrup airport; it's less than two weeks since I arrived there myself, but it seems much, much longer. We walk through the revolving doors and into the huge shiny concourse. The signs no longer look alien – I can even understand some of them. The people who pass us, drifting along with trolleys or hurrying by tugging wheeled suitcases, and their clothes – the way they dress – no longer seem so different, so utterly foreign.

As we hurry towards Arrivals, Anne rummages in her tote bag and produces two Danish flags, cloth ones with wooden sticks, and hands one to me. 'We must welcome my Karen,' she says. 'Always the flag.'

We wait together, the flags in our hands, and as we spot Karen hobbling through with a sturdy metal walking stick, her luggage hoisted on her back, we wave our flags, along with several other people beside us waiting to greet their own visitors. I think how extraordinary it would be if this were in England. Somehow it feels completely normal here. But I'm so excited to see her that I stop waving and dodge through the crowd and we hug, awkwardly because of the walking stick and backpack, and then I take the baggage off her back to carry myself.

'I'm not an invalid, you know,' she says, grinning, as practical and independent as ever, but she looks grateful.

'I've got *so* much to tell you,' I say, as we head over to where Anne is still waving her flag with increasing vigour. 'It's *amazing*. I'm so glad you're here.'

'*Velkommen!*' Anne is calling. '*Velkommen til Danmark igen, Karen!*' There's a pause while they hug and kiss, and speak Danish to each other. It makes me realise how hard the last couple of weeks must have been for Anne, struggling to talk in English all the time we were together.

'Well,' says Karen. 'I'm very glad to be here at last! And,' she points at her ankle and sticks out her leg, 'really, really sorry about this, Jess. I completely mucked things up for you.'

We walk towards the car park, her luggage stowed on a trolley that I push, and I wonder how I can begin to tell her everything that's happened since we last spoke. Our couple of phone conversations have been brief and centred mainly on her recovery and hopeful date of arrival.

'It's been good for me,' I tell her. 'In the end. Because I've had to do stuff on my own. Things I didn't think I could. But I'm really glad you're here now.'

She's smiling down at the flag which I've stuck on top of her backpack on the trolley.

'I see Mormor's got you introduced to the famous Dannebrog then.'

'The...? Oh, the flag, yes, I've been told all about that. Oldest flag in the world, comes out on all occasions – birthdays, homecomings, etcetera, etcetera. It is *everywhere*, isn't it? Weird! I'm getting used to it now, but at home it would be...'

'Really weird, in the U.K.' Karen agrees. 'And a bit overly patriotic. Nationalistic, in a not-good way.'

'But it doesn't feel like that here,' I say, as we reach Anne's small blue car. 'So something must be rubbing off on me, I guess.'

'It's your Danish roots.' Karen giggles again. She sits in the front of the car with Anne, the seat pushed back so that she can put her foot out in front of her, and she lapses into Danish. She and Anne chat all the way back to Frederiksberg.

I spend the journey staring out of the window and watching the streets of Copenhagen pass by: the yellow buses and the hot dog stalls; the big old-fashioned looking baby prams; the amazing flower shops and the konditori; the trees lining some of the roads, their fresh new green leaves just unfurled; and the rows of cycle racks. Tall, white painted buildings, their gable windows wedged high up into the grey slate roofs, no longer look at odds with the endless, elaborate graffiti on empty expanses of wall. A constant, constant flow of cyclists – young and old – streaming along. Many have baskets on the front of their bikes, with books or shopping or bags spilling over the edge, and some have an extra seat on the back, or pull a little trailer for small children to sit in.

We're driving along H.C. Andersens Boulevard, past Ny Carlsberg Glyptotek, where Anne took me two days ago because it's free on Wednesdays – and she'd asked if I was interested in art and sculpture – and Radhus Pladsen. I notice the signs for Tivoli, and as we turn into Vesterbrogade, Karen turns her head to say, 'Tivoli Gardens. We have to go there, Jess. It's great! Mormor has a special gold card so we can get in for free.'

I have to tell her that I've been already.

*

'Do you want we should go to Tivoli?' Kasper had asked. 'Do you know it?'

He was determined to show me everything that København can offer, he said, and that had to include Tivoli.

Now that I'd decided to postpone my search for Per until Karen arrived, Anne and Kasper were doing their best to give me guided tours of the city. All the sights. It was a wonderful way to spend my time and they both seemed more than happy to give up a few hours on different days to do it. The days with Anne were spent visiting very different places from those I saw with Kasper. Some days he and I just found a café or a bar and sat talking and people-watching.

'Don't you have work to do?' I'd asked him.

'Oh yes,' he'd shrugged in that carefree way of his. 'But I have time enough for that and time enough for this too. Tomorrow, for example, we cannot meet because I must go for a lecture.'

We'd already walked along beside the harbour, buffeted by the wind, to visit the Little Mermaid, and I'd had to agree with him that it had hardly been worth the effort. The statue was so much smaller than I'd imagined, smaller than it looked in the photos I'd seen. I'd felt sorry for her, sitting there sideways on her rock, forever stuck at the edge of the water with only cruise ships and merchant vessels for company. But not sorry enough to stay very long.

'I tried to tell you,' Kasper said as we headed back towards Kongens Nytorv. 'She is like that – what do you call him – Manneken Pis? Do you know this? He is also bronze.'

'The one in Brussels, you mean?'

'Pissing all day long, poor boy,' Kasper laughed. 'At least our *lille havfrue* is more polite.'

Two days later we went to Tivoli. We met on the corner of Bernstorffsgade and Vesterbrogade, and walked along to the main entrance to Tivoli. The smell of popcorn was sweet in the warm mid-day air.

'Truly you should be here at night,' Kasper said, guiding me through the elaborate gateway with its grand columns and dome, and TIVOLI announced in great gold letters on the arch. We passed an extraordinary building like an exotic white crenelated Moorish palace, which he told me was a restaurant. It reminded me a little of Brighton Pavilion. In front of it, just where we were walking, was a fountain with water bubbling up through an arrangement of Perspex tubes.

I felt a little overwhelmed by the place. I hadn't been sure what to expect, but certainly not the masses of spring flowers.

('The flowers are so famous at Tivoli,' Kasper told me, like a proper tour guide.) Certainly not this sheer relentless glitz, the unashamed sentimentality, all mixed together in a weirdly traditional way. The whole place had the atmosphere of an overgrown beer garden that had somehow lost its way and been transformed into something else. Almost like escapism.

We bought hot dogs from a stall and I said, 'So then maybe when Karen arrives, we could come again, but at night?'

He gave me an odd look and shrugged and said that yes, maybe we could. Then we tried as many rides as we could until we felt sick with the thrill of vertigo and ached with laughing. We walked back to Anne's place, and he took my hand loosely as we crossed a road and then didn't let go, and I realised on the way that I hadn't seen Sophie for several days.

All thoughts of finding my birth father were postponed after the disaster with the journalist who'd turned out to be too old and the wrong Per Jacobsen. The only other thing Kasper and I did was to locate the street whose name Mum had written down for me. It was the address she'd had for him, all those years ago, of where his parents lived. It wasn't far from Anne's apartment, which seemed too good to be true, and I'd already planned to go there with Karen, if she felt able to walk any distance.

'So now you have seen it,' Kasper had said afterwards, as we sat drinking hot chocolate outside a small café. 'And you will know where to go with your friend.'

That worm of anxiety began to wriggle inside me. All the time I was out and about, pretending to be a tourist, I didn't have to think about how I would cope this time with the possibility of meeting Per's parents and asking them about him. I set down my hot chocolate on the table, and watched the steam curling into the air. I pressed my hands between my knees, and tried to breathe normally.

'I can't wait,' I said, smiling with a fake brightness I borrowed briefly from Sophie. She wasn't there, so she wouldn't mind. 'I just can't wait.'

*

'I want to know all about Kasper!' Karen declares, when we're lying in our twin beds later, after the dinner that Anne had made in celebration of Karen's arrival, eaten at a table decorated with flowers and tall white candles and a now very familiar red and white flag on a small stainless-steel pole.

'To welcome my special granddaughter,' Anne had said as we helped ourselves to slices of roast pork and red cabbage and delicious tiny potatoes that seemed to have been caramelised in some peculiar way. There was a *lagkage* afterwards, full of cream, which we ate with our coffee.

'Traditional Danish cuisine at its very best,' Karen whispered to me with a wicked glint in her eye when Anne went out to make the coffee, and we started to clear the dishes. 'Its very fattening best.'

'*Tak for mad, Mormor*,' she said when Anne came back in, and the three of us went to sit by the coffee table.

('It's what you say,' she explained when she saw my frown, 'as you leave the table. Everyone does. Unless you're very rude or something. It means, "Thanks for the food", or maybe... the meal. Thanks for the meal. You must say it in future too, Jess. I'll be listening.')

Now I'm sitting propped up in bed leaning against the uncomfortable thin pillow so that the wall behind me feels very hard and unforgiving.

'There's nothing to tell,' I say. 'Anyway, you'll meet him soon, I expect, so you can see for yourself.'

Karen looks across at me, an expression of disbelief on her face.

'Nothing to tell? You spend nearly every day for two weeks with some guy you've just met on a plane, and there's nothing to tell?'

I shrug, and slide down beneath the duvet, pulling the pillow under my head at the same time.

'Only a few days, and he's just really friendly. You know – like you're always telling me how the Danes are. He likes showing me the city. I think he feels sorry for me, being on my own.'

'Of course he does!' There's a snort of derision from the other bed.

Then I add quickly, 'Anne's been great too, of course. Really great.'

Karen's voice drifts over, sounding half asleep, 'I'll make up my own mind about Kasper, then. Can't wait.'

*

Lucas had rung me the next day. I'd been in the middle of deciding whether I was going to pack only my usual jeans and T-shirts in my suitcase for university, or whether to include other things which would project an entirely new image of me when I arrived there: a smart, cool, altogether savvier type of person. Nobody would know. I could invent a whole different personality. I might even be able to stop counting.

'Hey. Jessie.' His drawl was spiked with sarcasm, and the low pitch of his voice potent with intent.

'Checking up on me, Lucas?' I didn't even try to avoid sounding cynical. 'No. I haven't delivered your thoughtful message of farewell yet. I somehow haven't found the right time to make my sister feel a million times worse than she already does. Funny, that.'

'You're too hard on me, Jess.'

'Really?'

'Yes, really.'

I allowed a silence, which stretched and yawned and folded in on itself until I almost wondered whether he'd somehow, ever so stealthily, hung up on me. Nothing would surprise me where Lucas was concerned. I was poised to drop, 'Well, if that's all...' into the unsettling pause when he spoke again.

'Wondered if we could meet.'

'Sorry?' This time it was too difficult to hide my incredulity.

'There's a couple of things for Sophie.'

'What things?'

'Stuff. And my uni address.'

'You could give that to her...'

'Leave it out, Jess. Can we meet or not? I'm not coming round again. It's too...'

'Too painful, Lucas? Too awkward? Too embarrassing? Poor you.'

I knew how hard he found it, not being in control. The conversation was slipping out of his grasp. He had to hang on to it with a consummate effort.

'Let's say this afternoon, then? Three. That playing field near you – what's it called?'

'Southfields.'

'That's the one. Three, at the far end. Under the trees.'

The conversation ended and the phone went dead. Round one to Lucas, I thought, and I had to admire his skill and strategy. He was going to make an excellent politician one day. I played with the idea of not turning up, but I had to admit to the tiniest bit of curiosity. And even if Sophie were to find out, it was only for her benefit I was going.

*

We stand in the shadows of tall apartment buildings in a small road off H.C. Orsteds Vej, and Karen says, 'Well, here we are! That wasn't far, even for a person like me of limited walking mobility!' She's leaning on her stick and breathing heavily as though the very effort of that half mile or so has added a year to her age for every ten steps.

235

I manage a small smile. 'Here goes, then.'

I unfold the scrap of creased paper that I've been gripping in my hand since we left Anne's flat, and check the door number again, although I know it by heart. Earlier we'd discussed whether to try phoning first, before we left, but I couldn't face all the potential difficulties that might involve. The thought of asking for Per by name, and then trying to explain who I was, and why I was looking for him seemed far more problematic than simply ringing a doorbell.

This is the moment I've been planning since November. I'm poised once more on the edge of this high board of uncertainty, gripping my toes and swaying to keep my balance before diving down. Down into the unknown. I'm hoping I'm going to surface with everything I want to know. Or maybe I'm going to plunge into a situation which is at best embarrassing, and at worst devastating? I hardly dare to imagine.

There's even a possibility – small but conceivable – that Per himself may be here.

The label by the bell push says "Grethe Skovgaard Jacobsen". So part of the family name is right at least, which is a relief. I'm not sure about the Skovgaard bit, but before I have time to ask Karen what she thinks, a voice crackles through the tiny grid by the doorbell.

Karen leans forward and says something, there's a click, and we push the heavy wooden door open and walk into a square hallway with a black and white tiled floor and a wide curving staircase ahead which we start to climb. It takes a long time, because Karen can only go very slowly, using her good foot for each step. We have to check three doors on each landing to read the name plates. On the second floor, we find the right one and tap with a door knocker. My heart is beating very fast. I'm sure Karen must be able to hear it, but she gives me only an encouraging glimmer of a smile.

It's a while before the door opens, and when it does, the person standing there is older than us – maybe in her thirties, with stiff clumps of orange hair, two rings in one nostril, and three studs under her bottom lip.

'Grethe Jacobsen?' Karen asks, with a polite but questioning edge in her voice.

The woman shakes her head. She's wearing slippers – those backless leather ones you push your feet into – and a white overall. After she and Karen have had a brief conversation, Karen says, 'This lady says she comes in to support Grethe Jacobsen so she can stay in her own home. She helps her with things she can't do any longer, like cleaning, and some shopping and cooking. She wants to know who we are and what we want.'

'Tell her,' I say. 'Tell her how I'm looking for, trying to trace, someone. His name is... well,' I end lamely, 'you know that bit.'

The woman is watching us, turning from one to the other.

'You look for somebody?' she says in English. 'Not Grethe Jacobsen? Someone who she know?' I notice a stud in her tongue as she speaks.

You're not being judgemental, are you, Jessie? She's finding ways of expressing her own individuality. Good for her!

'I think she may have a son,' I say, wishing we could be invited inside and not have to stand here on the landing. 'A son called Per Jacobsen. Could we... can we come in and see her? Maybe she can tell us where he lives.'

'Wait,' the woman says, after a long pause during which she regards us both with what can only be described as deep suspicion. 'I go and speak to her. Wait here please.' As an afterthought she adds, 'Who are you please? What are your names, and how you know this man?' She has a habit of screwing up her nose after she's spoken and blinking three times very fast. She continues, with a disapproving tone, 'He is not young.'

I explain that I'm on holiday in Copenhagen, and wish to find Per Jacobsen only because my mother knew him a long time ago – '*Very* long,' I stress.

'I'd be really grateful,' I reiterate, 'if Grethe Jacobsen could tell us anything about Per. My mother will be so pleased. They lost touch...' As the woman frowns, I say, 'Please... it's very important.'

She screws up her nose and blinks again, then turns with an audible exasperated sigh. Her feet flap and slap down the passage that's just visible glimpsed through the half-open door, and she disappears into a room out of sight.

'Stop looking so fierce and worried,' Karen whispers. 'I've got a good feeling about this.'

Time limps by. After a while Karen lowers herself onto the bottom stair of the next flight and we sit side by side. How long does it take to ask for an address, or some sort of contact details? I lean my head against the balustrade. We both jump when the woman appears again, soundlessly, at the doorway.

'Come, please,' she beckons. 'She says to come in. She wants she can see you.'

We follow her down the dark passage then she stops outside a room and says in a low voice, 'She has some...' She looks at Karen as if she's thinking of using Danish, of the familiarity of her own language, but then continues, '... Problem? Grethe has some problems.' She touches her ears. 'Not good to hear, and also,' she taps her head, 'sometime not so good to know what you mean. She forget some time also.'

'Oh great,' Karen mutters, right behind me. 'This should be fun.'

CHAPTER TWENTY-TWO

Lucas was already waiting under the trees at the far end of the field when I arrived. I'd made myself deliberately late, which was difficult for me. I was known for being the punctual one of the family. I'd dawdled down our lane, and then after glancing at my watch had walked up and down the High Street a couple of times to make sure it was well past three.

'You've come,' he declared when he saw me. I thought it was funny that he'd imagined I might not meet him. It was a small chink in the contrived and brittle invisible shell he wore like a bulletproof vest – his protection against the boring and trivial world where he seemed to assume most people lived.

I was determined to keep this encounter short and to the point. For some reason I felt nervous; I didn't know why. What did I think was going to happen? I didn't trust Lucas. I thought he tried too hard to be different, and clever, and individual. But nevertheless, he was just Lucas. I'd known him as long as Sophie had. We'd been in classes together; we shared the same friendship group.

'You said you'd got stuff for Sophie,' I said. I couldn't see anything he'd brought with him. He was lolling against the old horse chestnut tree. Every autumn its conkers had fallen wide and far, rolled under leaves that were scattered like sponge prints, yellow and brown and orange on the drying grass, and hidden behind tufts of greying stalks. As children we'd scurried to and fro, spotting and collecting them with whoops of glee. Now I could see some already, glossy brown or still snug inside their soft spiky shells, lying in wait to be found.

'Yeah, that's right,' he said. 'I did.'

'Well,' I said, 'come on then. Where is it, Lucas? I haven't got all day. I'm in the middle of packing for uni.'

He straightened unhurriedly. 'My address.' He dug in his pocket, and pulled out a scrap of paper. 'For my halls. In case Sophie ever manages to get around to wanting to make contact.'

'She's not doing this on purpose, Lucas,' I said. 'Do you really think she wants to be like this? It's an illness. Not a lifestyle choice.'

'Yeah, well, whatever.' His eyes travelled from my face, down my body and back, slowly. He allowed himself a brief, appreciative smile. 'Maybe it's me that made the wrong choice. Wrong sister. Wrong... twin.' He moved closer, and held out the piece of paper.

I snatched it from him. 'Shut up, Lucas. How can you talk like that? Sophie adores you – you know that? Once she starts to get better...'

'But who knows when that will be?' He held my gaze very directly. 'Could be months... years even. Not sure how long I can wait, to be honest. Not when I could be...' He shrugged. 'You and I, Jess. Don't tell me you've never wondered. Don't tell me it's never crossed your mind.' He dropped his voice, and murmured, leaning in close to my ear. 'She'd never know. Who's going to tell her?'

I took a step back. Every nerve in my body tingled. I wasn't prepared for this; I hadn't expected it. I knew he could read the confusion in my face. My hesitation, brief though it was, became my undoing. I should have left him then. Turned away, run back across the field, run home, kept safe, stayed true.

'Lucas,' I whispered. 'I don't think it's a good idea. I don't...'

He reached out towards me, and ran his thumb gently down my cheek. I felt a tremor run through me, a jolt, a sudden hunger, and the realisation too that I could be Sophie, just for a while. Just for today, for this moment, for an hour, nothing more. The old Sophie, that is, the Sophie who took risks, the quick, feisty, funny Sophie, the Sophie who could have chosen almost anyone but who wanted Lucas. Lucas, who now wants me.

'Well,' he muttered, 'if we only ever did the right thing... the good idea... What a boring life that would be.'

He had me then. I remembered when I was packing earlier, I'd been thinking how I could decide to be a whole different person at Warwick, and no one there would know the normal me. I could start now. I could stop being the careful, boring twin, the one who always chose the safe option, the one who did the right thing. I pushed Sophie to the very back of my mind; I ignored her startled, hurt expression. She'd never know. Who was going to tell her?

I let him kiss me under the tree, long and deep, and I kissed him back. I craved him. He led me into the wood, and a little part of my brain sang a quiet alarm: that he'd planned this from the beginning. That he'd always known what he could make happen. We lay down, unseen among the grass and the bracken, secret among the trees, and we both betrayed Sophie.

*

I arrange to meet Kasper in a bar in Vesterbro where he's spending an evening with some of his friends. Karen stays in the flat. Her ankle is aching badly after all the walking we've done today.

'Don't feel guilty,' she says. 'Just go and have fun. Go and enjoy telling him our news. I'll come next time. Definitely. I want to meet this guy, you know!' She looks very happy and relaxed lying there on Anne's sofa, drinking coffee with her grandmother, and watching an old episode of Mr Bean on television.

I'm longing to tell Kasper what we've discovered, but first I have to be introduced to his friends: Mads, Jonas, Rasmus, Daniel, Aksel. They each shake hands with me and appear delighted to meet me in that particularly friendly way of all Danes, or at least the ones I've come across. A waiter brings over beer, and we sit squashed in a corner. The bar is crowded and busy and throbs with noise.

I shout at Kasper, 'I think I know where my father is! I think I know where he lives!' but I can hardly hear his reply.

This is neither the time nor place to explain, I realise, and have a sudden overwhelming urge to phone home instead. To speak to my proper family. Not to be thinking all the time about whether people understand all the nuances and shades of meaning in what I'm saying. Kasper speaks English almost perfectly, but still I sometimes think he doesn't quite grasp everything I say to him. Right now, his friends are being brilliant at including me in their conversation, but it's exhausting, and after I finish my beer I make my excuses and leave. Kasper points to his phone and mimes speaking to me on it the next day, and I nod agreement.

Sophie trails back to the apartment with me. 'Walking on your own, Jessie?' she says. 'That's not very gallant of him, is it?'

'Don't be ridiculous. It's broad daylight.'

I'm speaking out of the corner of my mouth, conscious of other people hurrying home from work, or drifting into bars and restaurants. I want to get back to make my phone call home. I start to hurry, almost jogging.

'Hey! What's this?' she laughs. 'You trying to run away from me, Jess?'

I stop and turn round to face her, and she's brought to a sudden halt and looks unsure about what to do or say next. She tucks her hair behind her ears with that quick, familiar gesture, and then studies the rings on her fingers.

'Just this once, Sophie.' I speak out loud and ignore the astonished looks of passers-by. They skirt around me tutting with exasperation or, embarrassed, become very busy with their own conversations or peering at their mobiles. I move back out of the way to lean against a railing that marks the descent of steps from street level down to someone's basement flat. 'Just this once, can you let me do my own thing, please?' I'm whispering, furiously. Sophie has to edge closer to hear me. 'Why has it always got to be about you? What makes you think your opinion of everything is so much more important? I am capable of making my own decisions, you know, and now – right now – I just want to get back to Anne's and phone home and tell Mum what's happened today. I just want to hear her voice.'

My own voice trembles a bit, so I stop and breathe and count silently in pinpricked blackness. I reach twenty, and when I open my eyes Sophie is still standing there, wearing a pained and crestfallen expression. She drops her gaze and it lands at my feet and splinters into a thousand tiny hurt pieces, and I reach out for her, but she's untouchable.

'Sophie. Sophie, don't go. I'm sorry. I'm so sorry. I'm tired and excited – I'm not thinking straight.'

She levels her eyes and stares straight at me. She's so close I can see her pupils – huge in the blueness – but all I can feel is the chill of her breath and the coldness sliding off her skin.

'Why *did* you get your hair cut, Jess?' she asks. 'Didn't you want to look like me anymore?' She hesitates and frowns for a moment. 'Your eyes,' she says, 'are exactly the same colour as mine, aren't they? Kind of weird, isn't it? I liked being a twin. It was the best thing ever. You and me...'

'... Against the world.' I finish her sentence before she can. 'I think we've found him, Sophie. I think Karen and me may have found Per.'

I want to share everything with her all at once. It's as if she's never gone.

'I know,' she says, with a curious smile. 'You forget that I already know that. Even when you can't see me...'

I shiver. She's studying her fingers again with that careful indifference, that nonchalance.

'Even when I can't see you... what?'

Sophie raises her head.

'Oh, you know, Jessie. You know exactly what I mean. I'm here for ever, aren't I? Even when *you* can't see me. And before, when I was still... alive... well, I usually guessed. We always did, you and me, didn't we? Everything. Or maybe nearly everything. Sometimes we got it wrong. But it's OK what you did then, when I was... ill. It's really OK. It was just the once, I know. And it doesn't matter now, anyway. Does it?'

I've got some dust or something in my eye. I rub them both with my fingers, because Sophie's going all blurry. Like a ghost. I swallow down the threat of tears.

'It didn't mean anything,' I say, urgently. 'You do know that, don't you, Sophie?'

She doesn't answer.

'I'm sorry,' I whisper again. 'I'm so, so sorry. I just wanted to be you. And, for a while, I was. But then I realised I wanted to be me again, and now... now I can never take it back.'

I shake my head, and start to move away from her, to carry on walking home to Karen and Anne. I don't look to see if Sophie is still there, or following me. I know that other people are staring at me.

'I miss you, Sophie.' The mantra tiptoes through my head. 'I always will. But maybe it's time for me to just manage on my own. Don't you think?'

There's no sound. I have to turn round and look. She's vanished, but then I catch sight of her, crossing the street. Her feet are swallowed up by the surface of it and her hair floats in a wispy fuzz in the air. The pedestrian light shines red and the traffic moves constantly. She's untouched.

*

She wanted to tell Lucas she was pregnant. Or at least, she thought she was. Almost definitely. She wanted to ask him if there was something else that he needed to tell her as well. Something that might stop them staying together.

It all came out at the inquest. We had to sit and listen as Lucas gave his evidence in a low, barely audible voice. I could see Gran and Grampy concentrating hard in an effort to hear him. Even the coroner asked him to speak up. Lucas stared at the floor all through his mumbled explanations and answers.

He never looked over at me and my family, not once. He didn't raise his head; he couldn't meet my eyes.

I wanted him to. I wanted to call out, 'Lucas! Hey – remember me?' Then when he looked over, I'd have said, 'It's OK. I understand. You're an idiot and a coward and you're thoughtless, and you absolutely didn't deserve Sophie, but I forgive you – even though what happened is unforgivable. Because you're not worth it, I've decided. I've got more important things to worry about than hating you for the rest of my life.'

I'd had it all planned, but it never happened – only in my head. Lucas couldn't even face us across the coroner's court. He never kept his part of the bargain.

'And the Halloween mask?' the coroner said to him. 'Would you mind telling me about that?'

It was meant as a joke, Lucas had muttered. Yes, he realised now it wasn't really a joke, not at all, for someone who was frightened of people in masks. Anyone in a mask. Frightened nearly to the point of being phobic. He'd known this about Sophie. He just hadn't been thinking. He'd been trying to lighten the mood, he said. It had all got rather heavy, what with Sophie thinking she was pregnant and neither of them knowing what to do, and then on top of that, her accusations; they came completely out of the blue. Too much. It was all just too much. And of course, Sophie had been ill, and he hadn't realised how she might still be a little – he hesitated for a moment – a little unstable.

Gran's gasp pierced the room with outrage. Grampy took her hand, and on the other side of Mum, I could see how Dad's knuckles whitened on his clenched fists.

*

Karen and I stand on the pavement and look up at the building in front of us and then at each other. I nearly say, 'Fingers crossed', but it seems like tempting fate. All my hopes and fears are hovering over this morning. Its significance hangs in the air. I don't want to break the spell with some trite superstition.

Earlier this morning, Kasper had cycled over to Anne's and had a late breakfast with us. He had a lecture before lunch, he said, and then work to finish before the end of his university year.

'Or else I come with you, for sure.'

Karen had been thrilled to finally meet Kasper. She kept trying to catch my eye to register her approval, and I kept ignoring her with studied nonchalance. The truth was that as far as I could tell, Kasper and I were merely friends. He was a really lovely guy who was pleased to practise his already excellent English on me, and happy to show off his beloved Copenhagen. This is what I told myself, firmly. When he held my hand, or put his arm over my shoulder, my skin shivered as if it had suddenly become too delicate to hold me together, and my insides lurched, but I had no way of knowing whether he felt the same because nothing else happened.

He gave no sign of feeling anything other than friendly affection. He never mentioned whether he had a girlfriend, and I hadn't asked. I was too frightened of his reply, although common sense told me that I would have met her by now if she existed or he would have told me, because he seemed such an honest, open person. But who knows? People can appear to be all kinds of things and hide the truth if they want to. My problem with Kasper was that I could feel myself sinking under a spell, and I knew it was just going to complicate matters. I was in Copenhagen to find Per. I wasn't there to fall in love, or start a relationship.

Anne had bustled about with fresh coffee in her elegant thermos jug and warm rolls from the baker, and was revelling in this change to her normal routine. ('So nice. To see young people like this. Very good. I like to have all this life in my liddle house.') She was especially charmed to see Kasper again, and the two of them had some sort of riveting, animated discussion in Danish, until Karen intervened and said, 'Manners, you two! Let's all stick to one language. It's not fair on Jess.'

'I don't mind,' I said. 'It's good for me.' I'd started to recognise words and phrases, and even to get the gist of what people were saying sometimes.

I was desperate to learn as much of this awkward language as I could while I was in the country. I'd dreamt of the conversations I would have with my Danish father, and how amazed he'd be by my grasp of the language, and how I'd shrug and say, with a small, modest smile, 'Well, it must be my ancestry. It must be ingrained.' Now that seemed a completely unrealistic vision. Especially as Karen and I stand here, outside Per's apartment, and in a few minutes all those hopeful dreams may fizzle out and be replaced by bleak reality.

'Here goes,' I say, and I count my steps to the door under my breath. '... Six, seven, eight...' I peer at the names on the wall next to the apartment numbers. I breathe in and out with elaborate care. '... Nine, ten, eleven...'

There's no response when I press the bell. Karen has followed close behind without my realising it, and says very quietly, but right in my ear, 'Press again. Maybe it didn't work.'

Before I can, a disembodied voice crackles over the intercom, a woman's voice, and Karen leans round me and answers.

We push open the door.

'There's a lift.'

Karen points at an antiquated iron shutter, across from us in the dark entrance hall. It works like a concertina, and we push it open with difficulty, and cram ourselves into the tiny cubicle. How typical it would be, I think anxiously, if this suddenly broke down, and we were stuck inside. Or worse, if it plummeted to the ground, because it seems to me to be absolutely ancient and who knows... But with a clank and shudder, the lift stops on the third floor, and we squeeze out again.

There are two doors on the landing; one of them is already open, and a woman is standing just inside. She looks about my mother's age, maybe a little older, and she's very slim, with high cheekbones and a neat bob of sleek dark blond hair.

'*Per Skovgaard Jacobsen er ikke hjemme nu,*' she says, looking from one to the other of us, with an expression of mistrust.

'He's not here at the moment.' Karen translates for me. 'What do you want to say?'

'You are English?' says the woman. 'Of course I can speak in English to you. And you are...?'

I step forward to the doorway and hold out my hand. If I've learnt nothing else so far in Denmark, I know what to do whenever you meet someone.

'I'm Jessica Mortimer. From England. My mother knew Per Jacobsen many years ago, and I'm staying over here for a holiday with my friend. I thought I'd try to find him. To say hello?'

The woman shakes my hand and nods, but the doubt lingers in her face, and she doesn't offer her name.

'He is not here. He will not be here for some time. Are you sure you have the right person? Per Skovgaard Jacobsen lives here, and you say only Per Jacobsen. How do you find this address?' She has mesmerising ice blue eyes and a steely gaze. My new-found confidence begins to founder.

'We met his mother yesterday.' My voice sounds too quivery, and I cough in an effort to put myself back in control. 'She gave us this address.'

'*Mor?*' The woman gives a short sharp laugh. 'She doesn't know the time of day. How do we know you have the right person? I cannot believe she found this address and gave it to you. Just like this.'

252

'Per Skovgaard Jacobsen,' Karen interrupts. 'We didn't know about the Skovgaard at first, but now we're pretty sure this is his address, and that it's the right person. Do you know where he is? Are you expecting him home soon? Perhaps we could leave him a note or something...' Her voice trails away as the woman's grip on the edge of the door tightens, and she begins, very slowly, to start closing it.

'Please,' I say, struggling to keep the desperation out of my voice. 'Please, I'd really like to make contact with him. It's... quite important.'

The woman raises her eyebrows. 'I suppose it was that person at my mother's place who give you this address? Her... helper? She does not know what is confident, that one.' She sniffs with an unmistakeable air of contempt.

'Confidential,' Karen murmurs, unwisely, I think.

'What I say.' The woman directs a look of disbelief towards Karen. I'm half surprised Karen doesn't wither on the spot. 'This is what I tell you. She should not give away secret information to total strangers.' The door moves a little more. 'Like you.'

'My mother has something belonging to Per,' I blurt out, and fear of the hopelessness of the situation gives me words I hadn't known I was going to say. To have come so far, and to be turned away. I won't let that happen. Not now.

'They knew each other a long time ago. They were students together. He lent... gave her... something, and then... she never had the chance to return it, and so when I decided to come over on holiday, she asked me to please try and find Per. So that I can give it back.'

'After so long?'

'Yes.' I can hear how lame this sounds, how unbelievable, but I'll say anything.

Except the truth, of course. 'That's why we went to his mother's house. Because my mother found that she still had his parents' address, and she hoped that, maybe...'

'You say this to my mother?'

'Your...?' I'm tipped off balance for a moment. Only now do I realise that of course this must be Per's sister. 'OK. Yes. Your mother. Mrs... um, *Fru...* Jacobsen.'

We explain, taking turns to add different parts of the story, how we'd met the carer at the apartment, and she'd let us in only after first speaking to Per's mother, and how we'd followed her down that dark passage to a room lined with bookshelves and filled with light and photos and paintings and flowers and plants, where Grethe Jacobsen had greeted us with a regal wave of an arthritic hand. Communication had been tricky, given that she appeared to hear only about one word in ten, and everything had to be translated, and she kept losing concentration and drifting off into a world we couldn't see. ('Her English use to be perfect,' the carer whispered at one point. 'But she forget it all. So sad.')

Every so often it seemed as if there was a sudden flash, and whatever fog was clouding her vision and memory would lift, and everything became clear. It was during one of these moments that her face lit up and she talked rapidly and

254

enthusiastically for several minutes, and directed the carer – her name was Hanne, we discovered – to retrieve a beautifully bound address book from a drawer, and show us her son's address. ('But of course, I have this address also,' Hanne had whispered to us. 'For emergency. But it is not for me to tell you.')

While we're describing all this to Per's sister, it comes back to me with sickening clarity, that realisation that I'd had. The realisation, as I'd been standing in that light-filled room the previous day, that Grethe Jacobsen is almost definitely my grandmother. My Danish grandmother. And she will probably never know this. And the comparison between her and my English grandparents, my dear, darling Gran and Grampy, is too cruel to contemplate. But of course I don't share this thought with the woman standing in the doorway, the woman who must be my Danish aunt.

She's relaxing her hold on the door. Her face is softening.

'You must want to find my brother, to do so much work to discover him,' she says when we've finished our story. 'So. He is not here. As I say. He is away, at our summerhouse. Maybe you can phone him? If it is so important that you return what he give your mother.' There is still that small edge of disbelief in her tone. 'Sorry for my English. Sorry – I do not speak it so much now and I... forget word sometimes that I need.'

We both interrupt to reassure her that her English is fine. Excellent even. I'm hardly daring to hope that after all she's going to help me.

'Where's your summerhouse?' Karen asks. 'Here, on Sjælland?' She looks optimistic.

'I give you Per's mobile phone number. You first perhaps can speak to him? The... what you say... the line is not good, the proper phone that is in the house can be better perhaps. I can give you that also, that number?'

'Is it far?' I'm trying really hard to keep impatience out of my voice.

'Quite far. On Jylland – Jutland you call this in English, I think. Very far up, in the north, close to Skagen.'

I can see from Karen's face that this is not encouraging news, but I don't care. Whatever it takes, I'll get there. It can't be that difficult. It's still Denmark, after all, and Denmark's not a very big country. I have all the time in the world. I'll go on my own if I have to. My heart is singing again.

Then Per's still nameless sister does something that stops my humming heart for one brief second, and makes it skip a beat. With that quick, impatient movement that I've watched all my life, she tucks her hair behind her ears. Exactly like Sophie.

CHAPTER TWENTY-THREE

We drive to Skagen on a day of relentless rain. The days before have been warm and calm and spiked with sun, and it's felt as if summer might be around the corner.

'Just a blip,' Karen says, about the rain.

'And you know, often the weather is good in Skagen, even when it's bad everywhere else in Denmark,' Kasper assures us. We're not sure we believe him.

His father has a house in Skagen. It seems it's quite the place to go in the summer – only if you're Danish, I guess – but when I saw where it was on Anne's map, it looked as if it would take a long time to get there. Karen and I planned at first to go by train, and ferry, and another train. She was in the middle of looking for a place for us to stay when Kasper phoned.

'I can come with you.' It was a statement, not a question.

'Oh.' My heart did that double flip thing. I tried to sound calm. 'Can you? We're just trying to find somewhere to...'

He carried on speaking with that easy confidence of his, that blithe assumption that we would be delighted if he came with us, and that it would be fine, and what we wanted. It was, of course, or at least it was what I wanted, very much, but I was worried about how Karen might react. She had given up her time and spent her money to come over to Denmark to help me with what she liked to call my "quest". It seemed unfair if Kasper was going to hijack the whole enterprise. It made her own part in it look slightly unnecessary.

'Because as I tell you, my father has a house in Skagen. He don't use it right now. So he says, of course, that we can stay there.'

'Oh,' I said again, my mind racing.

'But of course you must talk to Karen. There is plenty of room enough, and I think you both will like it very much. It's good. There are three bedrooms. So, plenty of room for us. Talk to Karen. See what she think. It is for you two to decide.'

'OK. It's... very kind of your father, are you sure...?'

He made a dismissive noise down the phone. 'For him it is nothing. Truly, he is very happy of course. I'm his son. So why not?'

'And how much?' I spoke slowly, anxious not to seem too grabbing and over-keen. 'How much does it cost to rent?'

His voice over the line was amazed. 'But nothing, of course. That's why I suggest it.'

'That's very nice of him, your father, very kind when he doesn't know us. But – what about you, Kasper? What about university?'

If we could wait until the beginning of the following week, he said, then he'd be finished and it would be a holiday for him.

He loved going there, and it reminded him of summer family holidays before his parents divorced.

There was one more thing. His friend Mads – I'd met him in the bar at Vesterbro – would also like to come. That way, Kasper suggested, he and Mads could go off cycling, and fishing, and swimming, while Karen and I searched for Per. And Mads had his sister's car for the summer, while she was in South America for her studies, so Mads could drive the four of us to Skagen.

It all sounded too good to be true. Karen, however, didn't look in the least sceptical, other than to say, 'A-ha! I told you he was keen. On you, that is.' She thought Kasper's offer was wonderful, and made life much easier. Her ankle was still painful and stiff if she walked too much, so travelling by car was a good option. There was no trace of anything other than an upbeat optimism in her voice.

*

I loved being a student. I loved everything about it, apart from the fact that I couldn't share it with Sophie. By rights, she should be a student too. She'd been given a place at her first-choice university, but of course she was in no fit state to take it up. She had begun to respond to medication, but it was a slow, slow process, and every now and then she'd slip back down the slippery slope of despair. My mother told me that she'd been put on a list for a course of therapy, but she couldn't start until the drugs had produced a more significant improvement in her mental state.

I dealt with it by trying not to think about her, but that was difficult. It's almost impossible not to think about the person who's shared every bit of your life until that point; someone who knows you better than you know yourself.

This was how I justified – to myself – the fact that Lucas and I continued our affair. Sophie was oblivious to everything except the small and narrow parameters of her life just then. Lucas and I, at different universities, had each embarked on a great adventure. One which neither of us could properly explain to Sophie. In any case, she was simply not interested. It was beyond her comprehension.

For the first few weeks of that term, away from home, untethered from the constraints and necessary obligations of family, we had the illicit yet familiar luxury of each other. Lucas would appear in my halls on a Saturday, unannounced, once we'd both recovered from whatever we'd been doing on the Friday evening, and I would believe myself, for that short time, to be Sophie. I felt daring and reckless and brave. I never knew what he thought, because he never said. I believe now that he imagined he was doing me a great favour. He rarely spoke of Sophie, and there was no suggestion that I was replacing her in any way. He still loved her, despite everything he said; they had a profound and mysterious bond. I think we both always knew this was a temporary madness. Its flickering sparks were already dying.

*

'I feel bad,' Karen says, as we leave in Mads's old Fiat, our backpacks crammed in the boot and other things piled around us on the back seat. Anne stands on the pavement waving, until we've left her far behind. 'I arrived late, and now I'm already leaving.'

'I'm sure she understands.'

'Yes, I'm sure she does, but that doesn't make it better for her.'

We head west out of Copenhagen, this city which has already begun to feel so familiar to me. The rain falls harder, and it's difficult to see much outside, other than the lights of other cars as they pass us. Familiar music, all British bands, booms out of the radio. Mads strums his fingers on the steering wheel to the beat. The four of us are quiet as we leave the city streets behind and reach the countryside. Another chapter of my stay in Denmark is beginning.

I close my eyes and lean my head against the cool window. If I can count to fifty in French, and then backwards in English, it means he'll be there. Per will be somewhere in this unknown town called Skagen that's perched right up on the northernmost tip of Jutland.

'I've come to find you,' I'll say. 'And here I am. There should be two of us, but of course you didn't even know there was one. Now there's just me.' I squeeze my eyes tighter shut, and try to block out the sound of Kasper and Mads as they embark on a lively conversation in the front of the car. 'Be glad,' my inner voice tells Per. 'Please be glad I've found you. It's taken a long time, and I need it to be OK.' And silently, I begin: '*Un, deux, trois, quatre, cinq...*'

*

Mads has floppy brown hair that falls across his forehead and nearly into his eyes. He's calm and quiet and serious, but when he smiles his whole face lights up. He watches me, and he watches how I behave with Kasper, and he watches Kasper too. When he's not watching us he's looking at Karen. I try to gauge whether she's realised this. If she's just being cool, or whether she's genuinely unaware of his interest.

Now he asks me, 'Have you decided how to do this?' as we sit on the ferry at Kalundborg waiting to leave. The four of us are two each side of a table which we'd rushed to grab as soon as we'd come up from the car deck, and it's already littered with cups of coffee and hot chocolate, a couple of cans of coke, sweet wrappers and an array of pastries. We'd left Copenhagen early and without breakfast, despite Anne's entreaties.

I lean back in my seat and lick crumbs of pastry off my fingers.

'Jess, for God's sake!' Karen sounds quite shocked. 'Here – use this.' She hands me a paper napkin. Mads's intense gaze shifts briefly over to her and his eyes crinkle at the corners.

'What do you mean?' I ask him, as I brush more crumbs off my lap.

'How you will find this person you look for?' Mads explains. 'Will you phone him? Or, do you maybe have an address for him?'

'What I think is that we'll get to Skagen today, and get sorted, and then tomorrow, yes, I guess... I don't know.' I turn to look at Karen. 'What do you think?'

'How long can we stay there?' she asks Kasper. 'In your father's house?'

He shrugs. 'As long as we like. He's out of the country. Living in his other house in Spain, I think.'

The engine begins to throb and rumble, and the ferry moves slowly away from the dockside. Through the expanse of rain-spattered windows behind Mads and Kasper, I can see the buildings on the shore line as they dwindle in size. The wind, which had been merely breezy when we'd arrived at the ferry, has become stronger, and the sea looks choppy. People standing outside on the deck are holding onto the railing with both hands, and their hair streams wildly around their heads. Kasper stands, a little unsteadily, as the boat rocks with the motion of the water.

'*Mere kaffe?*' he asks, looking round at us all. '*Eller cola?*'

Karen flaps her hand at him. 'No – sit down for a minute,' she says. 'Let's think what we're going to do.'

*

What we do is become holiday makers for a few days. Karen has never visited Skagen before, and we both fall in love with the little town. I like the fact that it's the very northernmost tip of Denmark. How fascinating Grampy would find this, I think. When you look at a map you can see how it's planted on the nose of a long thin peninsula, sticking out into the sea towards Norway.

Kasper becomes our guide once more, delighted to help us explore. His father's house, contained tidily inside a white picket fence, is a neat fit in a back street of other similar houses, not far from the busy centre. It's indistinguishable from all the other houses around – yellow plastered walls and white lace-like trimmings on a red tiled roof. In the small back yard there's a paved area with a flaking table and some peeling wooden chairs and a flagpole. Kasper was right about the climate up here. While the rest of Denmark shivers under grey cloudy skies, we bask in warm sunshine.

We wander through streets lively with early tourists and snapping cameras, as well as locals – lots of them on bikes of course – busy going about their normal everyday activities. Down at the port we watch fishing boats return with their catch for the day, and admire some of the early yacht arrivals in the inner harbour. We eat fresh fish sitting at a long wooden table outside one of the many restaurants that line the harbour's edge, and drink lager late into the evening.

On our third day, Mads drives us a little way south to visit *den tilsandede kirke*. It's an ancient church that's been buried by migrating sand, so now only its tower is actually visible. For quite a long time the congregation had to dig their way into the church when they wanted to attend services.

'So devout,' Kasper says, and he can't keep the delight out of his voice. 'Is that the word in English? So devout. Quite funny.'

It's all very different from Sussex. I'm used to the rise and sweep and fold of the Downs, and fields of grass and crops; lanes that dip and curve between hedges thick with bramble and hawthorn. There doesn't seem to be any hedges in Denmark. When we'd driven across Sjælland from Copenhagen, and then north up here from Aarhus, the road had unravelled in front of us, and on either side, the fields stretched away so that you could see for what seemed like miles into the distance in any direction, your gaze uninterrupted by any sort of demarcation. Sometimes woods hugged the margins of the highway, often thick forests of pine trees.

We have proper old windmills at home that were once used to grind corn; not the tall, white, alien pillars with angular, rotating arms that populate this landscape. But the sand is kinder here. Brighton beach has no sand, only torturous obstacles of rounded pebbles and sharp stones.

We drive over from the buried church to Råbjerg Mile. It's like a giant sand dune.

'It's moving all the time,' Kasper explains, as we climb out of the car where Mads has parked it on a rough patch of flat ground. 'So much sand on this peninsula. Most of it is fastened by trees and grass, but this one, this is special. This moves about twenty metres a year.'

'Really?' says Karen, as she stands, leaning a little for support on the bonnet of the car, looking over at the huge expanse of dune. The word is whipped out of her mouth by the wind that's tumbling around in this strange, sandy place.

Mads locks the car and slips the key in his pocket. He seems to take sudden courage from this extraordinary landscape and holds out his hand to her: 'Come,' he says. 'I can help you. Hold my arm. I can show you the best way to climb the hill.' They set off together, slowly skirting round the bottom edge, and disappearing from view.

Kasper grins at me. 'There's a better way.' We take off our shoes and leave them by the car, and then he sprints across the flat ground before starting to climb straight up one side of the dune. I follow him, my feet sinking into the dry, warm, slippery sand with every step, but as fast as I try to go, I move only a tiny way up each time. It's incredibly hard work. He's waiting at the top, laughing, and reaches down to help pull me up the last few metres. I'm out of breath, panting, exhilarated with the climb. From where we're standing you can see over to the west coast and a glitter of sea. In every direction stretching away from us there's slope upon slope of undulating sand and other people, dotted about on the sides and the tops, like tiny black ants. Mads and Karen are nowhere to be seen.

Kasper keeps hold of my hands as I reach him. Our feet move and sink constantly in the shifting sand. It's a curious sensation; the grainy surface is warm with the sun but underneath is so cool. The wind moves the top layer endlessly, and the minute specks swirl around our legs.

He puts an arm round my shoulders and, when I don't resist, turns me to face him, hugging me closer.

'You know I like you, Jess,' he says, and he tips my face up so he can stare straight into my eyes. He looks very serious for once. A cold shiver runs down my spine. 'Very much. But, I think always you are holding back. There is something that stop you getting close, and I don't know what it is.'

I want to stay like this, wrapped close and warm and safe, for the rest of my life, but I know I can't.

'I need to find Per,' I mutter into the front of his T-shirt.

He steps back, but he keeps hold of my arms as if he can't let go. 'Yes. I know. That's why we're here. But,' he persists, 'it's not just that, is it? Is there something else? Is it because of your sister? You always seem...'

I wait. I'm not sure if I'm ready to tell him yet and I don't know if I want to, or what he will say if I do, but it feels as if Kasper's the only person in the world who matters enough. If I can't admit to him the treachery I've concealed in my head, the disgusting maggot of deceit that's been gnawing its way through my soul for so long now, then I might as well sink slowly into oblivion beneath the shifting sand.

*

'We understand each other, you and I, Jess,' Lucas said.

He was lying on my narrow, university-issue bed, and rolling a spliff.

'No we don't!' I exploded. 'I'll *never* understand you.'

I nearly added, 'Or what Sophie sees in you.' But lying next to him, minutes after we'd just had sex, it would have seemed a pathetic, ridiculous statement. I held myself taut with the effort of not rolling off the edge of the bed.

He said nothing. Just raised his eyebrows, his eyes narrowed as he finished working grass into the paper in that untroubled, indolent way.

'Pass my jeans, will you?' He groped in the pockets until he found his lighter. He inhaled deeply, and held out the joint to me, his face a mask.

'You know I don't,' I said, and stood up in one quick movement, and went over to push open the window.

'Oh yeah. How could I forget? Little Miss Goody Two-Shoes. Not like your sister, are you? Or not in that way.' He smiled lazily to himself as he took another puff. 'You should try it, you know. You might even like it. It would definitely help you... chill out.'

The reek was already affecting me, and I was frantic with fear that the smoke alarms would be activated, or that someone would smell the cannabis. What was I doing? Why ever had I let him be in my life like this? Just like that, I made up my mind.

'That's it now, Lucas. This has got to stop.' I spoke with my back to him, leaning out of the window, gulping in the cold November air.

'Done,' he said, and when I turned around, he'd extinguished the joint in the dregs of coffee pooled in the day-old mug on my bedside table. The sickly-sweet scent loitered in the air. He was lying back again, stretched out, one arm – the elbow bent – tucked behind his head, a look of smug triumph on his face.

'No.' I pulled out the chair from under the table that doubled as both my desk and a repository for make-up and books and mugs and CDs and anything else that had no home. I plonked myself down heavily astride the seat, my arms resting along the back of it. 'I mean it, Lucas. This is it. I don't want you to come any more. That's enough.'

Another sort of smile flitted across his face: 'But isn't that what's so good – when I come?'

I felt sick with disgust suddenly. What had I been I doing all these weeks? What had I been thinking? What sort of betrayal was this for Sophie? Her twin sister and her beloved boyfriend, sleeping together. That first time, in the woods behind Southfields when I'd agreed to meet him before we both left for university, that should have been the first and last time. I still couldn't understand what had happened to me then; I'd been appalled at myself afterwards. But the few weekends since then when he'd arrived in my halls, assured of his reception, he was like an addiction. I found it impossible to resist him, even though the overwhelming guilt I felt each time made me giddy with remorse. Was I flattered? Secretly pleased that someone so allegedly in love with my sister should in fact be attracted to me?

'Shut up!' I knocked over the chair as I jumped up. 'Shut *up*! Just fuck off, Lucas. We're finished! We should never...'

'Calm down, take it easy,' he said, swinging his legs off the bed and pulling on his jeans in one swift, fluid movement.

As he fastened them, his little dragonfly tattoo – a twin to Sophie's – disappeared under the waistband. 'What's your problem? Sophie? Is that it? How's she ever going to know?' He pulled his black T-shirt over his head and bent down to retrieve his purple brocade waistcoat off the floor. 'Are you going to tell her?' He straightened up and gave me a sideways look. Complacency and self-satisfaction oozed out of every pore; he was very sure of himself.

I could barely contain my fury. 'Of course not! God! Why would I do that? Can you imagine...'

I could imagine, only too well, what would happen if Sophie ever discovered the truth. I hated myself. I couldn't believe I'd ever allowed this to go on for as long as it had. 'And you're not to tell her either, Lucas! You wouldn't, would you? Lucas, promise... please, please promise me.'

He stood unhurriedly shrugging his arms into his elaborate waistcoat, and smiled again, slowly. 'What kind of a shit do you take me for, Jessie?'

The truth was, I didn't know. I'd realised I didn't know Lucas at all, let alone understand him. We slept together. That was all. It was the most deceitful thing I'd ever done, and each time, another band of shame stretched itself round the ever-expanding ball that weighed heavier and heavier in my heart.

I yanked at my door – or at least I tried to, but of course I'd locked it so I had to fumble with the key, and as I held it open, wide open, I said, 'Just get out, Lucas. Get out, and don't come back. It's over, it's finished. I don't ever want to see you...'

'Again?' He gave me that supercilious, raised eyebrow look of his. 'That could be difficult, don't you think?' He was pushing his feet into his shoes – curious green leather shoes with blue stitching – and fitting a fedora low over his eyes.

I almost spat out the words. 'You know what I mean. If you ever breathe a word... if Sophie ever hears... I'll kill you, I swear, I'll kill you.'

He picked up his long army greatcoat off the armchair where he'd flung it a couple of hours earlier.

'You know the trouble with you, Jess? Know what your problem is? You always take everything too seriously. You need to chill. You could learn a thing or two from your sister. Well, once upon a time, you could. Not now of course. Not now she's in need of the funny farm.'

I flew at him then. I hammered him with my fists and when he held my arms, laughing, I kicked him as hard as I could. He let go and rubbed his thigh. 'Bitch,' he said, a tinge of admiration in his voice. 'Little bitch.'

He'd dropped his coat in the scuffle. He picked it up and said, 'Well, see you around. Nice... having you. While it lasted. Who knows, Jessie? You may come begging me to have you back.'

'In your dreams, you bastard. Just get out. Get out!'

'Keep your cool.' He adjusted his hat, deliberately, nonchalantly. 'I'm going, don't worry. Plenty more fish in the sea as they say, and who knows?' He turned, half out of the door, as a group of students roared drunkenly down the corridor. 'Sophie may yet make a miraculous recovery. So

271

you're going to see me around, Jessie. No help for it. I'll always be there. You've not seen the last of me.'

*

When I finish speaking there is a silence. I've given Kasper an edited version of my relationship with Lucas, but a truthful one nevertheless. We're lying in a hollow between the dunes, and the little spiderlike figures of other people are still scrambling silently in the distance. I've never told anyone about what happened with Lucas – about my dreadful betrayal of Sophie. When my family heard about it at the inquest, I'd wanted to crawl away and curl up in a hole where no one could see me. It was the last time I'd seen Lucas, and he'd deceived us both.

I feel scraped clean now, and weightless, as if the guilt has unchained itself and floated free, but I've told the very last person I should've chosen to tell; the one person who shouldn't really know.

Scuppered your chances now! What were you thinking, Jessie? What a no-brain you are sometimes. I despair.

'I think that I don't deserve happiness,' I say. 'That I'm not good enough for anybody. I never will be. It meant nothing. Nothing. But how could I have done that? How could I? Even if Sophie didn't know...'

But I did. In the end, I did. We always knew each other so well, you and I, Jessie. I may have been a bit... loopy for a while, but I had plenty of time to think. I guessed your secret.

I sit up and scoop the soft sand between my cupped hands and watch the grains as they trickle through my fingers and disappear.

'I put up a barrier – I didn't want to let myself be that weak again. Someone like you who's just... lovely and... it was so terrible. What I did. How could anyone who heard that ever trust me?'

'None of that matters,' Kasper says, and he leans over and takes my face between his hands very gently. 'None of it. If that's the worst thing you ever do, you will be a good person. You *are* a good person. Already. It doesn't matter. It meant nothing to you and nothing can hurt Sophie now.'

His mouth is cool and tastes of mint, and his skin is warm and smooth under my fingers.

CHAPTER TWENTY-FOUR

'You'd love it here, Gran,' I say. 'Both of you, you and Grampy. Tell Grampy to look for Skagen on a map. It's kind of perched at the top of Jutland. It's amazing.'

I'm sitting outside on one of the old faded wooden chairs in the back yard while I speak on my mobile to my grandmother. As I twiddle my fingers through my hair I can feel, as well as see, that it's grown much longer since I've been in Denmark. I need to find a hairdresser, I think to myself.

'And you'd love the light, Gran,' I add. 'It's fantastic light for painting. Amazing. Huge clear skies. There was a group of artists who came here... can't remember when. Nineteenth century maybe? Anyway, we're going to see the gallery soon, where lots of their paintings are. It's just near here.'

'Sounds like you're having such a good time.' My grandmother sounds a little stilted. 'But what about your... father, Jessie? Are you any closer to finding him?'

That was exactly what my mother had asked five minutes ago when I'd phoned home. They both ask as if they hope I'm going to say that I've suddenly changed my mind, but I can hear them resigned to the fact that, actually, I'm going to answer exactly as they've guessed.

Kasper comes out of the house, a can of drink in his hand, and points to it with a questioning expression. I shake my head. As he walks past me his fingers drift over the back of my neck, and I reach up to catch his hand and squeeze it, gently.

'I'm just about to phone him, Gran. Wish me luck,' I say, and Kasper gives a slight nod and a thumbs up.

Last night we'd all four of us discussed the Per situation and agreed that I couldn't put it off any longer. Otherwise, what was the point of us being there – other than to have a kind of holiday? But the longer I've waited, the more uncertain I've become. Now that we know he's here somewhere, in Skagen, it all seems so immediate and attainable. I've even started to doubt my own motives.

And what are they exactly, Jessie? Didn't we just want to lay his ghost to rest? See what he looks like, hear his voice. All of that. At least you know he's alive. You've come so far – you can't give up now. He's our missing link!

I say my goodbyes to Gran, and then I fish in my jeans pocket for the slip of paper with Per's number that his sister had given us. His mobile doesn't connect. With a deep breath, I start to dial his landline instead.

*

'OK. This is how it's going to happen.' Sophie was lying on her bed, propped up on her pillows while she painted her nails.

275

'Of course it's against the rules, but that's why they have the rules. So we can break them! They're hardly going to stop me taking maths tomorrow, are they? Come on, Jessie! You're such a wimp!'

She'd adopted her usual authoritative tone, looking at me very seriously while waving around the hand she'd just finished, and then blowing on it. It was a rainy June afternoon during the summer term, the one when we were taking our GCSEs, and we had switched from our interminable discussion of which exams we were definitely going to fail, and which ones we hoped to get an A* for, into our more common theme of how and when we were going to find Per.

'I'll do the talking when we do meet him,' she said. 'Because we both know... well, that's best, isn't it?'

I was sitting cross-legged, my sketchbook in front of me on the floor, and I was leaning forward trying to capture the image of Sophie engrossed in her nail painting. But she kept moving; it was too difficult. I began to sketch her chair instead: a pair of jeans, a purple bra and a stripy top lying haphazardly over the back of it, three of her coursework files and a shabby copy of "To Kill a Mockingbird" piled on the seat.

I shrugged. 'I don't think it's something we can plan that closely, Sophie. Not once we've tracked him down. *If* we track him down. There's not going to be some pre-arranged script, is there?'

But I knew what she meant. She was afraid I'd have to count too far before I found the courage to speak, and even then, I might lose the words.

Sophie was peering carefully at her other hand, dipping the tiny brush in one of the three bottles lined up on her window sill, and painting alternate nails a bright green colour: her little finger, her middle finger, and her thumb. She held them out for my inspection. 'Red, do you think?' she asked. 'For the other two?'

'Well, you're clearly not going for the subtle, unnoticeable look...'

'Nah! What's the point? And I tell you who'll notice them.'

'Lucas Fleming?'

She grinned. 'Got it in one! He told me the other day that I was *the* most interesting, unusual, out-of-the-norm person in our whole year.'

'It must be true then.'

Sophie ignored me. She started to colour her forefinger nail a bright orange. 'Plus, he thinks I have more original ideas than anyone else. Plus, he told me he thought we were two of a kind.' She paused before starting to paint her ring finger, and looked up at me. 'I can't tell you how amazing he is, Jessie. When you talk to him. I mean, really, really talk to him. He has such... incredible ideas! *Incroyable!* Off the wall! There, I've even practised some French. And so *hot*! I mean really, really...'

I interrupted. I didn't want to hear any more of Sophie's comments on how wonderful Lucas was and how she knew they were meant for each other, and how it was only a matter of time. I'd watched him watching Sophie, and of course he wasn't only interested in her sparky ideas and unusual mind. Of course he wasn't. Apart from anything else, he was a normal, sixteen-year-old guy. I didn't know then that they were already having sex; had been since our sixteenth birthday back in February. It was the first secret Sophie had kept from me.

'If you can just get your head away from thoughts of Lucas Fleming for a minute,' I said. 'When, and if, we do find Per, how do you think he's going to react? That's the question. That's why you can't have some preordained plan about what you're going to say or not say, because we have no idea how he's going to react. He might not want to talk. At all. He might not believe us. He might walk away.'

Sophie swung her legs off the bed and studied her feet for a moment. Then she propped one foot on the chair next to her bed, and began to unscrew a different bottle of varnish. It was purple.

'You know your problem, Jessie? I mean, I love you loads, and all that, and being your twin is still the best thing ever, even now. But you're just too negative. You always think the worst.'

*

The woman who answers the phone speaks with a strong accent, and each time she replies to my questions there's a little pause as if she has to absorb the English and make sense of it.

Per isn't there, though, he's out. She thinks he will be back in the evening. She's only just arrived at the summerhouse, she explains, because he likes to have some time alone up here, but she's sure he'll be back soon. He's maybe gone for a run, down to the beach.

I feel as if I've already been given, as Alex would say, too much information. She's friendly, though, and eager to help. Why don't I give her my number, she suggests, then he can phone when he gets home? I hesitate, but only for a minute. What harm can it do? At least I won't have to keep ringing.

The others cheer as I end the call. It's as if there's been a united holding of breath the whole time I've been on the phone.

'Well done,' says Karen. 'So, you should know by the end of the day. Are you going to tell him when he phones?'

'Absolutely not!' I'm horror-struck by the thought. 'Hopefully I can sort out us meeting somewhere.'

'Tonight Karen and I do grill,' Mads announces. He has a habit of making completely unrelated comments in a conversation, which can sometimes be confusing.

'He means barbecue,' Karen explains. She's standing at the kitchen counter writing on a piece of scrap paper, her crutch propped beside her. 'We're just off to the supermarket. This is on us – it can be a pre-celebration of nearly finding Per. Just finishing the list – anything else we need?'

She looks up and her face is alive. I can't remember the last time she appeared so happy, yet Mads was the last person I would have chosen for her.

('He's so not your type,' I'd whispered to her early this morning. I was coming out of the bathroom, and she'd emerged, sleep-tousled, from the tiny room Mads had appropriated for himself when we'd first arrived. She'd grinned, and lifted her eyebrows, and whispered back, 'Surprises are always the best. And I'm sure it's not going to be long-term exactly.')

'I'll come with you,' Kasper says. 'We need more beer. I'll bring the – what do you call it? – kitty money. Maybe some wine could be nice too?'

I need to keep myself busy. It's early afternoon; this evening is several hurdle-jumps away. We all stroll down to the supermarket. The Danish summer has eased itself into June, the days becoming longer and warmer. The pink and blue hollyhocks flowering quietly up the front walls of houses in the old town lend it a strangely old-fashioned air.

Later, while Karen and Mads prepare for the barbecue in what seems to be some sort of ordered domestic harmony, Kasper and I – his arm flung around me as casually as ever – walk through the pedestrian area and on down Sct. Laurentii Vej to Skagens Museum. He wants to show me the famous Skagen paintings. As we wander hand in hand through the gallery, I'm able to lose myself for a while. Art is my comfort zone, especially paintings and drawings, and strolling around from room to room I relax a little and I think again how much Gran would love to come here. I spend some time wondering which artist she'd most admire, which picture would catch her imagination.

There's one I love which shows people at a bonfire on the beach. Gran would like the way the flames from the fire light up part of the crowd while the rest are in shadow. There's another one titled "Hip, hip, hurrah" – some sort of celebration in a garden – with people round a table. I'm suddenly homesick for my own family gatherings, not that they were anything like that. It's the wrong era for a start. I can't control the bubble of anxiety lurking in my head, the one that threatens to pop and spill out all sorts of potential problems about my eventual meeting with my birth father. What if my mother has remembered it all wrong? Perhaps he's never wanted to hear her name mentioned again. They'd parted on bad terms, and betrayal is the worst end to a relationship. They had both betrayed each other, unless there was some other explanation, but why would he tell me that? His daughter, yes, but otherwise a mere stranger.

*

We eat late, and everything is slightly burnt, but after a few glasses of wine we don't notice. Before the meal, Mads had said to me, 'I wanted to buy some delicious marzipan chocolates to have afterwards, but Karen tell me it make you ill.'

I'd fetched one of my EpiPens, because they all needed to know ('Just in case, Jessie, just in case,' Grampy's voice echoed), and I explained how it must be jabbed in my thigh, high up, as hard as you can, if I was in anaphylactic shock and beyond being able to do that on my own.

Mads said, 'What happens to you? When you're... affected?'

I explained how my face and airways would swell, and how breathing would become difficult and eventually impossible; how you'd gasp for air but there's none there, and everything would start to go out of focus. At least, I say, that's what I've been told.

'It's nuts,' I made clear. 'Definitely peanuts, but probably other nuts too.'

'Has it ever happened to you?' Kasper asked.

I hesitated, and glanced at Karen before saying, 'No, luckily, not since we... were both very little. That's when we were diagnosed, after we had some peanut butter. But there's always the risk. So I always have this with me, and one at home, and at uni, especially, I had to make sure there was always one in my room there, and one in my bag whenever I went out.'

'Hard for you,' Kasper said. 'Always to have to do that, always to remember. Also, to have always to be so careful about food. Not a good thing.'

'Better that, though,' Karen said briskly. 'Better that than the alternative.'

A small silence fell.

*

After we've finished eating, I stand abruptly and stagger for a moment as my head swims with the drink, and I say, 'Just going out for a bit. Just need to...' They watch me leave, and no one offers to go with me and I sigh with relief.

I wander through the nearly empty streets and hold my thoughts tight inside where no one can see them. I breathe, deep breaths in and out, and count to fifty. The nightmare pictures in my head fade, gradually.

When I get back to the house, Karen and Mads are sprawled half-asleep on the sofa. They look up at me with relief.

'Jess! Your mobile – it's been ringing and ringing.' Karen waves a hand in the direction of the kitchen.

I'd left it on the table. I pick it up and stare at the screen. No message, no voicemail. Just three missed calls.

'Someone, I think, is wanting to speak to you.' Kasper appears from upstairs. He holds the top of the door frame, and hangs there, stretching and swinging his legs before letting go, and flexing his arms. He gives me a grin. He shows no signs of having drunk too much.

I stare round the small kitchen. It's late now. Dread tugs at my heart. I take the phone and walk past Kasper, and out of the front door again into the sudden darkness of night. The evenings are lighter here than at home; it's nearly the longest day, but when night comes it's sudden and black. Candles flicker and glow in dim windows as I walk down to the harbour; people are still sitting at tables outside the fish restaurants. I lean against the harbour wall.

I can hear the chink of glasses, low murmurs, and sudden bursts of laughter from people sharing a happy evening. Cigarette smoke spirals up in the still air. I smell it as it floats and merges with the scent of cooked fish, and salt from the sea water. Behind me I can hear the creaking of masts and the gentle bumps and thuds of boats bobbing against each other on the water. My hands are shaking. I take a deep breath, and then another, and I press redial on the phone.

A male voice answers in Danish.

*

It's very late. I lie in bed next to Kasper and listen to his quiet steady breathing. I think how there's nothing worse than being unable to sleep and having to listen to someone else who is. Sophie was like that. When we shared a room, she would be fast asleep, her eyes closing as her head fell on the pillow, while I would be lying in the dark, a hundred thoughts and worries chasing themselves round and round my head. That's when I'd first started counting.

I turn onto my back. Everything is jumbled together. The tricky, stilted conversation on the phone with the nameless woman who must live with Per; the paintings in the gallery full of placid homely scenes, wide stretching skies and uncomfortable seas; the smoky charcoal taste of our barbecue; and lastly the phone call to Per, and the arrangement we'd made. How could I sleep? The pictures tumble and lurch and slide around in my head and I feel sick with apprehension. Or perhaps it's the wine. Tomorrow, I think. Tomorrow, I meet him.

Kasper says, 'You can't sleep?' His voice is blurred with drowsiness. He turns over onto his side, and drapes an arm across me.

'It's OK,' I whisper. 'Go back to sleep. I'll count sheep or something.'

There's a pause, and I think he's drifted off again, but then, 'Sheeps? You count sheeps?'

'*Sheep*.' I smile in the darkness. 'It's what people do in England if they can't sleep.'

He grunts a half laugh. 'Count in Danish.'

I roll onto my side too, my back against him. I'm wide awake now. 'I can't. I don't know how to count in Danish.'

'I think you count a lot. When you are... worried maybe?'

How does he know?

'Yes.'

'Maybe it help you to count in another language. I can learn you.' His voice swims out of the night shadows. There's another silence. I close my eyes. Then I feel his finger drawing on my back, warm against my skin, slow down my spine. One line.

'*En*,' he breathes.

Then a curved shape starting like a question mark but finishing with a straight horizontal line. '*To*.'

A half circle and another looped under. '*Tre*.'

He makes me repeat the numbers. I have to get it right. I turn onto my back again and I whisper the sequence to ten, and then he stops me with his mouth, and I wind my arms around his neck.

'... *en, to, tre, fire, fem, seks, syv, otte, ni, ti...*'

CHAPTER TWENTY-FIVE

We'd arranged to meet at a café in the main street.

As I leave the house, Karen is towelling her hair dry, ready to go off cycling with Mads.

('Cycling?' I'd said. 'You don't like *any* form of exercise!'

'Oh well. There's always a first time,' she'd shrugged. 'And it's very flat.')

'Sure?' she says now, folding her wet towel very precisely and hanging it over the back of one of the garden chairs. 'Sure you don't want me to come with you? Moral support? A bit of, you know, light relief? It might be less intense... I can meet Mads afterwards.'

Kasper says nothing. He wraps his arms around me, rests his chin on my head. I can feel the beat of his heart against me, slow and steady. He hasn't had a shower yet this morning; his hair and T-shirt smell of smoke from yesterday's barbecue and his chin is rough when he moves it against my cheek.

'I'm really, really frightened.' But I'm saying it in my head, where no one can hear. 'I wish Sophie...'

Frightened? Frightened of what? Think of the worst that can happen, Jess. Anyway, I'm here. Right here. He just won't see me. But you'll know, won't you. Know I'm with you.

The worst had already happened. Sophie was right, as usual. Nothing could ever be that bad again. Nothing else in my life would even come close to my feelings on the night she had died.

I say to Karen, 'No, I'll be fine. Of course I will. It's better like this. I have to do it on my own.'

I take Kasper's hand in mine for a second, and give it a squeeze. 'See you later. Wish me...'

Luck? Really? Where did luck ever come into it? This guy's your father. Our father! I can't wait!

On my own, in the street, I shake my head, trying to muffle Sophie's voice. I don't need her. I want to do this alone. I reach the café sooner than I expect, and hesitate at the doorway. A few people are sitting outside at small round tables covered in bright red gingham tablecloths, each one with its own pot of white daisies.

I can't believe it. I can't believe it. You're here, Jessie! Any minute now! Any minute now you'll see him.

A wave of panic rises, unbidden, and for a moment, a second, I sway on my feet. Then I push open the door, and walk straight over to the first empty table I can see. I sit so that I can watch the door, and glance around to check he hasn't arrived first. I start to shake, and press my hands between my knees to keep them still. I do need Sophie after all, I think.

'*God morgen!*'

It's the waitress. The little amount of Danish I've learned disappears in the fog of fear and anticipation clouding my head.

'I'm waiting...' I begin to explain, but she laughs, and waves her hand.

'No problem! I come over when your friend arrives. It's good.'

She moves away and there he is. I know in an instant. I've always thought he would look familiar, that if I passed him in the street I would realise that this was my father, but it's nothing like that. No sudden startling recognition. I can't say he looks like I'd imagined. I can't say what or who he looks like, but still I know with a complete and overwhelming certainty. Now this man is standing by my table, his eyebrows raised and his hand outstretched.

'You must be Jess?' There's hardly a trace of accent.

I take his hand. 'You must be Per.' We both laugh a little. Per pulls out the chair opposite me, and leans back in it as he sits down. He signals to the waitress with those fine questioning eyebrows, and then turns back to me.

'So!' he says. 'At last we meet. I am so interested, so... intrigued. Is that the word? I think it is. Because you were talking to me on the phone about Laura. Someone I knew so long ago. Really, a long time. And now, here you are... Laura's daughter.' He stares at me across the table, and his eyes crinkle at the edges. 'I think I can see that. You look a little how I remember her. How is she, your mother? Still beautiful?'

I put my hands on the table. 'Fine,' I say. 'She's very well, thank you.'

No, no! This is all wrong. Why do you always have to be like this, Jessie? He seems OK. Don't you think? Just tell him. Straight out. I would.

The waitress has arrived again, and some rapid Danish is spoken. I hear only *"kaffe"*, and say quickly, '*Kaffe, tak.* Nothing to eat, thank you.'

'So.' Per turns back to look at me. 'She is well, and what? She asked you to come all the way to Denmark to see if I was alive, perhaps? After so many years?'

I stare down at my hands, pressed onto the table. I'd practised my story with the others. Now I explain to Per about Karen, my friend, that her mother is Danish, and how Karen had wanted to spend some of the summer visiting her beloved Mormor, and had asked me to travel with her for company and so we could explore Denmark together. It's now beginning to sound as feeble and made-up a story as it really is.

A jug of coffee and two cups arrive.

'Oh, sorry – *undskyld*! – could I have some milk please?'

Per smiles: 'You English! Always milk in the coffee!'

'Then...' I finish pouring, 'when I told my parents I was going to come to Denmark, my mother said I could maybe look you up. Say hello.'

Even to my traitorous ears this has begun to sound unlikely.

Per takes a mouthful of coffee, and sets the cup back on the saucer. 'And did she tell you anything about me?' he asks. 'What do you know? You have come all this way to see a person she once knew. When we were both students. How did you find me? I live here just for some summer weeks, in my family's summerhouse. You must be a very remarkable person, Jess. You and your friend. Finding me up here, such a long way from my home.' He picks up his cup again, and studies me, pushing his thin rimless glasses onto the bridge of his nose with a long finger.

I look down at the table once more. This is so hard. I begin to shake again, and fold my arms across my body. 'I guess we've been a bit like detectives,' I say, 'following your trail. I had an address for you in Copenhagen, and somehow...' I reach for my coffee and breathe in the smell of it. It makes me feel sick.

'You know,' says Per, 'you remind me of my sister. She sits just like that when she feels uncomfortable with something. Just like you did with your arms, so. It's quite funny, I think. You met her, didn't you? At my apartment? She told me, of course. That there were some English looking for me. That was my sister.' He takes another sip of coffee and puts his cup down. 'Sofie.'

What's the worst that can happen?

The puddle of coffee spreads over the table, as my cup topples slowly to the edge, the handle stopping its flight. My hands grope at nothing in mid-air. I have no voice. My face is wet with soundless tears. I'm adrift in a sea of strangers with no map to guide me. There are no rules to follow.

I can see Per speaking, and I can sense his bewildered concern.

'I had a sister.' I have to speak slowly to form the right words, to force them out of my mouth in the proper order, to explain. 'I had a sister called Sophie, too. But she died.'

*

Somehow, Per has steered me out of the café, money's been left on the table, a wave of reassurance given to the anxious-looking waitress, and now he's holding my arm and guiding me down a side street towards the harbour car park.

'Usually I cycle in,' he says, 'but today, very luckily, I've driven.'

'I'm so sorry,' I'm saying, over and over again. 'So stupid of me. I'm sorry – it's just, Sophie died and – every now and then I get...'

I can't take in what he means about his car.

'Maybe you can come back with me now to my summerhouse?' he's suggesting. 'It's not in Skagen, exactly, but we can drive there in maybe fifteen minutes or so.'

He's not staying here in Skagen, then, but somewhere else entirely. We reach his car, a not very new Volvo.

'Then you can tell me about your mother.' And he adds 'Laura,' with that funny way the Danes have of not quite saying the "R" in the middle properly, so her name becomes "Lawer".

He seems to have taken charge somehow. Do I want to go back to his summerhouse? I don't even know him, other than

I'm as certain as I can be that, at last, I've found my missing father.

If I don't go, when will I tell him who I really am? My connection to him. When will I tell him, as I told his sister (Sofie!) that the thing my mother still had that was his is, in fact, me. Not strictly his, and not borrowed. Still. Half of my genes come from him. My blonde hair and my light blue eyes, all from him.

'Go back with you now, do you mean?' I ask, stalling for time while I try to assemble my thoughts into some sort of order and rank.

He looks amused. 'I haven't turned into a mass murderer since I knew your mother. Although, you of course only have my word about that. My... girlfriend is at the summerhouse. Also, I am expecting someone, so I cannot stay in Skagen for much longer today.'

Sometimes, you have to take risks. I'm not sure how much of a risk this is exactly, but why not go back with him now? Then I can tell him my news, quietly and privately, and maybe later Mads could drive over to collect me. If I can find out where we're going.

I phone Kasper as Per reverses through a narrow space, and then pulls out onto the road going south, the way we'd gone the other day to the buried church and the giant moving sand dune.

'It's in a place called Cannersten,' I say, so they will know where I am.

I can hear the smile in his voice. 'OK. Kandestederne. Very nice. I know it. You can tell us when we need to come over and get you.' Then, after a pause, 'Jess? Are you all right?'

*

Midsummer. Only a couple of weeks away. A time for celebration, Kasper had told me the previous afternoon as we'd strolled down towards the art museum.

'It's called Sankt Hans Aften,' he explained. 'Here, in Skagen, we all go to the beach. Very many people. All over Denmark, people is having these parties. We have a bonfire, a huge bonfire. Usually you can see a line of the fires, right along the coast. We'll take things to eat. And to drink, of course. I think you'll like it, Jess, if we're still here.'

The shops we wandered past were stocked full of things designed to help newly graduating high school students enjoy the end of their exams. There would be students at the celebration of course, Kasper said. They'd throw their lecture notes into the flames of the bonfire.

Sometimes I could hardly believe that only the expanse of the North Sea divided our countries of birth. It felt as if the gulf between our cultures was huge. So many customs and traditions that we didn't share and could probably never fully understand. The sort of rituals you needed to have absorbed, unwittingly, since the day you were born. Traditions that you took for granted.

Talking about bonfires reminded me of Guy Fawkes Night at home. How year after year we would go to the village bonfire. Exploding, distorted music blaring out from loudspeakers as we walked towards Southfields where it was held.

But this bonfire, this Danish bonfire, would have a witch on top, Kasper said. In England, I told him, witches belonged to Halloween. You might dress up as one to go and play trick-or-treat, or for a party. Witches were for the end of October, just before Bonfire Night, but nothing to do with that. Guy Fawkes burned on the bonfire; witches lived to tell the tale, linked inexplicably with pumpkins, carved out to leer gruesomely in the dark, with their sharp-angled slitty eyes and noses and gaping, toothy mouths, glowing from inside.

*

As we drive down the straight road southwards, Per is charming and friendly. I can tell he's trying very hard to make me feel at ease, after my embarrassing episode in the café.

'I'm sorry about your sister,' he begins. 'Was it sudden when she died?'

'Yes. Yes, it was.'

He glances over at me briefly as he changes gear. 'Is this difficult for you to speak about? Was it long ago?'

'Just over a year.'

'And you were close? The two of you?'

I nod, even though he can't see. 'Yes. Yes, we were, most of the time.' I can't bring myself to tell him we were twins.

Somehow this is mapping out all wrong. The point when I tell him I'm his daughter is receding into a blurred distance.

'So it must have been difficult times for you, and for your parents.'

He asks me about where I live in England, and whether I'm studying, and what I hope to do. He actually listens to what I'm saying, because he follows up what I say with relevant questions. Every now and then he glances over at me, sometimes as he's changing gear, and he nods as I speak. I can imagine people finding him very likeable. He must give the impression of someone who genuinely cares, who can be counted on when all else fails. He would watch the person he's talking to, in a room full of people, as if the speaker is the only one in the room worth listening to at that very moment. Without interrupting, or agreeing, or declaring that he knows exactly what they mean because the very same thing has happened to him.

And then I think how that's all hypothetical, and possibly rubbish. How can I tell having only met him an hour ago? The truth is I want him to be like that. I want him to be caring and thoughtful and charming. And the reason I want him to be like that is because that's how my real father is. Mike. I have almost no memories of a time when he wasn't part of our lives. When he wasn't looking after us both.

'And your mother?' Per asks, as he looks in the mirror before making a leisurely turn right off the main road onto a much smaller one. We drive past a small supermarket and a campsite, and then a hotel, yellow, and with the sort of red tiled roof that seems so popular everywhere. On either side of us the ground is a tangle of heather and low-lying bushes, with paths meandering through the scrub. Sandy dunes covered with rough marram grass are humped carelessly around us in the distance. I glimpse a few half-hidden roofs among them. We turn down a rough track, with grass growing down the middle. Clouds of dust advertise our journey.

'She's... fine,' I say, an inadequate way to describe the reality of my mother at the moment. What was I going to say? She's not coping very well right now with my sister's death and she's in the middle of bereavement counselling? Would he want to know that?

I'm rescued from any further disclosures as Per turns off the track and parks on a stretch of grass next to a sleek red car that looks rather expensive, gleaming in the mid-day sun. Alex and Toby would be able to tell me instantly what make it is. Per gives it a cursory glance, and raises his eyebrows.

'We've arrived,' he says, climbing out.

Ahead of us is a long, low, green planked summerhouse, with a roof that seems to be covered, inexplicably, in what looks like grass: wild, feathery, untidy grass. In front of the house is a decked area, with a table and chairs tucked into a corner. As we walk up the slope towards the house, a woman appears through the open door and steps onto the decking.

'Birgitte,' says Per, as we reach her. It's an explanation and an introduction.

She's wearing a long brown skirt, dotted with bright pink and orange flowers, and a yellow top, and a loose, black, slippery shawl draped over her shoulders, which she holds tightly with one hand. As she turns to talk to Per, I can see how her long rich apricot hair is caught up at the back in a shell-shaped comb, but bits have escaped and as she stands there, her pale face anxious, she keeps tucking in strands or winding them into the comb again. If I'd had to imagine what Per's girlfriend would look like, I wouldn't have chosen Birgitte.

She starts to speak, but Per says in English, 'And this is Jess. I knew her mother once a long time ago.'

Then, her ingrained Danish manners mean she must shake my hand, and say, '*Velkommen.*'

Per is gesturing for me to go into the house, but Birgitte grabs his arm, and continues talking, quickly, urgently, in a loud whispery voice, pointing both at the car and through the door as she does so.

'OK,' Per says, easily, calmly. 'Jess, we have another visitor, but that isn't a problem.'

He frowns briefly at Birgitte. To me he adds, 'Someone I was not expecting right now, not until later... but never mind.'

Through the door is a big, square living room, full of light, but before I can get any sort of impression of it, there's a shout.

'*Far! Far!*' Out of a door at the far end of the room runs a small girl, all legs and arms and long flying hair and hiccuping giggles.

Per bends down and scoops her up. '*Hej, skat!*'

His face is a picture of pride and delight. Love, too. That's what love looks like.

He turns to me, laughing, and says, 'I have two big sons, teenagers, you would say. They live with their mother in Copenhagen, but here is my little princess.'

CHAPTER TWENTY-SIX

Mai. Her name is Mai, Per's daughter, his "little princess".

Her words tumble out in a torrent of excitement as she talks to him, and he laughs and nods and looks amazed and interrupts with comments she finds hilarious. I stand for a while feeling foreign and foolish. Birgitte has drifted away into the kitchen through the half-open door on the right. I can see her filling the jug of a coffee machine. Oh great, I think, more coffee. Do they drink nothing else over here? I'm raw with resentment. I wish I hadn't agreed to come.

'Per?' It's a very officious voice. Another door opens and a woman emerges from what must be the bathroom. It's hard to imagine anyone more different from Birgitte.

Her hair falls in a glossy brown bob; I don't think it would dare do anything else. She's tall and angular: her collarbone juts above the neat neckline of her white dress, the dress skimming over tiny boobs, a flat stomach and slim hips. Her elbows are sharp, her wrists bony, and her long thin fingers have long shiny red nails. She's snapping those fingers now towards Mai and Per, talking rapidly in short, staccato bursts. Mai slides off

Per's lap reluctantly, and Per says, calmly, 'Lise. This is Jess. She's from England. I knew her mother a long time ago. Jess, this is Mai's mother. I think she is just leaving.'

Lise's gaze sweeps over me, and she raises her supercilious eyebrows and gives me a brittle smile which doesn't quite reach her eyes. Then she jerks her head towards the kitchen with a look of distaste and says something in Danish with a smirk on her face.

Per replies in English. I have to admire his composure.

'Yes. Birgitte and I are still together. Of course. Why not? We give each other time and space. I don't come home to find my books arranged in height order and my clothes colour-coded, and I'm allowed to eat what I like.'

'Your herring, you mean?' She gives a theatrical shudder. 'Those jars of herring! And liver pate, and salami, and blue cheese. *So* unhealthy. You would live longest if you had stay with me. I know what it is to eat healthy.'

'Hmm. Sushi, and tofu, and dry crackers, and...'

He glances down at Mai; her eyes are swivelling from one parent to the other, and they've gone swimmy with tears. He bends down and whispers something to her and she skips across the room and out onto the decking. I watch her through the window as she pulls a skipping rope out of a large plastic box and starts to untangle it.

Lise waggles her long sharp fingers at me. 'So! Nice to meet you...' She trails off as she clearly can't remember my name.

'*Birgitte*? *Jeg går*,' she shouts towards the kitchen and a muffled reply wafts through. She and Per have a brief cool exchange and, as they do, she's already taking car keys out of the neat leather satchel that's slung on her shoulder. Her feet, in their unforgiving shoes, snap briskly across the bleached wooden floor.

*

We eat lunch outside in the sunshine, a typical Danish lunch. Rye bread, herrings in a dill marinade from a jar, some other sort of fish, gherkins, slices of green pepper, and the pate and cheese that Lise had spoken of so scornfully. We drink bottles of Danish beer and Mai, who hardly stops talking between mouthfuls, has juice.

It's quite surreal.

I can't think how I'm going to tell him now. The afternoon is moving on and soon it will be too awkward. He'll wonder what I'm talking about, why I hadn't said straight away when we'd first met in the café. I could just leave. Perhaps I could write to him or something.

Karen and Kasper elbow their way into my head, and there's Mads too, just behind them, watching, waiting. What would I tell them if I go without saying anything? And my parents – they'll want to know – and Gran and Grampy, and Alex and Toby? This isn't just about me, I realise. It's not even about only me and Sophie. The repercussions spread out like ripples from a stone falling in water and all sorts of people are rocked.

Per stands up and is stacking plates together, and Mai says, '*Tak for mad, Birgitte,*' with that sweet smile that she flashes

301

indiscriminately. She leaves the table to run over to the plastic box again, and starts taking out more things: a Frisbee, two bats and several balls, spades and a bucket, and some of those plastic flowerpots you can balance on. She's exclaiming with delight as she discovers treasures she's forgotten since her last visit. She lives with Lise in Copenhagen, I understand, but she spends most weekends with Per. Staying with him in the summerhouse is her favourite thing, he says, and when he translates this into Danish, she nods her head vigorously. She's five and a half, but she hasn't started school yet. She'll go in August. That's the beginning of their new school year.

I squeeze out from the bench behind the table and ask about the bathroom, even though I'm sure it's the room Lise appeared from. As well as a loo, there's one of those showers in it which has a drain in the middle of the floor, and just a plastic curtain you pull across. The washbasin is wide and shallow, set in a long counter with cupboards underneath. Everything is neat and tidily arranged. Next to the shower, white towels hang from tiny steel hooks on the wall, suspended from loops of sewn-in tape. Neat and practical and organised. I could live in this country for ever, I think, with its white walls and wooden floors and tastefully designed furniture. I love the space, and the calm, and the predictability, and the friendly people who shake hands when they meet you.

But the minute that thought floats into my head, it's replaced by others. Who am I fooling? My life isn't here, not my real life. That's waiting for me, just across the water, the other side of the North Sea. It's waiting, patiently, for me to pick it up again where I left it all those months ago. It's going to be a different sort of life, because it has a future that doesn't hold Sophie, and that's a bit scary. That's what I've been avoiding all this time. My future, but not the one I always thought I'd have. Not our future, where Sophie would be somewhere and, if not actually with me, then not very far away.

What I really want, more than anything, is to go home – back to England. Not because I need my home and my family, although I miss them all, but because I understand with an unexpected jolt that this isn't where I belong. A random assortment of unfinished projects merges into an almost unwieldy cluster in my head: sorting out my return to uni, returning to Flowers' for the summer, checking the sunflowers – Bernard's sunflowers – which I'd planted in a pot before I left. But most of all, I must go home and help my mother sort out Sophie's room. I'm as sure as I can be that she'll have kept her promise to me and left it exactly as it was after that last dreadful occasion. We need to do it together. Hold Sophie's things one by one, keep the ones we want and put them safely in a box. All the things that make a memory of her.

With these myriad thoughts running full tilt through my mind, I wash my hands and I stare into the mirror above the basin. I'm looking for Sophie, but she's not there. My face is a little flushed with the sun, and the wind has raked my short hair into spikes. '*En, to, tre, fire...*' I whisper to my reflection.

When I've reached "*ti*" and can't stay in the bathroom any longer, I open the door, and find some sort of discussion taking place.

'Birgitte and Mai are going down to the beach,' Per announces. 'Maybe you and I can have the coffee we missed this morning?'

He's holding one of those stainless steel jugs, similar to the one Anne had but a sleeker, more modern, shape, and at the far end of the room, on a pale wood coffee table, cups and saucers and a plate of small biscuits are set out. He has it all planned, I think. We're going to have a polite chat over coffee about my mother, and their student days, and Brighton; no mention will be made of their love affair. Then I'll phone Kasper, or Karen, and Mads will come over and find me here, and take me back to Skagen. Per and I will say goodbye, and lovely to meet you, and *mange tak* for lunch, and coffee, and oh – remember me to your mother.

Birgitte and Mai will come back from the beach, sandy and wind-blown, bright with the sun, and Mai will run in to him, '*Far! Far! Look what we found!*' She'll open her hands slowly, and show him shells spilling soft sand all over the floor, and he'll laugh.

'*Careful! Careful, skat! What beautiful shells! And did you paddle in the sea? Was it cold?*' She'll climb on his lap, curled tight and snuggled in against him, and he'll hold her close as if he'll never let her go. Because she's his little girl, his princess, and he'll always keep her safe.

CHAPTER TWENTY-SEVEN

There are paintings, posters, and photos, hung with careful stylishness, on all four walls of the summerhouse. There's none of the random, eclectic mix of my home – my parents' home – and yet it doesn't look contrived. As I close the bathroom door behind me and walk into the living area to join Per, I glimpse an artful arrangement of black and white photos of two small blond boys, as well as some of Mai – just a toddler. There are a couple of posters, side by side, from art exhibitions held in Skagen with dates from a few years ago, and a beautiful painting of a beach and stormy sea with a ship tossed on the horizon.

Then I spot it. At the far end of the room, on a narrow expanse of wall next to a glass door that leads outside. My heart lurches. I walk over slowly and stand still in front of it.

'Will you have milk?' asks Per, pouring out coffee into the delicate blue and white cups, and he looks up. 'Ah! My mother's favourite!' he says, and comes to stand next to me. 'It's several years old now,' he tells me. 'But this photo was very popular in Denmark for a time. Do you know it? Many people

305

had a copy. It was an English photographer – here.' He points to the name under the title, "Michael Mortimer".

'That's my father.' My voice sounds very faint and far away. I cough to clear my throat. 'My father is Michael Mortimer.'

Per regards me with something like awe. 'Hey!' he whistles. 'Really? That is... extraordinary. My mother would have been *so* delighted to know that. It's a little sad that she... then... you must know all about it. Has he told you much? About the composition maybe, and the little...'

I swallow and interrupt him. 'It's me,' I explain and I avoid his gaze. 'Me and my sister – Sophie.'

'Oh?'

'We were twins.'

He studies the photo again. 'Some people now find it... hmm, what's the word in English? Trivial?'

'Sentimental?'

'Exactly. But for me, he has caught happiness, that way children have of finding happiness so suddenly in almost nothing, and it's very simple, but also I think there is something else.' He shrugs and shakes his head. 'Something elusive? I can't explain it. What about you and your sister? Do you remember the day? It was very long, waiting for the right shot, I suppose.' He peers at it again. 'You're quite small. It must have been difficult.'

The truth is, I tell him, that I no longer know whether I have any memory of that day, that hot, hot day. Or whether it's just the photo, the old familiar photo we've had forever, which makes me believe I remember. It was instant, I say, there was no setting up. We were just playing, and he captured it, and that was that. He's a skilled photographer, my father, and he knows a good picture when he sees one and, as he's always said, he was lucky. Everything else, the light and the shadows and perspective and subject all worked together, in that split second. A minute later, he'd say, and it could have been another story.

'And which girl is you?' Per asks. 'Can I guess?' He considers the picture for a moment.

I can't decide whether he's perceptive, or just makes a lucky choice. He's right, anyway. I nod.

You couldn't catch me, remember, Jessie? I was too fast!

Now he's moving back to sit down, and waits expectantly. I perch on the blue wool sofa opposite him and add milk to the cooling coffee.

'Was it only you and your sister?' he asks, sitting back, easy, very relaxed, one leg bent and hooked across the other. 'Or do you have another brother or sister?'

'Two younger brothers. But... half-brothers, really. You see, my father adopted us, Sophie and me. When he married my mother. So, we have his name, and he's always been my dad, for as long as I can remember really, but...'

Per leans forward and begins to pour himself more coffee. He pushes a plate of small biscuits towards me and I shake my head and he says, 'But?'

I twist my hands together in my lap, and stare at my feet.

'But he's not my biological father,' I explain, and my words start to catch in my throat. I look up and meet his eyes, his very clear, light blue eyes. 'I think that's you.'

*

Sophie's post-mortem had only confirmed what we'd already assumed was her cause of death. There had to be an inquest though, and waiting for that to happen was like waiting for the monster from a nightmare to pounce. It hung around in every corner of the house, it loomed over conversations, it skidded into our thoughts when we were least expecting it.

On the day, my father was brilliant. He had to talk about Sophie: what she was like as a person, whether she had any medical conditions, and her state of mind – "her mental health" is how the coroner put it. A deliberate attempt by Sophie to end her own life had to be ruled out. I understood that but I knew, had always known, that even in her worst times, when that black dog haunted her every waking moment, even then she had never been suicidal. So why would she have been that night, when at last she was heading upwards again, regaining her old self? Back with Lucas. Her whole life ahead of her. Everything to look forward to. Unless, the one thing he'd promised me he wouldn't do... Unless he'd told her that.

Lucas. He was the key. I hated the fact that he held all the answers. The fact that just as before, so much about Sophie still revolved around him.

The coroner was unreadable. He asked Lucas each question in a level, reasoned tone, and Lucas continued, as he had from the beginning, to answer in a low, barely audible voice.

'And you put on the mask?' the coroner prompted him.

'Yes, as a joke, and she'd screamed, and kept on screaming,' Lucas said. He didn't know how to stop her.

I pressed my hands over my ears; I could hear her screams echoing down all these months of waiting.

She wasn't in a very balanced state, Lucas said. She'd been unwell, and she was better, much better, but sometimes she got things out of proportion. The coroner reminded him to keep to the facts and not offer his opinions. What he needed to hear from Lucas, he said, was a straightforward account of what had happened that night, not a presumption or hypothesis based on his own interpretation of Sophie's mental condition.

I could see how Lucas steadied himself and took several deep breaths before he continued. I closed my eyes and started to count.

*

A bee bumps and buzzes against a corner of the glass door. The monotonous hum drones on and on. Sometimes the buzz changes pitch, or gets faster, but nothing changes the bee's fate. It's trapped, I think, and all it craves is an escape.

'I'm not sure,' says Per, and he speaks each word with deliberate slowness. 'That I know what you mean.' He puts down the coffee jug, and picks up his cup, and fixes me with an unnerving stare.

I pick up my own cup, but my hands are shaking too much and I have to place it back carefully on the saucer. 'My mother...' I start.

'Yes?'

'My mother always told us, from when we were really small, that our father's name was Per Jacobsen, and he was Danish, and that they'd been students together, at Sussex. He'd gone back to Copenhagen to carry on with his degree and he didn't know about us, because she didn't tell him. Then recently she did tell me...' I hug my arms around me. 'That he thought she'd had an abortion.'

It's all spilling out in a rush, a cork pulled out of a bottle. That's what it feels like. As if I've been storing it all up inside me, and now it's released.

Buzz, buzz, bump, goes the bee.

'I'm so sorry to tell you this, Jess,' Per says now, without changing his expression, 'but I think your mother – Laura – has not told you the whole truth.'

I squeeze my arms even closer. 'I know that you had an argument,' I say, 'if that's what you mean. I know there was a... misunderstanding, on your last evening. I know about that. She told me. But still...'

He's shifted his gaze now, and he's staring, blindly, at the table. 'Not a misunderstanding, no,' his voice sharpens. 'Your mother don't meet me like we say. As we agree. And I found her, she sleeps with someone else.' His wonderful fluent

310

English is slipping out of control, skewed off course by his desperation to explain. But the meaning is clear.

'No!' I cry. 'No! You've got it all wrong. She saw *you*, with another girl. On the sea front. Where you were waiting. You were... I don't know... hugging each other, or something. Mum was on the bus. She saw you! She was terribly, terribly upset. That's why she went off.'

I'm trailing away, my words dropping.

'And she didn't have sex with him,' I whisper. 'He was too drunk, and anyway,' I add, 'she was in love with you.'

I don't care anymore. What's the point?

Per is frowning at me, and he only appears to have heard one small part of what I've said. 'Girl?' he repeats. 'What girl?'

'Well, *I* don't know,' I reply.

The buzzing is furious now, loud and insistent in the corner against the glass.

Per stands up, very slowly, and moves over to open the door, and releases the bee. A jerky silence separates us.

'It was Sofie,' he says, suddenly. 'Of course.'

'What?'

'My sister, Sofie. I forgot. It was very long ago. She come... came over to tell me about Far. She flew over, and arrived that evening. I didn't know she was to come.'

He sits down again, and presses his fingers either side of his head, on his temples. 'I forget,' he says again. 'I forget she come. She... find me. She go to my house, where I live, and my friend tell her, I am to Brighton pier.' He looks up and straight

311

at me. 'Quite stupid.' He smiles now. 'Quite stupid she is... was, to think she can find me when so many... but she did.'

'I'm not sure...' I say. 'I don't...'

'Always she have been the big sister. Always. She... look after me, protect me, and my father – Far – they have just know he is to die, he is... was, very ill.'

'So she came over to tell you?' I prompt. 'Before you went back to Denmark? She wanted you to know?'

He nods. 'And I think she tell me then, in the street, not a good place perhaps. Maybe I ask her to tell me the problem. I don't know.' He shrugs. 'I can't know, I can't remember. It was a long time ago.'

And the picture I've been dragging round with me for so many weeks rearranges itself in my head. Per and his sister, Sofie, both upset by the news: she because she had to tell him, and Per because he hadn't known. He was holding her; they were hugging, comforting each other. That's what my mother saw from the top of the bus. My mother, late as ever, always chasing one last thing to do before she had to go somewhere, missing the point.

'What was the matter?' I ask, not even sure if I should ask. 'Your father – what was wrong with him?'

He had cancer, a tumour in his stomach. After Per returned to Denmark, he had only lived a few weeks.

'When your mother writes to me,' Per says, 'I was up here. In Kandestederne. We all came here: my mother, father, Sofie. My father loved it here.' He pauses. 'It's a good place to spend the end of your life.'

Sophie – my Sophie – spins in front of me. I'd tried to catch her that day, but the ground was crumbly and rough, and the yellowing stalks of corn scraped my legs, and she'd dodged through them, laughing, always just out of reach.

When I go fast like this am I all blurry? Like a ghost?

If you'd let me catch you, I think, just once, I would never have let you go.

Definitely buried. Under all that green grass and trees.

A good day was when she got up, and dressed. Sometimes she just lay in bed all day, her head turned to the wall.

Love at first sight. Anything else is boring. One day you'll know, Jessie. One day you'll find out.

Sophie, who liked Marmite, and the colour blue, and fudge, and running very fast through rain; Sophie who wore odd earrings and had a list of all the jobs she'd never want to do, whatever they paid her, and could swim like a fish; Sophie who died alone on some waste land behind the old telephone exchange in our village. Not very far from all the people who loved her best, but too far to be saved.

I stare over Per's head through the window behind him at the grassy, sandy hillocks and dunes and the wide, wide blue sky. I think of Per's father – my grandfather – spending his last days here, surrounded by his family. There are many worse places to die.

'I'm sorry about your father,' I say uncertainly.

He spreads his hands out in front of him in a futile gesture. 'It was many years ago now. But no, not so good at the time.'

He gets up abruptly, and goes over to open a cupboard door, and takes out two glasses and a bottle of whisky. He holds it up to me. 'I think I need a drink. Do you join me?'

I hate whisky, but it might stop my hands trembling and the shaky feeling in my legs. It might give me courage.

Just gets me through, baby, just gets me through. More on top of things.

'Yeah, OK. Thanks,' I say. 'But with water, please.'

He raises his eyebrows at that but goes off into the kitchen and comes back with a full glass that he sets in front of me. He sits opposite again and takes a couple of mouthfuls from his own glass with a funny sort of grimace, as if he doesn't like it very much but needs it, like medicine. He's leaning forward, his arms resting on his legs, cradling his drink.

'And your mother,' he says, at last, the words cutting the silence with a chilling directness. 'She told me she was getting rid of you. Having an abortion.'

I clutch the whisky glass between my hands, and take a gulp.

I'll do the talking, Jessie. Because we both know... well, that's best.

'Well, that would have been very convenient for everybody,' I say. 'But she changed her mind, and here I am.'

'When were you born?' he asks. 'What month?'

He doesn't believe you, Jess. You're going to have to try harder. Except... he's only got to look at you...

'February,' I tell him. 'The fifteenth. 1982.' I don't tell him that, being twins, we'd arrived earlier than our due date. What a relief, Sophie often said, that it wasn't the day before, because then our birthday would always get in the way of Valentine's Day. How clever we'd been to have waited. (As if we'd had any kind of choice.) Much better this way, she'd said, because we'd get all the Valentine stuff, and then, hey presto, all our birthday things the next day. Once she became involved with Lucas, all mention of Valentine's Day disappeared, because Lucas was of the opinion that anything like that was trite and crass and commercial, and Sophie agreed with him.

Per is silent for a while, presumably while he does the mental maths. I drink some more whisky and think I could begin to enjoy the taste. It runs down my throat, warm and soothing, while I wait for him to say something more.

'This is... a surprise,' he says, finally. 'You must understand this? More than a surprise, in fact. A shock. I don't know what to say.'

I can think of loads of things he could say! 'This is wonderful!' for example. 'I'm so pleased you've come all this way to tell me. Let's have some father and daughter time together, I need to get to know you.' What's his problem?

But he's Danish. He doesn't behave in any sort of way that we could have predicted. I've already discovered that the Danes, while being open and friendly and welcoming and helpful, are not particularly strong on sharing their feelings. Sophie and I had never taken into account the fact that he, up to this point, had no inkling of our existence.

And two of us! Poor guy...

What did we expect he would say? I've no idea. I'm just making it up as I go along. There's no script for this sort of thing. And I've never been very good at improvisation. I like to predict what's going to happen in a conversation, have some idea how things will pan out.

Then Per says, 'Why has Laura sent you now? Has something changed? She doesn't let me know I have twin daughters for... twenty-one years, and now she sends one to tell me? Just like this? It make no sense. Is it for money? Is that why you come?'

He shakes his head and pushes his glasses back up onto the bridge of his nose with his forefinger again. That easy, casual charm has vanished. He looks perplexed and unhappy. I find I don't feel anything for him. He could be a long-lost uncle, or some remote third cousin: interesting to meet, but nothing to discuss, no points of reference beyond the immediate polite family chit-chat. What could we share, after all? How he and my mother were lovers, over twenty years before? We have nothing in common, no shared history.

At the same time, I don't want him to be unhappy. I especially don't want him to have the wrong idea. About any of this. I put my whisky down on the table, next to three thin glass tea light holders of different heights, and a blue glass bowl with a collection of shells and pebbles in it. I seize my few remaining shreds of courage and stand up and move round the coffee table to sit next to him.

None of this had anything to do with my mother, I tell Per, apart from her telling us he was our biological father, and who he was, and how much she cared for him at the time. She'd never supported our idea to find him, although she never opposed it, either, but after Sophie died it had suddenly become the one thing I had to do.

I explain how we'd always planned this, Sophie and I, for as long as I could remember. We'd come back to it again and again and as we'd neared the end of school and Sixth Form, and were preparing to go to university, we'd talked about whether to go to Denmark before or after that.

Then Sophie had become ill, I tell him. No, that wasn't how she died, I add, noticing his expression. Not that sort of ill. Some sort of mental illness: depression, a devastating dive into some sort of murky underworld none of us could imagine. For the first time I'd been the one who had to make all the decisions, on my own, and take the lead and help care for her until I left to go to university. Slowly, slowly, with the help of medication and therapy she'd eventually turned a corner, I say, and the terrible darkness that had consumed her life for all that time started to recede, and daylight began to seem a possibility. There was a pinprick of hope that grew larger and larger.

After she died, I had no future I could imagine, because Sophie had always been a part of that future. Even when she was with Lucas. Isn't it important, I ask Per – almost unable to believe that I'm sitting here next to him, on a sofa in a summerhouse in Denmark, next to my father, this mythical person of my childhood – isn't it important to know about our roots? Who's made us? Why we are how we are? What have we inherited – which traits, which mannerisms, which

317

genetic imbalances, or disorders? Up to that moment I'd only ever known about one side of my make-up – my mother's side – but I really wanted to know what my other side was like too.

My mother doesn't want any money from you, I say, and I feel a little sad speaking those words. Why would she, after so long, when she's managed all her life without you? She didn't even want me to come over here, but my father understood. I imagine him at home: cooking Sunday lunch, a tea towel slung over one shoulder; kicking a ball about in the garden with Toby; emerging from his workroom, crumpled and bleary-eyed with strain from working on a new exhibition but exhilarated with the photos he'd got; holding back Sophie's hair while she was sick in the loo after too much drink one night.

I realise how much I miss him.

Per says, 'No. Of course not. I'm glad for that. It means my memory of that person – of Laura – is truthful. She was impulsive, I think, and always late to be somewhere, and when she had decide something, then that was that. That is what I loved in her, how she was.'

He looks at me then, but he doesn't reach out to me.

'I think she must be very glad you came to find me. She must be so proud of you. Isn't she? Proud of who you are and how you are. Both your parents must think this.'

He frowns as if he's just thought of something else, and then he adds, 'But I'm sad we parted in such a bad way. And maybe that is why she don't want me to know you were born, you and your sister.'

'Maybe,' I whisper, and I put my hand loosely over his. It feels warm, but unfamiliar. A stranger's hand.

I can't make it all right. I can't make any of it all right. My mother chose how she wanted her life to be, and Per has his own life too. All this time he hasn't ever known that there we were, Sophie and me, walking around in another country, connected to him by an invisible thread.

Nobody could ever have imagined that the photo my father took, that hot summer's day when we were four, would be chosen by someone living in Denmark, and hung in her summerhouse. A woman who was actually our Danish grandmother, only of course she had no idea about that, and that the man who was our Danish father, our biological father – although he knew nothing of our existence – would glance at it from time to time, notice it with affection even, and think: two lovely little girls, until at last, obscured by its familiarity, it had become wallpaper. It was there, and not there. A make-believe background to his real life.

CHAPTER TWENTY-EIGHT

All we can ever tell is our own version of a story. The facts become distorted by time and by the things we want people to think. We all have secrets, and some are closer than others, and some were never meant to be shared. How many people can you ever trust to tell you the truth, the whole truth? And how do you ever know? A lie can become a near truth, fiction a reality.

Per says he'll drop me back to Skagen. He leaves me alone in the summerhouse while he walks down to the beach to explain to Birgitte what he's going to do. I wonder, abstractedly, what else he'll tell her. I feel as if I've been wrung out, every last drop of emotion squeezed from me. My limbs appear so weak that even walking to the bathroom seems too much effort, and I'm strangely light-headed and limp.

I stare into the mirror again, and it's as if a whole lifetime has passed since the last time I looked, barely an hour ago. Sophie's face looks back at me and my heart misses a beat.

She says, 'Hey, Jessie, you're OK now, aren't you? I guess you can cope on your own. You don't need me anymore. You don't even really count much now, do you?'

'Sophie,' I say, lifting my fingers to touch the glass. 'Don't go and not come back, will you? Don't go and not say goodbye. There's still... things I need to explain.'

'Jessie, Jess, it's all right. It doesn't matter anymore. You don't need to explain. Or feel bad. It's not your fault, remember? It never was. I always knew – I always did. Peas in a pod, yin and yang, two sides of a coin... I can read you. Like a book.'

*

Lucas took off the mask and threw it on the ground. It glinted grotesquely in the murky dim light leaking round the edges of the waste ground from the High Street lamps.

'Happy now?' he said. 'Christ, Sophie, you can be so fucking melodramatic sometimes.'

Sophie sank down onto the ground and knelt there, in the long straggly grass, swaying on her heels. Her mascara was running in grimy streaks down her wet face. 'They just freak me out,' she hiccoughed. 'Masks. You know that, Lucas. You know that.'

'Yeah, well... just trying to lighten the mood. No need to go off on one.' Lucas rummaged inside the plastic bag he'd been carrying since he left the pub a while before, and pulled out two cans of beer. He shook one and tossed it onto the ground when he realised it was empty. He waved the other one at Sophie. 'Want some? Hair of the dog and all...'

Sophie shook her head. 'I'm not... drunk, Lucas. I can't be. You know that too. Not while I'm still taking those drugs. I just needed... to sort stuff out with you. That's all.'

Lucas squatted on the ground next to her, and pulled the ring off the can.

'Well, now you have, baby. Now you have.' He took several swigs. 'I've told you, there's no one else in my life. Hey, Sophe, what do you think I am? I wouldn't do that to you, would I?'

He avoided her eyes, took a few more gulps, and then put down the can and felt inside the bag again.

Sophie sat back and crossed her legs. She pulled off her shoes – the shiny ones with high heels she'd chosen that evening to wear with her jeans – and threw them behind her haphazardly. When she wore them they made her legs, thin after months of not eating properly, appear much longer than they were. They were classy but they were uncomfortable and made her wobble when she stood up. She used the heel of one hand to wipe away the last tears from her face, and sniffed. 'No. I know. I just had a feeling...'

Lucas was tearing open a packet of nuts, using his teeth to split the top of the bag.

'Yeah, well, it was a crap feeling, if you want to know. I'm quite hurt, Sophe. I thought you knew me better.'

He tipped the bag into his mouth, watching her face over the top of it. She was rubbing her toes where the shoes had chafed, and then stayed still, her elbows propped on her knees, kneading and worrying the hem of her jeans. He sat down too, gazing out into the blackness over the waste ground, chewing the nuts. There was a pause before the realisation of what he was doing swept over him in a bleak wave. 'Fuck,' he said. 'Shit, Sophie – I've just eaten these nuts – you going to be OK? Sorry, Sophe, sorry. Didn't think. Oh fuck.'

Sophie stared at him: 'What were they?' she asked. 'What sort of nuts?'

He picked the packet off the ground, turning it over to peer at the label. 'Whatever,' he said. 'Does that matter? Thought you were allergic to all nuts. Any nut. Full stop. Didn't think you were picky about which ones.' He took another mouthful of drink.

'Don't make fun of me,' Sophie frowned. 'I can't help it. It's not a choice, Lucas. It's not like it's me being fussy or something.'

'Yeah, well,' he muttered, his speech beginning to slur a little. 'Like I said, you do get a bit... over the top. Quite often. Specially since – you know, since you were... off. Down. Whatever...'

'Peanuts,' Sophie interrupted, a new resolution steeling her voice. 'Definitely peanuts, and probably others, but we've never been sure.'

'OK,' Lucas said. 'OK then,' and he looked at the bag again. 'OK. We're in luck. Says these are —'

'And it was anxiety and depression,' Sophie added. 'Get it right, Lucas.'

'Hey,' he said, 'let's not talk about it right now. Yeah? Look, I'm putting the packet safely away in the bag, and I'll swill my mouth out – is that enough? And over my hands.' He tipped the can to trickle the last few drips of the beer over his palms, but it was empty. He wiped them instead, with an uncharacteristic desperation and speed, down the front of his shirt.

'Yeah. That's OK.' Sophie shrugged. 'Just... don't get too close, that's all. You know I have to be really, really careful.'

'I do know,' he said, 'I do – you've told me enough times. Not likely to forget, am I?'

There was a pause. Sophie fiddled with her earrings. She had a stud and a silver hoop in one ear, and a trail of three little hearts dropping from the other. She tucked her hair back after a few moments and said, with renewed determination, 'But... I'm still worried, Lucas. Still worried I might be pregnant. What if I am? What then?'

'That's not going to happen, Sophie, is it?' he said. 'So don't try and freak me out, OK? It's just one of your little... fantasies, right? Just a load of shit.'

The unearthly cry of a fox sounded close by, and further away, on the edge of the village, an owl hooted.

Sophie shivered. 'Let's hope you're right, Lucas. Because I really don't need... I mean, what would we do?'

Lucas stood up in one slow, gracefully indolent movement. He reached down to pull up Sophie too.

'That's what you love about me,' he murmured. 'The way I'm always right, and... we won't *need* to do anything because it's not going to happen, right? You're not pregnant, no way. We've always been careful, haven't we? You know that, I know that. So just forget about it.'

He wiped his mouth quickly with his hand, and leant in towards Sophie. He held her upturned face between his palms, drink clouding his reason and shrivelling his caution.

She tried to tug away from him, shake his hands off.

'Don't touch me, please! Please don't! I need to go now, Lucas. I want to go home. I told Jess I'd only be...'

'Oh well, you'd better go then. If that's what you told Jess,' he smirked. 'Although... the stories I could tell you about that sister of yours... you'd never believe.'

She took a step back and stared at him.

'What? What are you talking about?'

'Nothing. Forget it.'

'It *is* true, isn't it? You *did* sleep with her,' she screamed. 'I knew it! I'd guessed! You slept with Jess!' The strength of her fury hit him like a physical force; he staggered back. She was shaking and crying. 'How could you? How could you do that? Get away... get *away!* I hate you! I hate you, Lucas!'

He moved towards her.

'Keep away! Get lost!' she shrieked.

'It wasn't just me, though, was it?' he said. 'What about little Miss Saintly? Just as much her fault, wasn't it?'

Sophie dropped down again onto the wet grass, clasping her arms around her as if suddenly frightened she might fall apart. She could feel the trembling in her legs and hands spreading through her whole body. She began to rock with an uneasy rhythm, back and forth, back and forth. 'She wouldn't,' she sobbed. 'She wouldn't. You must have... Jess wouldn't do that to me. She knew how...'

Lucas changed his tone. 'Sophie.' His voice had become that of someone reasonable and wise. 'Think about it. I was really worried when you were so... depressed. All that time. I couldn't get through to you. I thought we were over. I didn't want that, but still... what could I do?'

'Not fuck my twin sister,' Sophie said, her voice low and raw. 'Anything but that. I bet you told her, didn't you? I bet you said, this is just between us. What she doesn't know can't hurt her. I can hear you, Lucas. I know exactly what you'd say. Jess would never... She wouldn't want to hurt me.'

'Yeah,' Lucas replied. 'Well, you'll never know. In any case, it was only... the once, and I decided that was it. Finished it.' He glanced away from her. He wouldn't meet her gaze.

'Could never feel the same for her, Sophe. You know that, right? It's always been you.'

'So... just once?' Sophie sounded dull with pain. 'Is that it? Really?'

'Would I lie to you, Sophie? Would I?' His eyes slid over her for a second, and then away, up at the stars, as if seeking inspiration from the heavens. 'I just missed you, you know, that summer. Missed you so much, when... and, it just happened, with Jess. Just one of those things.'

Sophie scrambled up, careless of the wet grass cold and sharp beneath her bare feet. Misery and hope licked and spilled in equal amounts through every layer of her heart.

'It's only ever been you, Lucas. I thought you felt the same. Didn't think...'

'What? Didn't think what.' He was trying to focus on her, to stay alert, but the drink, together with the spliffs he'd smoked earlier, had begun to make him feel he was losing what little control of the situation he'd imagined he had.

She took a hesitant step towards him. 'I always thought you cared, Lucas,' she said. 'I know... well, I know you put up like, this front, this show, but I thought I knew you. I thought, deep down, you really cared. That you'd never...' Sophie took a deep, shuddering breath. '... Never hurt me. Not deliberately.'

Lucas made an effort to concentrate. He attempted to take a step closer to her, and lost balance for a moment. He straightened with a deliberate composure that he only summoned up with a struggle. The whole ragged conversation had started to waver in his mind. Nuts, he thought with sudden clarity, I must remember the nuts. But he knew he needed to win her back. Every part of him wanted Sophie very deeply just then, with a need and an ache that seemed both foreign and familiar.

'Only ever been you, Sophe, like I said,' he muttered.

'Really?' Sophie's voice shook. 'Do you really mean that, Lucas? Because, you know I love you, don't you, Lucas, don't you?'

She shifted closer, until their bodies were touching; she could hear his rapid breathing, and sense the life pulse in his chest, racing. 'I can feel your heart, Lucas,' she mouthed against his throat. 'I love you. I love you so much.' She pressed into him, reaching up to pull his head down towards her.

Lucas fought with himself to resist. 'Sophe,' he muttered. 'Those nuts. I didn't tell you... I'm not sure...' His mind swirled with foggy confusion.

She had pushed against him, her fingers winding through his hair. Had stretched up on tiptoe until he forgot – forgot about nuts, and his fear for her, for what he'd done – lost all concern, and grabbed her close and covered her open mouth with his, hands first cupping her face, and then moving down over her body. She clutched at him, holding him tight, tight. Her fingers snatched at his hair, stroked his neck, clawed his back, until when her arms fell away, he murmured, 'Hey, don't stop, baby.'

As she put her hands on her throat, wheezing and gasping, bending over, scrabbling for air, he said, 'Sophie! Cut it out! For fuck's sake...'

*

On our last day in Skagen we drive out to Grenen.

Later, in the evening, we plan to go to the Midsummer celebration on the beach at Skagen and meet Per and Birgitte and Mai there. It's all been arranged.

It's still quite early, the sky that milky blue that signals a clear day ahead, and only a few cars pockmark the sprawling parking area. The four of us walk out onto the long stretch of beach, and the sun is already hot on the back of my neck.

We take off our sandals and dangle them from our fingers as we amble along by the water's edge. A tractor pulling a trailer carries a few people who weren't prepared to walk the distance and passes us higher up the beach.

'It's called...' says Mads, and then has an exchange of Danish with Kasper which involves shrugs and head shaking, '... the Sand Worm. The tractor for people to ride on.' He's pleased with himself at the translation. 'The Sand Worm,' he repeats.

The sea breaks in small washing waves over thousands of tiny coloured pebbles and stones, sucking them with gentle hisses back and forth.

'Look,' says Kasper, 'look. Can you see now where the two waters meet? The two oceans, the seas. It's extraordinary, isn't it?'

Karen and I follow the two of them towards the spit of sand that fingers its way, thinner and thinner, out into the water. You can actually see a fluid ridge in the sea, like an invisible force, both seas fighting for supremacy. The Kattegat and the Skagerrak.

'We can stand at the edge of the water,' Kasper says. 'One foot in each ocean.'

'But it's too dangerous to swim,' Mads explains. 'Very dangerous. Every year, there are people who do, and it is unfortunate, a few don't survive.'

'Because...?' Karen asks.

'Because the strength of the current, the force of those two seas colliding, it's immense, very powerful.'

A few people are already wandering back along the beach. Others are strolling towards the end, like us, some at the water's edge.

'You watch,' says Kasper. 'Somebody will risk it.'

*

We sat completely still, my parents, my grandparents and I, and watched as Lucas finished telling his story to the coroner.

'I didn't realise,' Lucas said, with a break in his voice. 'I just didn't think. I told her, when I realised. I said sorry, sorry, Sophie. But I'd eaten the nuts by then and so...' He stopped. For a brief moment he looked appalled, as if the memory of that evening had ricocheted back to haunt him.

'And so...?' the coroner prompted, quietly.

Lucas took a breath. I almost felt sorry for him, but that sympathy didn't last long. 'She said – Sophie said – something about peanuts. She knew it was peanuts. That definitely affected her. And I looked at the packet, and it didn't say peanuts. Well, I thought it didn't say peanuts. I... um... I swilled out my mouth. I tried to wash my hands. With the lager. But... it was finished.'

'Can you tell us what you did then?' the coroner asked. 'What happened next?'

There had been a bit of a disagreement, Lucas said. Sophie had gone on again about whether she might be pregnant, and he'd done his best, he said, to reassure her. I closed my eyes then. I couldn't look at him. How would we ever know the real truth, when we'd always have only Lucas's own version of that night? The idea of him "reassuring" Sophie seemed so unlikely that I nearly laughed. I squeezed my eyes even tighter shut, and I counted backwards from fifty to try to stop myself shaking. My mother put her hand on mine and left it lying there, a gentle pressure.

But that wasn't all; of course it wasn't. Somehow he'd made the mistake, Lucas said, his voice dropping even lower, of telling Sophie that he'd slept with someone else. It was while she was unwell. It hadn't meant anything. But she'd become hysterical. He'd tried to calm her down. He'd thought it would help if he told her who it was. I opened my eyes then.

The coroner interrupted, 'For the purposes of this court we don't...'

But Lucas wouldn't be deterred.

I wanted to leave the courtroom. Nobody would believe him, surely. And we'd agreed. How would it have helped Sophie, if she'd known what had happened between us? I thought he'd given his word, and now, how was it going to help any of us? If I left, if I couldn't hear what he was going to say, perhaps none of it would be true. Or if I counted, in French, for as long as I could. How long would that be? My cheeks were burning; I felt shame spilling over me in an acid flood.

'I told her it was just the once. I tried to calm her down. I think – you know – because it was...' He paused, and then repeated, slowly and deliberately, 'Because it was... her sister, her *twin sister*, she found it... difficult.'

A low and indistinct murmuring spread through the courtroom. No one in my family moved. They all stared at Lucas, but they didn't look at me, not once.

Lucas coughed. Then Sophie had thrown herself at him, he said. Clung onto him, forced him to kiss her. He'd tried to tell her, tried to say it was mixed nuts, in the packet. Mixed nuts, and he hadn't been able to read which, because the bag was torn, right across the ingredients list.

He paused again, and this time reached for the glass of water on the stand in front of him. Not once did he raise his eyes to where we were sitting.

Soon it will all be over, I thought, and then we can leave Lucas, and the Coroner's Court, and the avid scattering of journalists; we can leave them all behind us, and we can try and replace these images – images of Sophie's last desperate minutes – with pictures of the real Sophie. The one who'll probably walk in any minute and say, 'Hey! What are you all doing here? I couldn't find you! You didn't think you could get rid of me that easily, did you?'

When he had finally understood that she was genuinely gasping for breath, that her airways were almost blocked, he began to search frantically for her EpiPen. The one she always carried with her. He knew about it, he said, how to use it; Sophie had shown him, and she never went anywhere without it. But she had brought nothing with her when she got out of the car.

He had put her in a recovery position on the ground, and then had rolled her onto her back again to give her mouth-to-mouth resuscitation, until he grasped the fatal implications of doing that. He'd propped her up then, frantically banging her on her back, but she'd lolled against him, boneless.

'And then I said...' Lucas stopped.

I held my breath. There was an utter hush in the room.

'... Something like... "Don't worry, Sophie, I'll get help. I'll be... right back. You'll be OK".'

He didn't have his mobile with him, he said. He'd left it charging at his home. He rarely used it, really, only – and he hesitated, and I could see how the awful connotation of what he was about to say dawned in his face – for emergencies. He'd not wanted to leave her, just lying there like that, but eventually he did. He'd run out into the road and then he'd seen Sophie's father.

*

'We were going to look out for some amber,' Karen reminds us. 'Have you ever found any, Kasper?'

The damp sand is like wet velvet under my toes. On the shoreline it's coarser, grittier. I crouch down to scoop up a handful and the tiny grains stick to my fingers. Among them are other, slightly larger pebbles. I catch one, a glassy yellow nugget. 'Hey! Is this amber? Does it look like this?'

Kasper and Mads both laugh. 'You'll be very lucky to find a piece so easy,' Kasper says. 'Let me see.'

We stand close together as he turns the small stone over in his hand and then flings it out to sea. 'Bad luck!' He grins.

I follow the line of his throw, and as I do I see that someone, just as he predicted, is wading out, close to the breaking line of the two oceans. I clutch his arm. 'Look!'

The sun is bright above us now, and it glints and dazzles on the water.

The others gaze out, squinting at where I'm pointing.

'Sun's in my eyes,' says Karen. 'Can't see a thing.'

It's someone with a long swing of blonde hair falling down her neck. She's staring out to sea, rocking gently with the force of the waves, and then she turns and stares at me instead. Only me. The sun's not in my eyes. I can see Sophie clearly. She stoops slightly, puts her hands down in the water, and flicks them gently. I walk very slowly to the edge, so the sea ripples over my toes.

'Why don't I come and join you, Sophie?' I call to her. 'It doesn't look that dangerous at all!'

Sophie moves back further into deeper water. I can only see her from her waist up now. It would be so easy for me to wade out to her, Sophie, who could swim like a fish but was always frightened of drowning. She lifts her arm and waves, merrily. 'Not dangerous for me!' she cries.

'If I reach you,' I shout, 'will you catch me? Keep me safe?'

I take another step forward. The water washes over my ankles; I flinch at the sudden coldness. There are sounds behind me, someone screaming my name. Karen, maybe? I shake the noises out of my head, and cup my hands behind my ears so I can concentrate on Sophie. Sophie, who liked Marmite, and the colour blue, and being first. Sophie, who wore odd earrings, and liked Peter Pan, but not clowns, or anyone in a mask; Sophie, who believed only in love at first sight.

'You said...' and her voice sounds thin and reedy now, as if she's slipping away from me, 'not to go, without saying goodbye. I always keep promises, Jessie, you know that.'

'Sophie,' I scream. 'Come back!' A sob catches in my throat. 'I didn't want you to go like this! Are you going and...' my breath is tearing in my chest, 'never coming back?'

The wind snatches my words and flings them far, far out to sea. A huge ship, reduced to a toy, moves slowly across the horizon. The screeching of gulls rises and falls like the birds themselves, dipping and soaring, floating on the currents of air.

'You've found him now, Jessie.' Her words pitch with the rolling water, coaxing and seductive. 'Per – you've found him. All on your own. You didn't need me after all!'

It's getting more difficult to make her out now. There's some sort of sea mist drifting in, so she's wavery and indistinct, and yet I have to put up my hand to shield my eyes from the sharpness of the light.

Just a few more steps, that's all it would take, just a few more steps and I'd reach her, and this time I'd hold on tight. I'd never let her go. We could watch E.T. and eat the Christmas tree chocolates and leave the empty wrappers hanging. We could read Wuthering Heights and war poems, and dance in the rain. And I've forgotten to tell her that I believe in love at first sight too, only I know it gets better and better.

'I miss you, Sophie.' Tears are running down my face. 'You know I do.'

335

Some people reach death in their own time. For others, death comes to find them. It's never a question of rightness – it never seems quite fair. Often the wrong people get chosen.

I take another step forwards. I can feel the current now, churning against my legs. I stagger a little, and force my feet on through the water. I almost lose my balance. As I take my hands away from my ears and stretch out my arms to steady myself, I can hear more indistinct shouting and commotion behind me. I stop. I try to keep my feet anchored in the shifting gravel but the sea is too strong; it sweeps and sucks, high up my legs, pulling my feet away from under me. I'm frightened now. My fear is as strong as the sea. I don't want to reach Sophie after all. I don't want to die.

Sometimes the only choice you have is how you'll carry on. You may not have had an option in what happened to you or what someone else did to your life, but you can decide whether to keep that inside you for ever and stay in one place, or to take it with you, alongside you, and move on.

I'm grabbed from behind. Someone yanks me back, arms round my waist. Kasper and I flounder together in the shallows and then he pulls me away from the water's edge, and we fall onto the beach. He's shaking his head, looking bewildered.

'Jess, oh my God!' Karen is shrieking. 'What were you doing? That was so scary!'

I glance at her for one brief moment. She looks hysterical, her face white with fear as she grips Mads's arm. I don't understand.

Kasper stands and pulls me to my feet. We're wet with sea and sand and shingle; the mixture clings to our legs and shorts. We make futile attempts to brush it off, but I'm shaking, shaking too hard to use my hands properly. He folds his arms round me, close, tight. His voice is hoarse, his breath warm against my ear. 'Are you OK? You frighten me.'

Sometimes, the choice is made for you, but it's the one you'd pick anyway.

We turn away from the water, all four of us, and head back along the beach. We walk in a row of sombre silence.

'Sorry, everyone,' I say. 'Sorry. It was just...'

I stop and look back towards the two oceans, and the line of foam where they crash against each other. But Sophie has disappeared. Maybe she was never there.

*

We'd agreed to meet them in one of the harbourside cafés. It's already incredibly busy down there; lots of people are gathering. Some are students, just as Kasper had told me, clutching great wads of paper. Other people carry baskets, and bags of food and drink, and those disposable barbecues you can get. When we stroll through the café door, I can see the three of them: Birgitte, her hands raised, her fingers tucking stray wisps of hair into a green, butterfly-shaped comb, and Per, with his back to us, in solemn conversation with Mai. As we reach their table, he notices us and stands up with a slow welcoming smile.

'*Hej!*' we all say at the same time, and everyone shakes hands, even though we'd only seen each other a couple of days ago. Birgitte leans in to kiss me on both cheeks, gives me a small, encouraging nod, and points to the chair next to Per for me to sit on. More chairs are dragged over, and everyone is talking at once, in Danish and English, discussions on what to order, and how hot is the sun, and how we didn't find amber.

'*Nej!*' Per exclaims. 'Oh, no! For amber you need the west coast. You will be lucky to see amber here.' Something like a shadow flits across his face as if he's dislodged a long-ago memory, but then he touches Mai on the arm.

'*Mai? Kan du husk hvad jeg fortalte dig? Her er Jess igen. Og hun er din nye storesøster.*'

He looks at me, and says, 'Do you understand, Jess? I ask Mai if she remembers what I tell her, that she has a new big sister. That's you.'

'*Hej igen, Mai,*' I say. Mai is sitting opposite me and she stares across very solemnly and then her face breaks into one of her widest smiles.

'*Hej!*' She nods energetically, and speaks in her usual rush of incomprehensible words.

Kasper laughs. 'She says yes, she knows. And she knows you don't speak Danish so good so she wants to help you. Oh, and what's your favourite colour? Hers is blue.'

All this time Mai has continued to study me carefully, and now she holds up her hand in a fist and starts to raise the fingers on it one by one. '*En, to, tre...*' she says.

I smile back and carry on, '*... fire, fem, seks...*'

Mai's face is a picture. Together we finish, '... *Syv, otte, ni, ti.*' She claps her hands with delight.

She leans onto the table from where she's kneeling on her chair, her long hair swings forward, and with one quick, impatient movement she tucks it behind her ears.

EPILOGUE

I never saw Sophie again. She disappeared. She'd vanished in Grenen, and when Karen and I flew home to England a week later, she wasn't there either.

I'd stopped counting. It was several weeks before I realised. I was at home with Toby, and he wanted to know how much Danish I could speak.

'Hardly any,' I said. 'It's *so* ridiculously difficult, Toby. None of it sounds like it looks, none of it resembles *any* other language I've ever known. I did start to understand little bits of conversation, but it's just...'

I high-fived him. 'Oh – except – I can *count* in Danish, Toby! I'm quite good at that. I'll teach you to count to ten, if you like.'

As we began I thought, this is the first time I've counted since... I don't remember when, and anyway, it's not in my head. It's not in my head, because I don't need to do that anymore. I felt liberated, free. Strong. Not counting made me feel strong. I could do anything I liked without craving that crutch and without needing Sophie.

My Danish grandmother, Grethe, died before I ever saw her again. She had never known about Sophie and me, of course, and by the time Per knew about us, she was too frail to be told, too ill to understand.

'But that was probably for the best,' Gran said. 'And don't forget, Jess, in a way she knew you, because she had the "Corn" print, didn't she? Didn't Per say it was always a favourite of hers?'

Those typically comforting words from Gran didn't stop me feeling sad, and regretful, but nothing more. You can't grieve for someone you never had a connection with, someone you never knew. Grethe was just an old lady I once met, very briefly. My sadness could only be for not meeting my Danish relatives earlier in my life.

Per was my father, and yet he wasn't. I was sure that over the years we'd keep in touch, and I hoped the cautious bond would strengthen, but it would never be the same bond as the one that tied me to Mike, to my English father. How could it be – what had I expected? Per was still a stranger. Or if not now exactly a stranger, then more like an uncle, or some distant relative. We had started to get to know each other, but there were years and years of my life – all those lost years of my childhood – that neither of us could ever recapture. And the most poignant thing was that he never met Sophie.

I listened for her voice then. I glanced round but she wasn't there. I had to imagine in my head what she might say. 'Yeah, kind of sad, Jessie. Heartrending, even. But you can't miss what hasn't happened. And you know what? You've met him now, you've found him. You did it!'

What had I hoped would come about when I found Per? Would how we were, Sophie and I, become explained? How we were so different, and so alike. Yin and yang, peas in a pod. Perhaps everything would fall neatly into place, and the missing jigsaw pieces would complete me? And who I am would fold into a book, the pages a thesaurus that slowly uncovered my life.

*

The morning light filters round the edges of the blind and I lie still, listening. Kasper is asleep beside me, his breathing regular and calm. I think I can hear gulls in the distance. Nothing else, only silence. At this time of year, not too long after Midsummer, darkness barely falls. The greyness of night lasts only a few hours. I have no idea what time it is, only that it's very, very early.

We arrived yesterday. I flew to Aalborg, and Kasper was waiting for me. I hurried out of Arrivals and ran towards him, the bag in my hand bouncing against my leg, and I dropped it as he pushed his way through the little knot of people waiting there, and hurtled into his arms. We stood, wrapped together, as if we would never let each other go, until too many other passengers had shoved and tutted their way past us.

As we drove north, in the car borrowed from Kasper's mother, I had to keep touching him. My hand rested on the back of his neck where his hair brushed his T-shirt, my fingers stroking his skin. The sun had come out by the time we reached the turn-off for Kandestederne, and we followed the road and bumpy track to Per's summerhouse. There was no one there, just a note, pinned to the door. Kasper scanned it. 'They've gone into Skagen for shopping. We can meet them there – phone, and meet them for coffee. Or we can stay here and wait. Our room is ready. The one at the end.'

We already knew where the spare key was hidden.

We looked at each other and grinned.

'Do we need to discuss that?' I asked, and Kasper moved towards me.

'No discussion,' he said. 'No choice, actually.'

Now I swing my feet onto the bleached wood floor, pull Kasper's abandoned T-shirt over my head, and tiptoe out of the bedroom. He doesn't stir.

Outside, I stand in the chill dawn air and breathe in the quiet. The absolute peace.

I walk to the edge of the decking, my toes curling, surprised by the unexpected cold of the dew. The sun has already risen behind the summerhouse, the first shafts streaking the grassy sand in front of me and shining faintly on the roofs of the other summerhouses just glimpsed peeping from behind the dunes in the distance. Another good day.

Mai will arrive later, with her two teenage half-brothers, Jacob and Martin. They're coming by train. I've not met them yet, but they're my half-brothers too, of course. I'm imagining that they'll be typical teenage boys like Alex and Toby, off-hand, non-committal, underwhelmed by meeting me. The summerhouse will be quite crowded. Per had shrugged when I said that last night. The boys would camp outside, he said, they loved that. The only problem would be preventing Mai from joining them.

A year has passed, a whole year, since I was last here, and yet how familiar it seems. As if, while my life raced forward, time here has stood still. Last night the four of us had eaten out on the decking, the wooden walls of the summerhouse and the boards beneath our bare feet still warm from the day's sun. Birgitte placed a little wooden flag in the middle of the table, and small glass bowls flickered with candlelight on the table and round the edge of the deck. It felt like a homecoming.

In that year, so much has happened. I'd helped Mum sort the rest of Sophie's belongings, soon after I arrived home. We made a memory box and filled it with all the small things that had defined who she was, how we remembered her. I kept her diary safe in my own room, though. Some secrets are still best never told.

Grampy had already planted out Bernard's sunflowers for me, and he made sure I watered them regularly. They grew, tall and cheerful, a lofty and optimistic yellow in the bright sunlight when we held the garden party event in Sophie's memory, with cakes and a raffle and tombola, and games for children like hook-a-duck and a treasure hunt and lucky dip. Most of the village seemed to cram into our garden that day; it was humbling to realise how many people wanted to come and honour Sophie's memory. It was so successful that we agreed we should hold one every year. We gave the money we raised to what Toby called, 'that Allergic charity.'

Through all these months, since my return to my family in England, Kasper and I have tried to snatch what time we can to be together. When we're apart his absence is so painful that it's like being bereft. Except that, unlike with Sophie's absence, I know of course that I will see him again. I can talk to him, for hours sometimes, on the phone, and I know he's there, just across the sea and land; he's not a figment of my imagination. Or a ghost.

The best news is that he's coming to England in the autumn. He's joining me at Warwick. I'll be in my final year, and he's applied to be a student there for his second degree. We're going to share a flat. Every now and then, when I remember this is going to happen, bubbles of joy rise and fizz inside me, and I feel as if I could float with happiness.

Tomorrow – a quiver of anticipation spears my heart, and makes me tremble for a moment – tomorrow my family arrive from England. They're renting a summerhouse near here for a few days. I'm both excited and anxious. My birth parents meeting again, after so many years, seems like the most significant event I can imagine. I'm fearful and hopeful in equal measure. Last year, I think, I would definitely have needed to count.

*

After all, it's an ending and a beginning.

I close my eyes and I think I will always remember this moment. This moment and this day. I shall wrap it in gold tissue paper and tie it with gauzy ribbon and, for safekeeping, I'll bury it, deep in my mind. Inside the shiny package will be the sound of the surf, sucking and breaking and falling, and the harsh screech of gulls swooping overhead. There will be shouts and sudden loud laughter from the football game being played on the sand – England versus Denmark, of course; Kasper, Jacob and Martin against Mike and Alex and Toby, and the murmuring of shared discovery as Birgitte and Mai look for shells along the water's edge. I'll add precious pictures: my grandmother, perched on the rocks at the top of the beach, doing her best to sketch, with her hat abandoned, weighed down under a stone for safekeeping from the sudden gusts of wind from the sea. My grandfather, struggling to unfold one of the maps he'd been so delighted to discover in the summerhouse, their huge scale charting the curve and alignment of the coast. ('I'll bring it with me down to the beach, if that's all right?' he'd said to Per. 'Just in case.')

My parents, my birth parents, sitting side by side a little way apart from everyone, high up on the dry, shifting sand – my mother propped on her hands, her legs stretched out in front of her and Per with his arms resting on his bent knees. They're close in conversation. I long to hear what they're saying, but they're too far away. Anyway, it's just for them. Are they remembering their last day together in Brighton, all those years ago? Did they sit together, like this, but on the shingle? Perhaps he told her about this beach. The white sand stretching into the

346

distance, so different from pebbly Brighton. The possibility of finding amber, if you were unbelievably lucky. Has my mother held that memory deep inside for all these years? When do you let go of something like that? Perhaps you never do.

I sit cross-legged on the sand and my fingers sift through the fine grains, searching for shells. Kasper and I had looked for shells when he came over to visit me in the spring. We'd sat, just like Per and my mother are now, but on Brighton beach, and we'd arranged our finds in a pattern around us: chalky spiralling whelks, ridged limpets and scallops, striped razors, inky mussels. We'd added misshapen stones with holes in the middle, and rounded coloured pebbles – red, coal black, pink, and tawny. We'd sat holding each other close inside our magic seaside circle, and I'd thought I could stay like that forever.

But nothing is forever, and you wouldn't want it to be. I can feel the day slipping out of my grasp, floating, like the bubbles that Mai had blown earlier from a tub, dipping and hovering and finally splintering into a dozen blurry pictures. I want to grab each one before they burst, like the bubbles, and vanished for ever. This day, these remembrances, they'll stay inside me and they'll become part of who I am. Who I'm going to be.

I want Kasper to stay with me forever. I look at him, or I think of him, or I hear his voice, and my heart still skips a beat. But if nothing else, I've learned that you can plan your future – you can decide how you want your life to be – but nobody can ever be sure any of it will come about. Nobody knows.

You've only got one life, as my father – Mike, my real father – has always said, so enjoy. Enjoy the moment, and keep it safe.

*

Now I stand in the doorway of the summerhouse. The shadows lengthen on the decking, as the smoke from the barbecue drifts in the still air. It's being jointly supervised by both my fathers, while they also consume quite a lot of beer. Birgitte and my mother rustle past with other food in bowls – salads and potatoes and bread – and place them on an already crowded table.

Later, we all sit together eating and drinking, and I think: I've made this happen. This has occurred because of me. I tuck the image inside the golden parcel. I found Per, and along the way I found Kasper too. I've brought these different families together, just for a short while. I did this, and I did it without Sophie. She's somewhere else now. She's with me, and she's not with me. I never glimpse her disappearing round a corner, or just out of sight down a road, but her essence is with me, the memory of who she was, and that's all right. That's nearly enough.

Now Per raises his glass and looks around the table. '*Skål,*' he says, lifting his drink to each of us, meeting our eyes, the Danish way. The Vikings used to do it, Kasper had told me, but I have no idea why.

'*Skål,*' we raise our own glasses to him, and while the moment is with us, while we're replete with food and drink and large amounts of goodwill and politeness, I scramble to my feet, and I look around the table at them all, my English family and my new, Danish one, and at Kasper, who has caught my free hand in his.

'And this is for Sophie,' I say, and I hold up my wine and take a sip. We may never do this again, we may never meet all together like this, so it's important.

'Sophie,' they echo, and everyone drinks. It's very simple.

It's a beginning, and it's an ending too.

ABOUT THE AUTHOR

After studying English and Education to degree level and then teaching for many years in Sussex, Hampshire and London, Celia Berggreen retired from teaching to begin writing in earnest. She'd been writing short stories, novels and poetry since she was a child, but life had got in the way and she'd never had the time to devote to it that she'd have liked. She joined The Creative Writing Programme, based initially at the

University of Sussex, and threw herself into writing the novel that would become "Counting in Danish".

Celia completed the two-year course and then a further year of Advanced Writing Workshops while continuing work on the novel. She was a member of New Writing South and, later, of the Chalk Circle writers' group. She contributed short stories to Chalk Circle's 2021 collection "Shadows on the Path", and to the literary magazine *Mslexia*.

Celia lived in Sussex with her Danish husband, Kristian Berggreen, whom she met on a blind date when she was a single parent juggling three teenagers, full-time teaching and a house move. Happily, he was undaunted, and they married shortly afterwards. With her trademark curiosity and zest for life, Celia embraced Danish culture, and her large, extended family of Danish in-laws and regular trips to Denmark provided some of the inspiration and background for this novel.

In 2022, Celia died of ovarian cancer. She'd continued writing until the cancer treatment got too much for her, starting work on a second novel while seeking an agent for "Counting in Danish". Sadly, she ran out of time. She was never to see her first novel in print, or complete the second. "Counting in Danish" has been published on the initiative of her husband, who was determined that her long-held ambition should be realised.

ACKNOWLEDGEMENTS

Publishing a book without the author available to liaise with the publisher and support marketing and sales activities is certainly a challenge. Thanks to Annemarie Berggreen, who helped with this as well as proofreading the novel and assisting with editing.

Thanks also to all of those who nurtured, encouraged and guided Celia in her writing career, including Susannah Waters and Mark Slater, her tutors on the Creative Writing Programme at the University of Sussex, and all her fellow Chalk Circle Writers.